WE'RE NOT HAVING S.E.X!

VENEZIA PHILLIPS

VENEZIA PHILLIPS

Copyright © 2020 by Venezia Phillips. Venezia Phillips asserts the moral right to be identified as the author of this book.

All rights reserved.

No part of this book may be reproduced in any form or by any electronic or mechanical means, including information storage and retrieval systems, without written permission from the author, except for the use of brief, attributed quotations in a book review.

All characters and events in this book, other than those clearly in the public domain, are fictitious and any resemblance to real persons, living or dead, is purely coincidental.

*To all you girls out there.
Forget the guy who makes you laugh.
Find the man who thinks you're funny.*

1

12 FEBRUARY – BATTERSEA BRIDGE, LONDON, UK

Myname.sNotConnie *@FitnessPhilly289 – Hi Philly! Any smoothie tip for a truly sh**ty, wet English afternoon?*

FitnessPhilly289 *@Myname.sNotConnie – Sure honey, check out my recipe for 'Grapefuit and Guava Sunshine' on my FitnessPhillyBlog. Truckload of Vit. C! Top of the morning to you!*

Myname.sNotConnie *@Fitnessphilly289 – That's what they say in* Ireland. *Not England. Seriously Philly, do your research.*

FitnessPhilly289 *@Myname.sNotConnie – Don't get your knickers in a knot, darlin'! Swap GGS for 'SmoothMood', berry-static and dopamine, xoxo*

Myname.sNotConnie *@Fitnessphilly289 – Thanks, will do xx*

Two days before Valentine's, Constance Wilkinson is well and truly stuck. The traffic on Battersea Bridge is just as fluid as dried-up Weetabix.

Mist rises from the Thames, and much like the temperature, Constance struggles to stay positive.

She has passed the time messaging the fitness guru she follows on Instagram, but now her phone is flat, and her berry-tastic smoothie is still waiting for her in her kitchen fruit bowl, two hours of logjam away.

She scrapes the bottom of her mental chatter barrel and thinks about her brand-new client – a children's author fond of talking donkeys – as she scans the London skyline.

On her left, the river winds towards Fulham, Hammersmith, and Chiswick. On her right, 4x4 car doors in shiny black or showy white block her view, because Oggie, her 1996 left-hand-drive Twingo, is dwarfed by the line of Chelsea tractors exiting their SW3 mothership.

The traffic stops again, and Constance catches a glimpse of a tall man hunched too low over the bridge's Moorish balustrade.

His clothes are dripping wet, and he looks into the greenish water below with such intensity that she becomes convinced he's about to jump.

She couldn't say why, but she leaps out of her car. And although she is much smaller than he is, she manhandles him into the back seat.

Then, still wondering what she's doing, she climbs back into the driver's seat and catches up with the slow-moving traffic.

She chances a glance in her rear-view mirror. *Holy Bikini! Yes, it really* is *him. Oh my heart!*

2

12 FEBRUARY – OGGIE THE TWINGO, BATTERSEA BRIDGE, LONDON, UK

Choking on her surprise, Constance forgets how to swallow.

At first neither of them speaks. She struggles to catch her breath while her new passenger squelches like a floor mop.

On impulse, she hands him her coat. 'Lie low and cover yourself.'

When he moves to obey, he smells like rain and exhaust fumes. His russet hair is plastered to his forehead. It drips into his green eyes and down the field of freckles that is his face.

Constance has never seen a more gorgeous face and her breath hitches, but she does her best to sound confident. 'You're going to be fine.'

He makes a sceptical noise.

'At least, no one else noticed you,' she continues.

'I wouldn't care if they had,' declares the wet man.

Constance, never a great one for small talk, cannot think what to say next, and heavy silence settles into the tiny car.

After a few minutes of awkwardness, Constance tries again to lighten the mood. 'Well, you'd really do anything to be in the papers tomorrow!'

Of course, her ill-thought-out attempt to cheer him up fails dramatically.

From underneath her wool and cashmere coat – the one she chose because it was the only one not dragging on the floor–, the would-be drowner snorts.

Red-cheeked, she gives up on conversation. 'Where can I take you?'

'Next bridge,' he says.

'Okaay…'

Constance controls her irritation, but she is already making all kinds of mental notes never again to get involved in a drowning.

To her credit, she can't help feeling sorry for the man behind her.

Last chance.

'I'm on my way home, would you like to tag along? Dry your clothes, etc.'

'I don't care,' replies the man. His American accent is hardly noticeable, not like it was on TV where his Southern drawl, bordering on cowboy, was on full display.

'Okay then,' says Constance, cursing her better nature.

In complete silence, she drives past the Chelsea and Westminster Hospital and along Earls Court Road, before turning left onto Cromwell Road. The traffic eases up as they head west through outer Kensington.

Constance slowly comes to terms with the complete bonkers-ness of the situation: she's driving home in her ancient green Twingo with a haggard and soaking-wet American movie superstar in the back.

How could they miss that out of my horoscope?

She glances back. 'Hey.'

'Mmmmh?' says the actor.

Constance enunciates carefully. 'Are you cold?'

She gets no answer. Because *she* is quite cold actually in her thin blouse, she turns the heating to max. The antique '*chauffage*' jumps into hyperdrive and the resulting hum covers the sounds of traffic. The temperature rises quickly.

As she goes up the Hammersmith flyover, Constance experiences a brainwave. 'You must be in shock. I'd better take you to A&E first.'

Once he translates A-N-E into 'Emergency Room', the man comes out of his torpor. 'No! No hospital,' he declares firmly.

Great. What now? I'm in sole charge of a suicidal A-lister?

'What about a couple of coffees at least?' she offers, still conciliatory. 'I'm going to pull up here for a minute.'

She's left behind posh South Ken and its coffee boutiques and has to make do with an A-road greasy-spoon café. She parks Oggie on the double yellow lines right in front of it, then almost jumps out of her skin when the man sits up abruptly.

He shoots her a look of pure hostility she feels is frankly undeserved.

'What? What have I said?' she huffs.

Gawd, he's got something against coffee as well as dry clothes and hospitals.

'Don't go in there and tell everyone I'm in your car!' he threatens in his longest utterance to date.

Who does he take me for?

Affronted, Constance snaps back, 'Oh mister, don't get your wet boxers in a twist! Not everyone's got the tabloids on speed-dial, believe it or not.'

Suicidal and paranoid!

The man slouches back in his seat, her coat on his lap still undergoing its transmutation into a wet rag.

'"How I Saved Suicidal Seb!!!" in big fat headlines, with out-of-focus photos? Not for me, thank-you-very-much,' says

Constance. She pictures it in her mind. 'I'll tell you one reason why I won't sell my story to the papers.' She air-quotes 'story'.

He looks up, an arched eyebrow challenging her to make that reason a good one.

She regrets her rash announcement, but bravely ploughs on, scrambling for something, anything, to say. When she does find her 'reason', she struggles to keep the triumph out of her voice.

'Dark hair, dark eyes? I'm at a disadvantage in black and white. Cheap tabloid photos would look no better than mugshots. What do you say to that, Mr Big Movie Star?'

'Tabloids are in colour.'

A full Technicolor blush creeps onto her cheeks.

Constance, you muppet!

Keenly aware she's made a fool of herself yet again, she shrugs, 'Whatever, mate. *I* need a coffee.'

Before she can exit the car, he says, 'Mine's black. No sugar.'

Raising himself on one elbow, he watches her gingerly negotiate her way across the flooded pavement in her girlish patent ballet flats.

With her scrawny limbs, dark hair, wide brown eyes, and sharp features, she looks like a younger, prettier Edith Piaf. He corrects himself. *The Marion Cotillard version. Not the original.*

It takes a while until his heart remembers how to beat.

3
12 FEBRUARY – COFFEE SHOP, GREAT WEST ROAD, LONDON, UK

The all-day-breakfast coffee shop is overheated and smells of fried eggs and bacon fat. The music has been tuned to Heart Radio since its first ever broadcast in 1994.

Constance marches up to the counter. One glance at the smudged blackboard confirms there's not a snowball's chance in hell of a smoothie, berry-tastic or otherwise.

'One skinny soy latte with cinnamon and one black Americano to go, please,' she huffs, grabbing a handful of sugar packets from a grubby bowl on the side of the till.

The waitress has blue hair, which one might – erroneously – assume guarantees a certain cheerful disposition.

'That'll be two coffees, luv. One white, one black,' she mutters.

Then, she does a double take and stares at Constance's usually unremarkable bosom. Constance looks down at her cleavage and discovers she has lost the two top buttons of her shirt in the scuffle at the bridge. She rolls her eyes.

Bloody brilliant.

'£5.20,' the waitress demands.

'What? £5.20 for two instant coffees?'

'This is London, luv,' replies the waitress, unapologetic. 'Want them or not?'

'I *need* them,' sighs Constance. She looks around at the formica tables and mismatched chairs until she sees what she was hoping for – an ageing tartan blanket draped over one of the cracked leather armchairs. 'How much for that rug?'

'Wha—?' asks the waitress, finally interested.

'I need that rug. How much?'

'Fifty quid, luv. It was me nan's, innit. Sentimental value and all that…' Which of course is a fairly inelegant fib.

'Twenty, plus the coffees, and you throw in two muffins. Take it or leave it.' Constance is not normally this forceful, but the day is taking its toll.

The waitress doesn't miss a beat. 'Twenty-five.'

'Done.'

The waitress hands over two styrofoam cups with ill-fitting lids and two random muffins in a grease-stained paper bag. 'You're a nutter, you know that, don'cha luv?'

Constance grabs the blanket, shakes the dust out, and pulls three ten-pound notes out of her 'Hello Kitty' purse.

'Keep the change,' she smiles.

Outside, the rain is hitting the pavement like bullets. Her shoes get soaked as she runs back to Oggie. Her heart beats a stampede at the thought of seeing the Adonis in the back seat again.

4

12 FEBRUARY – OGGIE THE TWINGO, M4 MOTORWAY WEST, UK

As she struggles to open the Twingo's door, clutching the coffees and muffins with a blanket tucked under her arm, she has no hand to hold her shirt together and part of her bra is on display.

She throws the blanket at the man, who has been staring at her with interest, and climbs into the driver's seat. A black cab hoots, and the cabbie shouts something Constance rightly imagines to be extremely abusive.

She settles behind the wheel and pours sugar into her white coffee. 'Hey, you could have told me my girls were hanging out. You must have got quite an eyeful, you perv.'

The man hides a smile. 'Never noticed,' he lies. He grabs the black coffee, and Constance forces three of the sugars into his hand. He refuses.

Constance is unmoved. 'You're in shock, you're having sugar.'

Without further protestations, he pours the three sugars into his watery Nescafé. 'I'm only seeing your back,' he says.

Constance turns around, affording him a front-row seat to the globe of her left breast. 'What?'

'I *was* only seeing your back,' he corrects. 'You know, your shirt.' His eyes are glued to the line her push-up bra forms in between her breasts.

Constance covers herself with two hands. 'Wear your blanket and zip it,' she says, her cheeks scarlet.

He starts peeling off his expensive-looking – and soaked – grey marl cashmere jumper and designer shirt.

She watches him in the rear-view mirror.

The square of his jaw is in perfect proportion with his carefully trimmed eyebrows; his nose is straight without looking fake, and the bow of his lips seems computer-generated for kissability. And his eyes – his eyes are his most recognisable trait, not to mention utterly spectacular. They're a light blueygreen that reminds Constance of the colour of tropical seas in BBC nature programmes.

He catches her checking him out. 'Who's the perv now?' he smirks, not unattractively.

Constance, eyes-front and indignant, replies, 'I'm a lady, I couldn't possibly be a perv.'

'Only English girls and Southern belles can get away with saying "I'm a lady". And in neither case is it true.'

'Behave or straight to the hospital,' threatens Constance, flattered by the implied compliment and keen to dispel an inconvenient flutter.

'Yes, ma'am.'

As she rejoins the traffic, her hazard warning lights still on, to the loud annoyance of the white van behind her, Constance takes the opportunity to watch him again in the rear-view mirror.

He looks dishevelled and has purple shadows beneath his movie-star eyes, as if he's been punched. Substance abuse of every kind, suspects Constance. He's a 10/10 nevertheless.

Suddenly, Constance feels self-conscious, despite her carefully chosen 'client meeting' outfit consisting of her best cream silk blouse, her favourite Claudie Pierlot black tutu skirt and *plumetis* tights.

I must look like a waitress.

'I'm not exactly your A-list hook-up material anyway,' she says out loud.

'If you say so,' he grins.

'Eat your muffin, Blanket Boy.' She's never spoken to anyone like that before. Not once, not even in primary school, not even when drunk.

He laughs, pulls the blanket closer and sips his coffee.

'What on earth is this dadgum brown stuff?' he exclaims. 'Is it what passes for coffee here? Still stuck in the Blitz, aren't you? What's next, food rations?'

'I don't know what you mean, instant in styrofoam is the nation's favourite,' she smiles. 'Do you want mine? I've got milk.'

'You're sweet, but no.' He sips from his cup with a small frown, perfectly in line with his symmetrical features.

After two cars flash their full beams at her, Constance switches off her warning lights.

She gets onto the M4 and picks up speed. The Twingo is shuddering with the effort, but it's seen worse.

The actor sits up. 'You don't talk much.'

'No, often I don't.'

'Do you think I would have died?' he asks, nonchalant.

Constance's reply is equally casual. 'I didn't have time to look down. How high was it?'

'Maybe forty feet…'

'What's that in metres? I don't speak Victorian.'

They exchange a smile in the mirror.

'About four stories.'

'Twelve metres? Then probably not. Unless of course you'd got hypothermia and drowned.'

'I think I would have drowned.'

'Or maybe you would have swum.'

The man is dubious.

'Hmm,' he says and his low vibrato make Constance's insides melt a little.

Still wrapped in the blanket, he lies back down underneath her coat and smells it discreetly.

The silence returns until he pops his head out. 'What's your name?'

'Constance. Constance Wilkinson.'

'Do you know who I am?'

'I know your *name* – Sebastian Anders.'

Sebastian smiles because he likes her answer. 'And what I do for a living?'

'Yes, obviously that too,' she answers.

'It's refreshing.'

'That someone should recognise you?' she teases.

'No squealing, no asking for autographs or selfies or celebrity anecdotes…'

Constance shrugs and turns on the music. It's an Eminem song. She raps it under her breath. 'Now hush, little baby, don't you cry. Everything's gonna be alright—'

'So, you're a lady who likes Eminem?' says Sebastian, who has a sudden vision of church-going girls slumming it with rappers.

When Constance doesn't answer, he presses, 'Are you deaf as well as mute?'

Constance deadpans, 'I'm blind too, I drive following my sense of smell.'

Sebastian laughs, and as if by magic, one of the knots in his chest loosens.

'You're pretty cheerful for a near-suicide,' remarks Constance. After a pause, she adds, 'Eminem is a poet.'

'He's offensive.'

'Sorry, granny.' She winks. She can't remember the last time she winked at anyone. She hopes it came out okay and not like she had something in her eye.

'I just didn't have you down as a ho from the hood.'

'And I didn't have you down as a prude.'

She finds his eyes in the mirror. His answering smile is surprisingly gentle.

'I'm a lady of loose morals,' she says.

Sebastian chuckles. 'Now who is speaking Victorian?'

She smiles at him again.

As they pass Windsor, he restarts the conversation. 'So, who's home?'

'My home, obviously! Dummy.'

Sebastian articulates exaggeratedly, 'No. Who is home, at your home?'

'No one today.'

Sebastian rolls his eyes and detaches the words. 'Do. You. Live. Alone? Do. You. Have. A roommate or. Perhaps. A boyfriend?'

Constance replies quite seriously, 'I'm in an open relationship with my grandad's best friend.'

Sebastian chokes on his 'What?'.

But Constance grins. 'Goodness, you're too easy! However do you get on in Hollywood? If you must know, I have a boyfriend who lives with me when he's not working abroad. He does humanitarian work.'

'And he's away at the moment?'

Constance doesn't like where the conversation is going.

'Why? You're thinking of moving in? He comes back next Wednesday. Gawd, you're creeping me out. Why are you so interested in my living arrangements? Are you planning to murder me?'

'Who's being naive now?' Sebastian retaliates.

Constance's cheeks are burning. She turns off the music for better effect.

'Look, I'm helping you here. I saw you about to jump, and I stepped in. I'm taking you to my house so you can dry your clothes, call your people, whatever. But then you'll be on your way. No sexual favours included, thank-you-very-much.'

Sebastian manages to look chastised. 'I'm sorry, you're right. You saved my life, and I offend you. I'm a dog.'

Constance's good mood returns. 'Exactly. And if you're not careful, I'll abandon you on the side of the road.'

Sebastian catches her eye in the mirror and says, 'Woof!'

Constance shakes her head and her dark curls start a jaunty dance. 'You're the funnest suicide I have ever rescued. You're not eating your muffin?'

'It's not wheat-free.'

'So, you'd jump into the Thames, but you're scared of *gluten*!'

Sebastian smiles apologetically, and a bubble of warmth spreads across Constance's chest.

As she veers left onto the A404, she can be heard muttering to herself, 'Cup of tea, taxi company, end of story. He's deranged. I'm deranged. Gawd, what a day!'

5

12 FEBRUARY – CONSTANCE'S HOUSE, HENLEY-ON-THAMES, UK

*C*onstance's house is a Victorian semi-detached on a tree-lined street near the centre of Henley-on-Thames, a quiet, well-heeled town on the border between Berkshire and Oxfordshire.

It is early afternoon when she pulls into her drive, and she does a quick 360-recce for nosy neighbours.

All is quiet on the home front. Everyone's at work, and the dog-walkers who march up and down her street both mornings and evenings have taken their perfectly groomed pooches home for their afternoon brush.

Throwing wary looks around him, Sebastian shuffles out of Oggie's back seat. Constance didn't expect him to be so tall. How she managed to fold him into the back of the Twingo will remain a mystery.

She jangles her keys while he waits behind her, his all-manness making her hands shake and her cheeks flame up again.

When the scuffed, pebble-grey door finally opens, she stands aside to let him in, and braces herself for the brush of his body against hers.

'Shoes off please,' she says, working hard to seem unaffected by his oh-so-sexy aura.

'My socks are not much better, I'm afraid,' he notes.

Constance shuts the door behind them, and her heart sounds like a washing machine on a spin cycle.

'The dryer is this way.' She indicates the narrow utility room that runs alongside the main corridor.

He follows her meekly.

While she fusses with the dials and wonders whether his expensive threads are 'Do not tumble dry', he removes his clothes.

When she turns around, he hands her his trousers, his jumper, and his shirt. He's in his wet boxers, golden skin and hard muscles everywhere.

Her throat explodes with an emotion overload.

She rallies quickly. 'Gawd, you've no decency! Cover yourself please.'

Sebastian shrugs. 'Sorry. I spend most of my life half-naked on sets manned by fully-clothed people. Doesn't bother me any more.' He throws his black socks into the drum.

'Well, I'm so glad you're comfortable,' she gripes. 'Why don't you sit next to that radiator over there. The heating's on.'

Obediently, he sits on the floor by the living-room radiator she indicated.

'Not on the floor, on the armchair of course!'

What a complete fruitcake, she thinks, but the way he looks up at her through his lashes releases a kaleidoscope of butterflies in her stomach.

'Look,' she says, trying to sound cross. 'You're comfortable with your body and that's great, but I'm not entirely indifferent to the fact there's a naked movie star in my living room, so could you *please* wear something?'

Sebastian shrugs in a mock display of helplessness.

As she leaves the room, Constance grumbles to herself, 'We are *not* having S.E.X!'

She returns with a thick cream angora blanket that looks like the foam on the perfect cappuccino, and she drops it in his lap, making a show of averting her eyes.

'What is it with you and blankets?' he asks, but Constance is already in the kitchen, and the kettle starts whooshing.

She blitzes a handful of frozen blueberries and the bruised remainder of her fruit bowl – stalks, pips and all – with some coconut milk, and tips the purple sludge from her NutriBullet into a Mason jar.

The dryer, the kettle, and the liquidiser blend into a deafening concerto of hospitality that removes all possibility of non-telepathic conversation.

When she comes back with two cups of tea – both white – and two straws in the smoothie jar, she sits on the carpeted floor next to him.

This could have done with a quick hoover, she frets. *But then our eardrums wouldn't have survived, nor the fuse box.*

Sebastian takes a sip of the proffered berry concoction, and wrinkles his nose, before turning his million-dollar green eyes on her. 'Is this a little awkward?'

'Yes, this is definitely a little awkward,' she admits, soldiering through her smoothie.

His face is so serious she can't help smiling, despite the tart taste that makes her eyes water. He blinks and a beat too late, he smiles back. They drink their tea in silence.

Thank you, God, for the distraction, thinks Constance when her phone rings. The screen says 'Mark' and shows an out-of-focus selfie of a dark-haired man.

'Hey, you!' she greets him extra-cheerfully.

'Hi Connie, how's you?'

'Great, thanks. Where are you calling from?'

'A hell-pit of a refugee camp near Mafraq, at the Jordan border. We've got an outbreak of the shits. I'm up to my elbows here. Tell me something normal. What have you been doing with yourself?'

'Actually, I've just saved someone's life.'

'Really?' he says as if she'd mentioned a trip to Tesco. Then it reaches the brain. 'What? In Henley?'

'In London.' Constance's ego is scratched, and she adds a bit sharply, 'There are lives to be saved here too you know…' There's a silence, and she continues, 'Someone who was about to jump off Battersea Bridge.'

'Battersea Bridge?' repeats Mark, as if that's the bit he's struggling to believe.

'Yes. A famous actor. I can't tell you who.'

'Ha ha, you almost had me,' laughs Mark, relieved to retain the life-saving upper hand. 'I never know when you're joking.'

'I'm not joking.'

'Okay, so where's that actor you saved? Did you take any pictures?'

'I didn't take any pictures, but I took him home.'

'Well, that's exciting,' he says in a voice that means it isn't. 'I'm sorry, I have to get going. It's costing me an arm and a leg to call you.'

'All right, go save the world then.' Her tone is the same as always, cheerful and easy-going, although she feels anything but.

'I will. You keep on saving Hollywood!' he quips.

'Bye,' repeats Constance, but the line is already dead. The phone screen returns to an illustration of a hibiscus flower.

'What a D.I.C.K,' frowns Sebastian, although no one's asking him.

Constance bristles. 'Shut up. You're the dick.'

'True, takes one to know one.' After a pause, he adds, 'That was a fantastic lie, by the way. "I took him home"? Classic. You ladies are something else!'

Constance gets to her knees, and her eyes narrow. '"We ladies…"? Because men never lie of course!'

'Oh we do. It wouldn't surprise me if Dick was calling from a gas station somewhere near… Oxford perhaps, on his way to see his wifey and his kids.'

'You are incredibly jaded—' Constance ripostes, but Sebastian talks over her.

'And I don't understand true love?'

Constance gets to her feet, kicking him in the shin in the process, not too accidentally.

'Shut up! You're an idiot.'

'I love you too, sweetheart,' Sebastian responds flirtingly.

This is too much for Constance, who loses what's left of her composure.

'Fuck you, Mister. I don't know you from Adam. I'm helping you, and you're making fun of my crappy relationship? And when exactly was the last time someone had sex with you without expecting payment? Or a selfie with a celeb? Or a VIP invite to a club? Or whatever passes for reward in your crazy world?'

She storms out and can be heard still ranting from the utility room.

'I don't care if your clothes are still wet. I don't care if you're suicidal. I don't care if your life is so disappointing you don't want it any more.'

As Sebastian, still in his boxers and six-pack, corners her by the dryer, she jabs him in the chest so hard he flinches.

'Don't you dare make fun of me!' She throws his damp clothes at his face. Then she remembers her under-performing shirt and crosses her arms over her chest.

Sebastian has one trouser leg thrown over his tanned shoulder with the crotch neatly circling his neck, but nevertheless mounts a spirited defence.

'Look, I'm sorry. It's just that you're beautiful, kind and funny, and I hate that your boyfriend is a self-absorbed son of a biscuit who doesn't appreciate you.'

Constance dismisses the exotic cuss-word and the trio of compliments as *a load of tosh* and counter-attacks without a moment's hesitation.

'Well, that's my life, and it's not that crap that *I* would want to end it. So, shut up and get out.'

Sebastian doesn't move, attempting to read her expression. He gauges correctly that the best part of her anger is for the gallery.

She stares at the floor sulkily, committed never to look him in the eye again.

Sebastian's voice drops an octave. 'Can you feel it?' he asks, as if the previous exchange never happened.

'What now?'

'You know what. The sexual tension. The attraction between us.'

'Yes, I feel it,' she answers begrudgingly. 'But that's what you do, right? That's what you get paid for. Attract women, like a Venus trap!'

Constance has no idea this is the name of a carnivorous plant that eats insects; she thinks it's what you call a man a bit too lucky with the ladies.

Sebastian grins, sending his freckles into a merry dance across his face. 'I prefer "heartthrob", or perhaps "sex on legs", if you must…'

He winks, and her temperature rises by a factor of two.

Constance fights a smile. 'More like the fake rabbit thingy at the dog races.'

He lets out a musical chuckle. 'Awesome. I preferred when you called me a dick.'

Constance still cannot meet his eyes, but she returns once more into the breach.

'You know who make people fall in love in a matter of hours? Manipulative narcissists! People who get their kicks from emotionally abusing others.'

'So... are you saying I'm a narcissist or that you're in love with me already?'

He really hopes this will mollify Constance long enough so he can finish drying his clothes. It doesn't work.

'I'm not playing any more. I want you out of my house. Now.'

She stabs at his naked chest with her index finger and her nail leaves a red crescent behind.

'You're dangerous; one minute you're suicidal, the next you're flirting with me. I've known you less than two hours, and already I don't know which way is up.'

'Hey, I'm only flirting because you're gorgeous, because I was at rock bottom and in two hours, you've made me want to live again.'

'What. A. Lot. Of. Rubbish!'

'No, it's not. I really want to stay here with you for a while. I don't want to return to my hotel, to my agent, my personal assistant and my bodyguard, and feel so utterly alone I want to kill myself. Can't you understand that?'

She can.

Sebastian continues. 'Look, I just want to stay with you. Even if we don't talk. I want to sit in a normal house, in a *home*. And be with someone real. Talk about something – or nothing – with someone who isn't fake.'

Constance sighs, staring at her wet plumetis tights. 'Okay. But we're *not* having S.E.X!'

'You keep saying that. I heard you the first time.'

'And don't flirt with me.'

'You're flirting with me too, you know.'

'I'm not, I was just trying to cheer you up.'

Sebastian smiles at the top of her head. 'It's working.'

This brings a bashful smile to her lips.

'You're beautiful,' says Sebastian.

'Stop it,' she bites back. 'I don't even believe you. You're not that great an actor. You can't even sell me "you're beautiful".'

'Damned if I do, damned if I don't,' concludes Sebastian philosophically.

Constance moans in exasperation. 'Oh, do shut up.'

Sebastian recovers his playful mood. His pecs ripple as he laughs. '"Shut up!" and "We're not having S.E.X!" Why do you have all the best catchphrases?'

'Make your own,' she smiles.

Sebastian shoves his clothes back into the dryer and turns the knobs at random. Constance tut-tuts and resets the timer.

'They'll be too small for a hamster once you're done with those.'

He politely lets her out of the kitchen first and takes the opportunity he's created to check her behind, but the tutu-skirt leaves too much to the imagination.

She feels his gaze on her back and shivers, but she recovers quickly and says over her shoulder, 'Anyway, I shag nothing below Oscar-level.'

'Are we talking McConaughey here?' jokes Sebastian.

'We're talking Colin Firth. I don't do Americans either.'

'Is that because we count in feet and inches?'

'Yes, too much length lost in translation.'

'Ooh, saucy!' laughs Sebastian, charmed. 'You could do stand-up, you know.'

'Yes, and you're still mostly naked. Wear something. The cameras have gone home.'

As she climbs the white wooden stairs, he calls after her mischievously, 'Says the woman with her *girls* hanging out.'

Constance turns red and locks herself in the bathroom for a much-needed self pep-talk.

> ***Myname.sNotConnie*** *@FitnessPhilly289, that berry-static stuff was bl**dy awful, thanks for nothing, tooth enamel all but gone. Plus-side, got to share it with IRL celeb. I hope you're jealous.*
>
> ***FitnessPhilly289*** *@Myname.sNotConnie, no need to pitch a fit, Missy. I never said it tasted nice! Unless it's @donnyosmond, not interested.*
>
> ***Myname.sNotConnie*** *@FitnessPhilly289, how old are you exactly?*

6

12 FEBRUARY – CONSTANCE'S HOUSE, HENLEY-ON-THAMES, UK

Sebastian reinserts himself into his now-dry jumper, but the sleeves end mid-arm and his pecs look moulded-on.

He is by a long stretch the handsomest man Constance has ever seen. And right now he is lounging on the floor of her sitting room, his long limbs stretched in a relaxed pose.

She admires him from the sofa, where she is curled up in a blanket. She's buttoned up a flannel pyjama top over her struggling blouse.

Candles glow in the dim light, throwing soft shapes on the magnolia walls and filling the air with the sweet scent of vanilla.

They are channel hopping until *Celebs Go Dating* comes on the screen.

'Were you ever approached to go on one of these?' asks Constance for something to say.

'I don't know, Regina deals with that.'

'And Regina is….?'

'My agent.'

'So you're too important to answer your own phone?'

Constance says with a pinched look. She shuffles her weight and sits up straight.

'There are dozens of calls like these every day,' he says. 'I would never get off the phone. In fact, it's probably my PA Brandie's job. Regina hasn't got the time either.'

On the TV, celebs are still dating. Constance is feeling inadequate, and she doesn't like how nonchalant Sebastian is about the team of people who work for him.

'That must make your life a bit simpler,' she comments.

Sebastian turns around and understands what she's not saying. 'I was serious about ending it today.'

'Why?'

'My life is crap, that's why.'

Constance rolls her eyes. 'Is it the money? Or the awards? Or the famous girlfriends?'

'All of it,' replies Sebastian. 'And I've never had a famous girlfriend, contrary to what gossip bloggers say.'

'If you say so…'

'Yeah, I do say so.' Sebastian's flash of irritation does something to Constance's stomach.

She dials down the sarcasm. 'All I know is that when I've had a shit day, I love curling up on the sofa to watch a movie. Even if it's a bit shallow or not very funny. The way I see it, you actors provide a public service, and you do a far better job than the buses or the internet companies.'

Sebastian hears this as an apology and leans his designer stubble against Constance's dangling knee. The bristles scratch at the plumetis tights she's still wearing. She shivers.

Neither of them speaks for a while.

As the emotions swirl and build, Constance is the first to cave in. 'What is it like having a team of people looking after you?'

Sebastian scoffs. 'They're not looking after me. They're

making money out of me. I live in hotel rooms. I'm told where to be, what to wear, what to say, what to eat, what jobs to take, how much to train, in what gym, and which muscles.'

His voice rises, 'I can't move without people taking photos of me on their dadgum phones, sharing them with all the other butts of the world, and commenting on how buff, fat or old I look. That's not counting speculations about me being gay, a drug addict or a paedophile. Or even an alien from outer space.'

He takes a breath, but she watches him open-mouthed so he continues his tirade.

'People give me stuff I don't want, stuff I couldn't possibly want. What twenty-six-year-old guy wants flowers, teddy bears, or unwashed underwear? I get boxes of chocolates I'm not allowed to eat. I'm hungry all the time.

'When I don't work, I'm bored, and I obsess over not working. When I do work, I'm permanently exhausted and/or jet-lagged.

'My last girlfriend, I thought she was a sweet girl-next-door from Alabama, but within six months, she'd turned into one of them. She was jealous as a tiger: constant drama, slammed doors and snooping on my phone. When I left her, she threatened to sell her "story", and my lawyers had to pay her off.'

Constance doesn't know what to say, so she just listens. Sebastian is still not finished.

'My brother can't stomach that I've left Tennessee for Hollywood. I haven't spoken to him in years. My parents are both dead, and I haven't had an actual friend since childhood. And now *he* is married with a kid. He's active at his church and he has no time for the God-less craziness that is my life.'

He's almost crying now.

'So yes, today I wanted to be done. If you hadn't stopped me, I would have jumped.'

Constance has tears in her eyes too.

He takes her hand. 'But you grabbed me. You're half my size and somehow you pushed me into the back of your toy car.'

She giggles.

'I liked that you took charge,' he continues. 'I liked that you didn't bombard me with questions, and that you were kind to me. Even if there was no room for my legs and my knees were under my chin, your car was the nicest place I'd been in ages.'

Constance rests her fingers lightly on his hand that's holding hers, and she's hyper-aware of the warmth spreading up her arms. He can tell she's dropping her guard.

He says finally, 'So excuse me if I'm a bit smitten with you right now, okay?'

'Wow, that was quite the monologue,' says Constance. 'Do you write your own lines? Or do you have someone do it for you?'

Sebastian smiles with all his perfect, porcelain-veneered teeth and Constance is dazzled. 'Shut your pie hole,' he says.

'No, that's my line.'

'See, you're a tease.'

She shoves him in the shoulder, amazed at her bravery, and squeals when he grabs her around the waist in his strong arms and upends her on the sofa.

As she tries and fails to punch him in his rock-hard stomach, he laughs, flattens her and climbs on top. But when he sees her smile vanish, he freezes.

'Don't kiss me,' she says. 'And get off. We're *not* having sex.'

'I've never wanted a woman more,' says Sebastian in low, husky voice that makes her tummy tremble.

But she recovers herself quickly. 'Tough. Add that to your list of woes.'

Sebastian climbs off her and settles next to her on the sofa, rearranging himself discreetly.

She sits up and ties her hair while he watches her.

'You smell real good,' says Sebastian.

She smiles, the awkwardness forgotten.

'I make it myself. Like a hobby. I give some to neighbours and clients for birthdays and Christmas. This one is orange blossom and vanilla. It's my favourite it because it smells a bit like cake.'

'It's really neat. I could smell it on your coat earlier. I don't think I'll ever forget that fragrance.'

'You're so smooth.'

He looks at her, her hair up and the downy nape of her neck. 'And you're very elegant.'

Constance sniggers. 'It's the pyjama top… it's designer.'

'Is it?'

'No, of course not! I don't have money to burn on stupid things like that.'

On the screen, the Celebs are deciding whether the plain Janes and Joes they've been matched with are worth a second date. Constance is suddenly uncomfortable.

Sebastian yawns with extra gusto. 'If we're not having S.E.X, do you mind if I have a sleep before I go?'

Constance throws him a suspicious look. 'Not on my bed?'

'Sofa will be fine, you can even leave the TV on, I don't like the silence.'

'It's not long enough for your legs.'

'I'll live,' chuckles Sebastian with a hint of bitterness.

'Don't be silly, I have a spare room. Just need to remove a few boxes. It'll only take a few minutes.'

Sebastian's green eyes sparkle. 'I should mention I can't be trusted to sleep on my own. You know, suicide risk etcetera.'

Constance actually wonders whether he has a point. *Can't have him throwing himself out of the window in the middle of the night.* But she soon realises he's joking. 'No, sorry. I can't have you sleeping in my bed. Sex risk etcetera.'

Sebastian grins. 'You're obsessed with sex, you know that?'

'Yeah, right.'

After she's changed the spare bed sheets, she sprays some of the perfume he liked on the pillows.

Downstairs, Sebastian watches the end of the TV show, muttering 'poor nutsos' under his breath and inhaling the scent of Constance's cream blanket.

7

13 FEBRUARY – CONSTANCE'S HOUSE, HENLEY-ON-THAMES, UK

*S*ebastian, who's hardly slept during the past week, is fast asleep in Constance's spare bedroom.

It is a box room, two by two metres – or by Sebastian's reckoning – seven feet by seven). The bed – not quite a double – is clean and comfortable, and Constance's soothing smell emanates from the sheets.

In his dreamless sleep, Sebastian has kicked off the covers, and his toned, tanned body is stretched out like a cat's.

Constance creeps into the room and watches him sleep by the light of the moon that peeks through the chintz curtains.

When she turns to leave, she stubs her big toe on one of the boxes. Her muffled 'ouch' is enough to wake Sebastian.

As he sits bolt upright, he mumbles, 'What? What? What is it?'

'Nothing,' whispers Constance. 'I hurt my foot. Never mind. Sorry to wake you. Go back to sleep.'

'Don't worry, I'm awake now. What's wrong?'

'Nothing. I was just checking you— checking on you.'

'You can stay. You know, to monitor me more closely.'

He realises she's wearing a white nightgown a Victorian

lady would have deemed perfectly appropriate. Apart from her head, hands, and the tip of a bleeding toe, there is nothing to see.

It looks like a costume for a period gothic horror movie, and he's expecting Count Dracula to grab her from behind at any moment.

'I'm going back to bed. I'll see you in the morning.'

As she's going through the door, he calls after her. 'Constance. I really like you. *Really* like you.'

'Good night,' she says stubbornly.

'Hey, one last thing. Why are you insisting we shouldn't have sex? It's not like you're in a serious relationship, is it? We're both consenting adults. I know you want me too.'

She is facing a choice. Do what she's always done and get what she's always got… or change.

She stands frozen and supports herself on the doorframe while very big thoughts are churning in her mind. She couldn't explain why she says what she says next.

'I'm not very good with sex.'

Sebastian thinks he's misheard her. 'What do you mean?'

Constance looks like she's been drained of blood, and she whispers to her feet. 'I don't enjoy it. It makes me feel anxious and awkward.'

There is a silence as Sebastian tries to distil her words into something he can relate to.

'Are you still there?' asks Constance in a tiny voice.

'I'm thinking about it. It's the first time I've heard anyone say that.'

Constance retorts, 'It's not that uncommon; lots of people feel like that, but they just don't say it!'

'What happened?' says Sebastian.

This question annoys Constance. She crosses her arms over her chest to stop shivering.

'Nothing *happened*! I just don't like it. It's sweaty and grunty and tiring. It's not for me, okay?'

Sebastian looks at her with concern. She looks so pale and fragile in the moonlight that he wants to rush to her rescue. But she doesn't let him.

She shouts, 'Look, I don't need your sexual healing. I'm not even sure what you're still doing in my house. I don't want to talk about it. You don't have the monopoly on crappy lives!'

With that, she finally walks out of the room, and the moonlight seems to leave with her.

The darkness sharpens Sebastian's hearing and through the wall he can tell she's crying quietly in her bed.

8

13 FEBRUARY – CONSTANCE'S HOUSE, HENLEY-ON-THAMES, UK

The next morning, Constance is clanking pans and emptying the dishwasher none too gently.

Sebastian enters the kitchen, smelling of her Atlantic Kelp shower gel, his hair just as wet as when they first met.

He's fully dressed, but she's back in her pyjama top now accompanied by its matching bottoms.

He wonders what happened to the Victorian nightie and whether it would look sexy or anachronistic next to the open dishwasher.

'How did you sleep?' he asks, to spare her the effort of finding something to say.

'Fine, and you? Bed okay?' Her politeness showcases her irritation.

'Yes, ma'am. Thank you.'

'Coffee?'

'Yes, please,' says Sebastian as he pulls a white, wooden chair away from the diminutive kitchen table, which is painted in a baby blue and, for some unfathomable reason, reminds him of baby rabbits.

Constance spars with the coffee machine, her back to him.

'Are you from London?' he asks.

'No, I was born in Oxford, and I grew up in this house. My parents signed it over to me in the divorce. In theory, my mother still lives here, but she's gone on an endless cruise with boyfriend #25. So I'm here on my own most of the time.'

'Have you got free rein on the decor?'

'Why do you ask? You don't like my style?'

'Lots of neutral colours.'

'Good job! You've managed to insult me and my home in one fell swoop.' She slams a cup in front of him and a tsunami of coffee lands on the table.

He pulls some kitchen roll from the dispenser on the side of the microwave and mops up the spillage.

Constance is surprised to find him so house-trained. She softens her tone. 'So, do you have several homes?'

'I don't even have one.'

'Where do you keep your stuff?'

'In storage. In LA.'

'Don't you have a car or a bike or something?'

'No, I rent or I'm driven around.'

'You really don't have a normal life then, do you?'

'I wasn't lying.'

Constance sits opposite Sebastian at the small table, and she places a plate of buttered toast between them.

'Maybe that's something to think about. You know, buying a house, and perhaps also a car. For in between jobs. A bit of normality?'

He holds her gaze, and her eyes make him think of dark chocolate, but he can detect a certain puffiness that betrays her nightly tears.

She breaks the silence first. 'It could help to have somewhere to go when it gets a bit too much.'

'I'll think about it,' he promises.

They sip coffee and Constance munches on a piece of toast. 'You're not hungry? We didn't even eat last night.'

'Gluten,' says Sebastian with an apologetic smile.

'Oh dear, I'm sorry. What a rubbish hostess. I thought you were joking yesterday. Would you like some eggs, or perhaps some yoghurt?'

'*YOGhurt* please, ma'am,' he replies, mimicking her British pronunciation.

'I could have you talking like a normal person in no time,' she teases.

'That'd be a good reason not to kick me out.'

She sighs and stands to prepare a bowl of yoghurt for him.

'I just don't think we have anything in common, Sebastian. You're a famous actor from LA and I'm an illustrator from London. We don't exactly move in the same circles.'

'You're an artist?'

'I illustrate books. I'm not some big artist or anything.'

She deposits in front of him – gently this time – a bowl full of Greek yoghurt with chopped fruit and nuts.

'Thank you, ma'am. What kind of work do you do?'

'Anything that pays – children's books, book covers, marketing material and the like.'

'Sounds neat. I didn't realise you were a dyed-in-the-wool hipster.'

She smiles deprecatingly. 'I like it. Some clients are nice.'

'Do you work in a studio?'

'Sometimes, but most of the time I work from home. I have an office upstairs in what used to be my mother's room.'

'Isn't it a bit lonely?'

'No, I like it. It's quiet.'

Sebastian lets out a huge sigh. 'Your life sounds like the exact opposite of mine.'

'It does rather, doesn't it?' She crinkles her nose in a lovely smile that goes straight to his heart.

She finishes the plate of toast while he devours his yoghurt, his first food in two days.

She's drumming her fingers absent-mindedly when she notices how the sunshine coming through the Venetian blind is lighting her knuckles.

He's watching the sunlight turn her loose hair the same chocolate colour as her eyes.

For the first time, he takes in the shape of her nose and the flare of her nostrils. By his account, it is a very pretty nose.

'It's a beautiful day today. After yesterday's deluge,' he says to stop his thoughts from wandering towards the more inappropriate end of his daydreams.

Constance just smiles.

'Are you working this morning?' he asks.

She's about to lie but admits the truth instead. 'My new client hasn't yet sent me the brief.'

'Wanna go for a walk? In the countryside, I mean. Somewhere quiet.'

She cocks her head, and heavy curls roll down her arm. Sebastian sets his face in a hopeful yet determined smile. It works.

'I know where we could go for a quick stroll before you leave. It's secluded and at this time of day we shouldn't bump into anyone. Too late for dog-walkers.'

Sebastian gets to his feet. 'Perfect. When do we leave?'

'Hold your horses, cowboy!' giggles Constance. 'I'm still in my pyjamas. Give me ten minutes.'

'Is that some lady dialect for an hour and ten?'

She laughs. 'No, ten minutes tops!'

While she's gone, Sebastian puts the dishes in the dishwasher, wipes down the surfaces, and rinses the coffee machine.

9

13 FEBRUARY – CHILTERN HILLS, OXFORDSHIRE, UK

Seventy minutes later, they're sitting on an engraved oak bench ('in memory of Tabitha "Tibs" Montgomery 1928–2007 who loved to walk these woods'), bleached by the sun at the top of a steep hill overlooking the Chilterns.

'This is stunning,' marvels Sebastian. 'The landscape is so soft and green. All these trees, and wild animals… We can see for miles! Or it is kilometres with you? I could sit here all day.'

'I'm glad you like the view. The weather's pretty decent for the season.'

'I can't remember the last time I was surrounded by nature. This is magical.'

'You sound like you've escaped from prison!'

'That's exactly how I feel. And I'm just so happy to be sharing this with you.' He breathes in deeply and beams at her with a beatific smile that leaves her lost for words.

She blushes and stares at her shoes. This time, she's wearing an old pair of Converse high tops, in a creamy off-white that reminds her of his remark about her house. She tucks her feet under the bench out of his sight.

He only has eyes for her face and wouldn't have noticed if she wore open-toe combat boots. 'You're so beautiful,' he says.

She turns away and takes a keen interest in the nearby woodland.

'Don't be embarrassed,' Sebastian whispers.

'No, it's not that,' she lies. 'I've just seen a squirrel.'

'Liar,' he murmurs with a tenderness she's never heard before.

She pretends to be absorbed in the landscape, but in fact she's trying hard to keep her eyes dry.

'So, I'm getting a house and a car. While we're fixing each other's lives, when are you going to give Mr Bleeding Heart his marching orders?'

He braces for an angry outburst, but she only sighs. 'I should. He definitely could have a secret family somewhere. He supposedly spends all this time in warm countries, but he never gets tanned.'

She can't help throwing a swift glance at Sebastian's perfect Californian glow. Her eyes linger on the tan line of the TAG Heuer watch he advertises in the fashion magazines Constance reads at the hairdresser's.

'Why haven't you ditched him yet if you don't trust him?'

'He doesn't ask much.'

Sebastian makes no comment, but what he is thinking is clear to her.

'And I like saying I have a boyfriend,' she continues. 'Otherwise people think you're a pathetic spinster or all kinds of weird.'

He gives her a pointed look.

'You're right,' she huffs. 'It's such a terrible excuse.'

He turns to her and a little cloud of Atlantic Kelp travels towards her.

'Look,' he says, 'I really like you, and I feel we have this natural... rapport.' She nods. 'So I'm going to ask you again. What happened to you?'

She speaks to her Converses.

'You know, the usual. Bad start, too young. The first boy I went out with kind of forced my hand. Then he dumped me, saying I was frigid. I wanted to prove him wrong, so I had sex with a couple of other boys, although I didn't really want to. I was really put off. I was having nightmares.

'Then I didn't do any more than kissing for a few years and even that was making my skin crawl. I've been with Mark for nearly two years, and we've only had sex half a dozen times. I didn't like it, but doing it with the same person more than once turned out to be easier.

'I do it for the sake of the relationship, for birthday presents and phone calls. He can be very sweet.'

Sebastian sits up straight, his shoulders rigid under his shrunk cashmere jumper.

'That is so freaking sad. It's twisting my gut just hearing you say it, if you wanna know the truth.'

'You think I'm pathetic?'

'No, but I'd love to punch a few faces.'

'Including mine?'

He takes her chin in a gentle grip and makes her look at him. 'No, not yours.'

They digest the conversation in silence until Constance speaks to the row of beech trees to her right. 'I always worry people can tell. Could you tell?'

'Nope. With all the sass and banter, I had no clue. I thought you just were not into me. That was a surprise, because it doesn't happen often, but you're full of surprises anyway.'

Constance's soft chuckling lightens the mood. 'You mean no woman ever turns you down?'

He grins. 'The few I asked said yes.'

'I would have thought a man getting lots of sex wouldn't get suicidal...'

'I'm not having *lots* of sex. I just said I've never got turned down.'

'Well, obviously, on top of the house and the car, that's something else you will have to change. I hear sex is good for depressed types such as yourself.' She gives him a cheeky smile.

'I *was* planning to change that, but I've hit a roadblock.'

Constance's smile turns sad, and he takes her hand. For a while they both stare at their interlinked fingers as if a second set of digits had suddenly sprouted out of their respective palms. 'Is that okay?' he asks eventually.

'Yes, that's surprisingly okay.'

'And yesterday, when we were fooling around on your sofa, was that okay?'

'That got a bit too close,' she admits, her cheeks heating up at the memory.

'I noticed something was off, but I would never have thought... I'm sorry, I'm really sorry.'

'It's alright, no harm done.'

Sebastian returns to his thoughts, a frown on his handsome face.

'Don't be such a sour puss, it's fine,' she says.

He gives her hand a squeeze. Hers is a tiny hand with short, round nails painted in a clear light pink.

Sebastian feels a sudden rush of love and wishes he could hold this hand forever.

He makes a spur-of-the-moment decision. 'I'd really like to

spend the rest of the day with you. I don't want to go back to London.'

Constance can't help feeling flattered and likes how warm he keeps her hand. 'Aren't they going to be looking for you?'

'They're probably losing their minds. I walked out of a meet-and-greet, or a meat-and-greed as I call them. It was the night before last, I spent the night walking in the rain. Forgot my coat somewhere, lost my wallet and threw my phone in the river.'

Constance's eyes widen. 'Well, that's some bells and whistles meltdown.'

'Even by Hollywood's high standards, it was a pretty decent performance,' he agrees.

Constance lets his revelations sink in. She hadn't quite measured the depth of his distress, and wonders what could possibly drive anyone to such self-destructive lengths.

She wonders why she, a complete stranger, was the only one to offer him a helping hand. Surely, he must have friends, colleagues, people looking out for him.

Apparently not.

'I can't believe no one recognised you. You have such a famous face. Even looking like a drowned rat, I knew who you were straight away. I bundled you up in the car to save you the embarrassment of someone noticing you and making a fuss.'

'That was very thoughtful.'

'I couldn't believe my eyes. I saw you on Graham Norton last Saturday night, and you seemed so confident and radiant. And there you were two days later, ready for the great jump.'

'I'm not confident,' says Sebastian. 'I'm an actor.'

'You really did sell me the "perfect guy with the perfect life" spiel.'

'Just doing my job, ma'am,' says Sebastian with bitterness.

This shakes Constance's world view. 'Is it the same for

every actor? Every celebrity? Are they all basically lying to our faces with their TV appearances and their Instagram stories?'

'You have to be pretty shallow to fully enjoy the lifestyle. I think most people struggle with it once the glitter's run down the shower drain. But the money is real good.'

'A gilded cage.'

'You have to be passionate about the work, the craft, if you're going to survive long-term. Maybe I'm not passionate enough. I thought I was, but perhaps not.'

'You need a good long break to find your passion again.'

'The problem is you're on this treadmill and you can't stop, because if you do, there's no guarantee they'll let you back on.'

'Who's "they"?'

'The producers, the big studio execs, the money men... And what's definitely worse than being a popular actor is being an out-of-work, blacklisted has-been. One wrong word to the guy I'm working for and my career goes up in flames.'

'Really? Who's he?'

'Tony Da Ricci. You must have seen his name on the credits for half the movies you watched this year. He's a big shot.'

'Never heard of him,' says Constance, who would have denied knowledge of him even if she had. She refuses to lend this man any more power over Sebastian than he already has.

'Take it from me, nothing happens in Hollywood without his say-so, and he holds my future in his hands. I'm only twenty-six, so the best scenario is I'm looking at another fifty years of nothing but the same.'

Constance suddenly feels very cold.

Sebastian feels her shiver and lets go of her hand whiles

she zips up her khaki hunting jacket, and pulls on her – cream – woolly hat.

She worries that his jumper and shirt are not warm enough and offers him her scarf, which he takes for the simple pleasure of smelling her sweet perfume.

During this exchange, time suspends its flight, and both keep their eyes cast down, afraid of the vulnerability they know is painted on the other person's face.

In the ensuing silence, the birds twitter to their hearts' content, and the chill February wind plays cat and mouse with the few leaves remaining on the boughs.

This perfect Oxfordshire morning is nevertheless laden with unexpressed feelings and frightening desires. Constance is the first to surrender to the need for distraction.

'Are you rich?' she asks, hoping his life of bondage has at least some monetary upside.

'Yes.'

'How rich?'

He shrugs. 'Richer than I set out to be.'

'Couldn't you just not work any more? Live on what you have? Retire somewhere exotic, drink piña coladas on the beach for the rest of your days?'

'Sounds boring to me,' he says. She can't help but agree.

'What about a log cabin in the Canadian wilderness then?' She chuckles. 'You could wear some of those racquet shoes, and a dead fox on your head?'

'More tempting, but still a bit lonely.'

'You're a grumpy so-and-so!'

They laugh and for a moment both look young and carefree. But soon Sebastian's face returns to his anxious frown. He takes her hand again.

'Hey, Miss Constance; just a thought: you wouldn't fancy

coming back to London with me, would you? I could show you the sights.'

'A Yankee could show me the London sights?' she scoffs.

'I'm *not* a Yankee!' he laughs. 'I'm from Tennessee.'

'Same difference! Would you make me eat greasy, overpriced fish and chips? Drag me to Madame Tussaud's? I don't think so, thank you!'

'What about room-service in a five-star hotel and a face-to-face with an angry Hollywood agent?'

Constance smiles. 'Pass.'

'And if I threw in a limousine ride?'

'What kind of bimbo do you think I am?' she laughs.

'Okay, hardball, what would it take to get you into a black cab?'

'Dinner somewhere nice,' replies Constance too quickly, as the warmth of his hand on hers is impairing her critical thinking.

Sebastian raises a perfectly arched, quizzical eyebrow. 'Like a date?'

'No, like a civilised evening with someone not dripping water in my hallway.'

Sebastian gets to his feet and pulls Constance to him. 'I would love to take you on a date.'

'It's not a date,' protests Constance, pushing away from his chest, but Sebastian grips her hand and starts towards the car.

As she's being led briskly through the rust and copper woods littered with holly bushes and rotting branches, she repeats several more times that it is in no way a date, but it clearly is too late.

10

13 FEBRUARY – M4 MOTORWAY EAST, LONDON, UK

*I*n the back of the hackney carriage, Sebastian looks at ease and Constance nervous.

She clutches her handbag and rifles through a weathered Louis Vuitton overnight bag she found discarded in a corner of her mother's wardrobe.

The glass partition is shut, but the cabbie – a stereotypical East End geezer, complete with a cobra neck tattoo – steals compulsive glances at them.

Constance plumps her curls with a trembling hand. 'I could have just gone home tonight. No need for you to book me a room in your hotel. I'm sure I've forgotten half my things.'

He runs a hand through his hair, and Constance is suddenly jealous of his fingers.

'I've told you a million times,' he smiles. 'You don't need anything. It's all there in the hotel. Anything you could possibly want – dress, shoes, toothbrush, dental floss… The concierge could probably find you the exact replica of your stripy pyjamas if that made you feel more comfortable.'

'Oh, no need. I've got those.'

Sebastian's cheeky grin makes him look like a teenager. A

very well developed one at least. 'You're so funny, ten minutes to get ready and two hours to pack an overnight bag.'

'I'm nervous,' she pouts.

'No kidding.'

'And I really don't want to meet all these horrible people who make your life hell.'

'You won't have to see them. You can go straight to your room. I'll face the music and meet you there afterwards.'

Constance is still fretting. 'What about the paparazzi? What if they take pictures of me? What if people want your autograph while we're eating?'

Sebastian stares out of the window at the Audi car dealership on his left. He's just spotted a car he likes and commits its shape and colour to memory.

Then he replies nonchalantly, 'What if people want *your* autograph while we're eating?'

Constance gawks at him until he bursts out laughing. 'It's not funny,' she says.

'Stop worrying, just a normal day in the office. Plus, it was your idea.'

She sniffs. 'I freely admit I didn't think it through.'

She looks out the window at the glass-fronted artist studios of Talgarth Road and wonders whether one of them could ever be hers one day.

Then her mind returns to her present predicament, and she declares, 'They'll just think I'm your PA or something.'

As the cab speeds through Hammersmith, Sebastian repeats soothingly, 'Yes, absolutely. My PA. Or something.'

11

13 FEBRUARY – LANGHAM HOTEL, MARYLEBONE, LONDON, UK

*A*s they're pulling up in front of the Langham Hotel on Portland Place in Marylebone, Constance and Sebastian are met by a sea of photographers and press.

In a well-practised move, Sebastian tucks Constance under his arm and drapes her coat over her head. Engulfed in his manly scent, she prays her feet will remember how to walk.

It is in this undignified fashion that Constance makes her entrance into the world of the – mildly – famous.

The hotel porter, in his light blue-grey livery, fights the crowd towards them and takes Constance's bag out of her hand. Blind as she is, she thinks it's been snatched, but she's too overwhelmed by the bouquet of Atlantic Kelp mingled with Sebastian's own smell to complain.

The reporter closest to Sebastian shouts over the noise. 'Mr Anders, Mr Anders! Where were you during the last thirty-six hours? Can you confirm you entered rehab? Was it the Priory?'

He's interrupted by a second man shouting louder. 'Seb! Seb! This way! Is that your new girl? What's her name?'

Another voice further back bellows, 'Is it true you rushed to your sick brother's bedside? Is he dead?'

'My brother's never been better, thank you,' says Sebastian in a voice hardly audible over the din.

'Aren't you estranged?' asks someone else. 'How long is it since you last saw him?'

The first man pushes his way through the crowd. 'So, were you in rehab, Mr Anders?'

Sebastian and Constance are nearly at the door; he turns around to face the army of photographers launching their zoom lenses at his face, like so many air-to-surface missiles.

'I'm absolutely fine, so is my brother. I'm really excited to be in London to promote my new film, *Zombie Attack*. I love London!'

A man calls, 'Is that because your new girl is from here?' He grabs at Constance through the coat and ends up with a handful of boob. 'What's your name, sweetheart? Give us a smile!' Sebastian karate chops the invading arm, and Constance bleats incoherently in response, her breast throbbing and her heart racing.

She becomes aware the rest of the commotion originates from a squadron of young women screaming Sebastian's name, as well as 'Seb, marry me!' and 'Seb, I love you!'.

As she is ushered through the revolving doors, she can hear a young girl yell, 'I'm expecting your baby,' before bursting into tears.

Constance reaches safety, and a uniformed employee leads her to a high-back armchair tucked between imposing marble Tuscan columns.

Before joining Constance in the hotel lobby, Sebastian speaks to the crowd. 'Thank you, everyone! I'll come back and chat soon.'

The girls' screams reach a crescendo, and Sebastian is pelted with teddy bears and flowers. For the first time in three days, he misses his usual pair of bodyguards.

As the hotel security officers place their considerable bulk between the glass doors and the melee, Sebastian finally makes it into the lobby and the noise suddenly fades, as if he's entered a wormhole to another galactic plane.

12

13 FEBRUARY – LANGHAM HOTEL, MARYLEBONE, LONDON, UK

A few minutes later, in a room behind the vast hotel reception desk, an ashen-faced Constance collapses on a taupe Bergère armchair.

Sebastian leans against the wall. 'Holy moly, that was bad.'

Constance has lost the ability to speak. She clutches her crumpled coat and stares open-mouthed at Sebastian. As their eyes meet, her lips move but no sound comes out.

'You okay?' he asks, although he already knows the answer. He crouches close to her and waits for her to find her words.

'I want to go home,' she warbles.

Sebastian's eyes are soft, but he doesn't reply.

'This was the worst idea I've ever had,' she continues, nervously smoothing beyond-repair creases in the thickly woven cloth. 'I want to go home now. Please.'

He takes her hand delicately as if it was made of precious china and gives it a little shake of sympathy. Whatever he is about to say is cut short by the thunderclap of a door slamming open.

A large woman, overly made up and dressed in a magenta

trouser suit in stark contrast with the muted tones of Sebastian's and Constance's clothes, steps in and, without warning, unleashes her fury.

'Where the fuck have you been?' she bellows, her eyes bulging. 'We've looked everywhere. We've searched ever single tittie-bar, every seedy fuck-hotel! We went to the fuckin' morgues!' Her face now matches the colour of her pantsuit. 'You dickhead!' she continues without drawing breath. 'You entitled little fucktard! I'm gonna ruin your career, that's what I'm gonna do. You won't even get a limp-dick advertising gig. You'll have nothing, N-O-thing! I can take it all away! I'm gonna take it all away, you talentless jerk!'

Sebastian listens patiently to her ranting, and it is Constance who jumps to her feet and comes toe-to-toe with the new arrival.

She shoves her overnight bag against the woman's ample bosom. 'Don't you dare talk to him like that, you ugly cow!' she shouts just as loud. 'You're nothing but an overpaid pimp! A horse trader! You soulless loser!'

As she flares her nostrils angrily, Constance gets a lungful of the woman's strong chocolatey perfume she knows she'll recognise later, but that for now makes her wave at the air around her to dissipate the smell.

'Who in the fucking hell are you?' the woman responds. 'His latest lay? You know how many of you I've seen? Just on the wrong side of pretty, easy and desperate for their three seconds of fame? Dozens! So, get the fuck out of my face and let the grown-ups talk.'

Nostrils flared, they exchange death-stares, and neither of them backs down.

Sebastian steps in between them. 'Okay, ladies. Let's all just calm down. I'm here. I haven't missed anything. We're still on schedule.'

'And what about all those press junkets yesterday? Huh?' shouts the woman. 'You owe me three hours! The things I've had to do to rearrange it without telling Tony or starting a nationwide search party! But no, you think it all revolves around you, you jumped-up redneck. You're a star because we're all doing our jobs. And you'd better start to do yours! Because otherwise we'll all move on to the next pretty face with a sprayed-on six-pack and you'll be left holding your dick in hillbilly land!'

She storms out. Sebastian and Constance look at each other.

She can't believe what she just heard. 'So, you weren't exaggerating.'

'Nope.'

'Who was that?'

'Her name's Regina. Regina Havilland. She could start an argument in an empty house, but she's one of the best in the business, and one of the few who can deal with Tony, the producer I told you about.'

'Is she always like that?'

He grins and his eyes crinkle. 'Only when I don't do exactly as I'm told.'

'She's a bully.'

'In an industry full of bullies, it's not always a bad thing to have your own. And anyway, my previous agent looked sweet-as-pie but was meaner than a wet panther. I prefer Regina. She's straight, and she gets the job done.'

'While leaving behind a trail of casualties scarred for life!'

Sebastian runs a hand through his auburn hair. His boyish good looks do something to Constance's breathing. 'Are you scarred for life?' he asks with a grin.

She can't help but smile back. 'Like I've been beaten up in a back alley.'

'I'm sorry, I really didn't think it would go that way. The crazies at the front, Raging Regina... I thought I could sneak you in quietly, let her taser my privates behind closed doors, and meet you for dinner afterwards. Do you still want to go home?'

He feels he has to ask, but he's praying she will say no, and she does.

She shakes her head. 'Nah-ah. I'm going to do some reconnaissance here. Check out the battlefield, but I'm warning you. At this point, I'm setting up a black-op to exfiltrate you before 0200 hours.' She crinkles her nose in a grin.

Sebastian's gut relaxes. 'Who talks like that?' he laughs. 'Even in my crappy war movies, no one talks like that.'

'Shut up, you jerk,' retorts Constance.

Sebastian's deep belly laugh fills the opulent room with a new ease and comfort. 'Look at you,' he says. 'You've gone native already!'

13

13 FEBRUARY – LANGHAM HOTEL, MARYLEBONE, LONDON, UK

Constance's room is a symphony of tasteful cream and mahogany with a lovely view over the Marylebone roofs.

> ***Myname.sNotConnie*** *@FitnessPhilly289 – About to go on date with IRL Celeb, no smoothie ingredients to hand… any other tips?*
>
> ***FitnessPhilly289*** *@Myname.sNotConnie – Yes: no sex before marriage.*
>
> ***Myname.sNotConnie*** *@FitnessPhilly289 – Really? Really! That's it? That's all you're going to give me?*
>
> ***FitnessPhilly289*** *@Myname.sNotConnie – You sound like a sweet girl (apart from the occasional foul language). You deserve a godly young man who's going to respect you, so yes. That's my tip to you. Have a blessed day, xo*
>
> ***Myname.sNotConnie*** *@FitnessPhilly289 –*

Stick to smoothie recipes, Philly.

Constance lays her dress out on the giant white bed. She's chosen a green, knee-length Bardot that flatters her shapely shoulders and elegant neck.

Philly would approve.

She's paired it with cute, silver-heeled Mary-Janes which lend her some extra height without compromising her comfort.

Currently though, she's wearing nothing but her simple black strapless bra and a matching thong she wishes was a good old pair of granny panties as she absolutely hates strings running between her bum cheeks.

She is doing her hair with a look of fierce determination and talking to herself in the mirror.

For once, you like a guy. Really like a guy. And he's übergorgeous. He's got dreamy eyes. And freckles. He's super-respectful. And funny. And he's got this scalding-hot body. And he's rich and successful. And he seems to like you. So what, if he lives in hotels and doesn't have a life? So what, if he's surrounded by psychopaths?

He doesn't scare you. Even when he talks about sex all the time. Don't be a wuss. Don't be a scaredy cat! Constance, grasp the nettle! Man up.

When you go back to your shitty life tomorrow, you'll just have to deal with it. You'll dump Mark with his secret wife and his secret kids...!

It is completely possible to stay single. You can be celibate. It's a thing now. So tonight you can have fun with your new movie-star friend, and sod the consequences.

She continues muttering to herself along the same lines while marshalling her curls into a semblance of order.

There is a knock at the door and Sebastian whispers a bit

too loud, 'Constance, it's me.' She slithers into her dress and opens the door.

'I'm ready.'

Sebastian emits a low whistle. She blushes to the root of her hair but manages to hold his gaze.

He looks like a fashion model in an exquisitely tailored suit and open white shirt, and the sweet herbal scent of his aftershave, which she recognises as Chanel's Egoïste, threatens to make her swoon.

'You look pretty as a peach,' he says. 'Just perfect.'

'Thanks. You too. I mean, you're really handsome in real life too.' *Well, how's that for a compliment? You're such an idiot, Constance!*

'It's just a pretty face,' says Sebastian dismissively.

'Better than an ugly one, no?'

'Not always.'

The tips of his fingers brush her right elbow as he leads her out of the room and down the heavily carpeted corridor towards the lift.

This time, he gets a good look at her backside draped in green satin and finds it much to his taste.

The Sisyphean effort she's made with her hair is consequently lost on him.

14

13 FEBRUARY – ROUX AT THE LANDAU RESTAURANT, LANGHAM HOTEL, MARYLEBONE, LONDON, UK

*D*ownstairs, in the wood-panelled comfort of the Roux restaurant, Sebastian and Constance sit on lilac leather seats at a discreet table.

No one has come to bother them yet. They're eating. Every single time Constance looks up from her food, she loses track of time, awe-struck by his virile beauty.

Still, her mother didn't raise a rude girl, so Constance beams a smile at Sebastian. 'Thank you for inviting me here. This sea bass is delicious, and it's perfect with celeriac. It's even worth the trauma to get here.'

'I'm glad,' he says, and dazzled by her radiant eyes, he blinks twice.

Gosh he looks tired, thinks Constance, mistaking his fascination for exhaustion. She leans over the table and unwittingly gives him a good view of her cleavage while asking in a lowered voice, 'Do you normally sleep well?'

He's taken aback, but he's used to all sorts of odd interview questions and answers smoothly, although with much more sincerity than he would normally allow himself. 'No, not really.'

After a short pause, Constance says quite seriously, 'I think you have PTSD. Like soldiers.'

'What?'

'You know, trouble sleeping,' Constance whispers. 'Depression, suicidal thoughts… Because of what they put you through – the shouting and screaming, the shoving, the rules. It's like being a hostage in your own life. Perhaps you even have Stockholm Syndrome.'

Sebastian rubs his reddish stubble. 'I can't decide if what you're saying is clever or crazy.'

Constance shrugs, her point made. She returns to enjoying her dinner.

Sebastian watches how the tip of her nose wriggles when she chews. He really loves her nose, a little long, straight and round. He notices she is wearing hardly any make-up. Just some smokey eyeshadow, pink blush, and a nude lipstick.

Silence settles over them like a cashmere blanket, warm and sensual. They are dimly aware of the restaurant soundscape, baroque choral music and soft-spoken conversations, but listen only to the chords of their own duetting breaths.

'Did you go back to see your fans?' she asks as the waiter removes her empty plate.

'Of course I did.'

'That's nice.'

He takes a sip of his Graves Bordeaux white and dabs at his lips with his cloth napkin. 'Not what you were thinking earlier…' he smiles.

'It's a lot for an outsider to take in. Some of them are so young, they were there with their mums. No more than twelve or thirteen. What would they even do if they actually got their hands on you? Play hopscotch?'

She chuckles at her own witty remark and brings her glass to her lips.

'Once there was this girl,' Sebastian explains, 'she had braces. Maybe fourteen?' He pauses for effect. 'She was taking pictures of my crotch.'

Constance daintily chokes on her wine. 'Goodness! I must have been a very innocent fourteen-year-old.'

Sebastian gives her a look over the rim of his glass, and she starts to squirm. 'I wasn't quite that young when... Not much older, but older,' she answers his unspoken question before pursing her lips.

The muscles of Sebastian's jaw jump in a nervous tic. 'You did nothing wrong,' he says with feeling.

Constance pulls herself together and soldiers on. 'I made a mistake, and I reaped the consequences.'

'Don't talk like that,' pleads Sebastian, reaching for her hand. 'If I'd smuggled that fourteen-year-old into my room, would it have been her fault?'

Constance evades his manoeuvre and clenches her fists in her lap. 'I don't like where this conversation is going.'

'I'm sorry,' he says, and Constance rewards him with a forced smile.

When their desserts arrive, they eat in silence, letting the wine and the music heal the rift between them and restore their easy companionship.

It is Constance who speaks first. 'So, are you going to have to... you know, sick up your food afterwards? For your diet?'

Sebastian almost spits out his mouthful and coughs loudly. Around the room, eyes turn to him, some with a glint of recognition. 'I can't believe you've just said that,' he splutters.

'Oh, don't be coy! Don't you all do it in LA?'

He wipes tears from his eyes and struggles to catch his breath. 'No way.' Then he adds with a wink, 'The people I know there don't eat enough to have anything to... bring up.'

Constance looks disappointed. 'Oh.'

'Why? Is that something you do?' asks Sebastian, suddenly suspicious of her thin arms and the clavicles showing at the base of her neck.

'Me? Do I look like I would? No!' She waves her hands for extra effect. 'I don't know why I said that. I'm just nervous.'

'Why? We're all friends here,' he says, scanning the room with good humour.

She pouts, and he loses a moment admiring the curve of her bottom lip he finds eminently kissable.

When she speaks, she pulls him out of his pleasant thoughts. 'I feel you're judging me…' She mouths, 'Because of my sex problem.'

Sebastian's eyes widen. 'You don't have a sex problem. You were raped and now you're traumatised.'

He's not ready for Constance's reaction. The colour drains from her face, and she looks like she is indeed about to be sick. Then her eyes well up.

Sebastian suddenly has a bad feeling about the next few minutes. 'Look, I'm sorry, but we're being honest here,' he says so that his previous words no longer hang between them like a bad smell.

When she recovers the power of speech, he is braced for the worst.

'That wasn't honest. That was brutal. I'm going to leave now. Don't get up.'

She gathers up her silver sparkle clutch and walks away with as much dignity as she can manage. *Don't cry, don't cry, don't you dare cry*, she chants inwardly.

Sebastian watches her as she goes, and his gut wrenches with every receding step.

He drops his head into his hands, but a second later he gets up with a loud scrape of his chair that draws all eyes to him again.

Then he hurries after her.

15

13 FEBRUARY – LANGHAM HOTEL, MARYLEBONE, LONDON, UK

*H*is footsteps follow hers in a staccato of marble down the length of the crowded hotel lobby. He grabs her by the arm, but she shakes him off and continues to walk.

The full impact of the bomb his careless words have detonated is on display across her face. Her features have crumpled in on themselves, her eyebrows and mouth pulled downward into a mask of desolation and distress.

His breath catches in his throat, and he scrambles for something to say.

'Please don't let this be the end. Don't go. Give me a chance to make it up to you. Please.' The veined marbled walls amplify the anxiety in his voice.

'There's nothing more to say,' Constance hisses, struggling to keep her balance on the swirly black and white floor patterns that make her feel dizzy.

'Please give me five minutes. Please, I'm begging you.'

'No.'

She wrenches her arm from his grip and strides towards the

taxi rank outside the hotel. She disappears inside a cab in every way identical to the one that brought them here.

As Sebastian watches its rear lights throw fiery reflections onto the wet pavement, he is spotted by his fans.

They start screaming.

16

14 FEBRUARY – CONSTANCE'S HOUSE, HENLEY-ON-THAMES, UK

A few hours later, Sebastian stands outside Constance's house in the rain, with her monogrammed overnight bag clutched in one hand. With the other, he makes a soft fist and knocks gently at the door.

'Constance. It's me,' he calls sotto voce.

There's no reply, but he keeps calling and knocking.

'I have your things,' he says after a while. 'Your bag – with your favourite pyjamas. It took me half the night to rent a car and find your house. Please, Constance, let me in.'

Nothing.

He is still talking through the door. 'I'm sorry, forgive me. Give me another chance. I'm an idiot. I'm the dumbest, biggest fool that ever was. Don't leave it like this. It was so great meeting you, so unexpected. You're wonderful. Please don't let it end with me saying the most insensitive thing I have ever said. Open the door.'

Finally the door flies open, and Constance stands in the doorway like a vengeful angel in her white Victorian nightie.

She's been crying. Her voice is hoarse and her eyes puffy and red.

'You can't come in,' she says through her teeth. 'The worst thing is you're right. You're right and it hurts. It hurts more now than when it happened. It hurts like crazy. And I cannot bear to see your face right now. So go away!'

As she tries to shut the door, he jams his foot in the gap, but on seeing fear creep onto her face, he feels like a stalker and removes it.

He gives her her bag, and the door is slammed in his face.

He speaks through the brass letterbox. 'Constance, please. I'm not going anywhere. I'm not leaving until you give me a chance to explain.'

He wipes the rain off his face with the back of his hand.

'Explain what?' shouts Constance from behind the door. 'There's nothing to explain. Go away!'

'I'm not leav—'

Constance reopens the door and squares up to Sebastian. 'Do you really want to be one of the men in my life who couldn't take no for an answer?' she says, her tone glacial.

Sebastian recoils as if he's been slapped. Constance stares him down and shuts the door.

'I'm going,' says Sebastian, devastated. 'But please believe me. I've never been sorrier in my twenty-six years of apologising for myself. If I could take it back, I would. I would give anything to make it better.'

'I know,' whispers Constance, feeling more forgiving for the protection of the heavy door. 'I'm sorry too.'

'You have done nothing wrong.' He watches the door for a minute and remembers how he felt when he first went through it yesterday.

This door was opening a new chapter of his life; now it is very firmly shut.

Oblivious to the puddles pock-marking her drive, he staggers back to his rental car – perhaps a Ford, he's not sure.

Through habit, he opens the door to the passenger seat, before going round and finding the right-hand driver's door.

Finally out of the rain, he leans across the steering wheel. For long minutes, he doesn't move.

He's thinking of that bridge with the dark water below. Battersea, she'd called it. He doubts he could find it again, but there's another perfectly good bridge nearby, the one that says 'Welcome to Oxfordshire', although his own invitation has been rescinded.

He knows the way: down the street, across the traffic lights, and turn right. It's not as high as his original suicide spot, but the Thames is strong and can do the same job in Henley as she can in Chelsea.

Unbeknown to him, Constance is watching him through the heavy cream curtains of the upstairs bow window. By the shape his rigid body forms hunched over the dashboard, she knows he's in pain.

She too is in pain, but strangely his feels harder to bear. She has carried her own burden for years and has grown used to it.

It wasn't so much his words she objected to, but the new intimacy they suggested. Her bare feet worry the shag-pile carpet as she hangs on to the double-lined curtains for ineffective moral support.

After much debating, she creeps downstairs and opens the front door.

Barefoot and still in her nightie, she opens the Ford's rear door and gets into the back seat.

Sebastian is watching her over his shoulder, speechless and bewildered.

'Drive,' says Constance.

17

14 FEBRUARY – SEBASTIAN'S RENTAL CAR, HENLEY-ON-THAMES, UK

In a trance, Sebastian starts the engine, but it splutters and stalls. 'Sorry, I'm not very good at driving stick,' he cringes.

He tries again and the engine springs into life. Forgetting to indicate, he reverses out of the drive and onto the deserted tree-lined street.

He joins the silent main road and heads at random towards a stretch of Victorian terraces named after Canadian provinces.

No chance of a late-night cafe around here.

Then he remembers Constance is in her nightie anyway.

'Talk to me,' he says, but she doesn't speak.

'Are you cold?' he asks, and without waiting for an answer, he turns on the heating and passes her his coat. She brings it to her face and bursts into tears.

Sebastian stops at a traffic light. 'Hush, don't cry. Everything's gonna be alright. I'll make it better. Just let me park somewhere.'

'No,' says Constance sharply. 'Don't stop, keep driving. And don't say anything.'

Sebastian finds a route through the one-way system and

twice ends up in front of Manitoba Terrace. The mood in the car is heavy.

'Remind you of anything?' he asks, breaking his vow of silence.

Constance snorts through her tears and pulls the coat closer.

'Yesterday, you made it all better for me; I'm sorry I can't do the same for you,' he says.

In a voice muffled by his thick coat, Constance says, 'You are.'

'What?'

'You are. Making it better.'

Sebastian is incredulous. 'I am?'

'Shut up and drive,' orders Constance.

'Yes, ma'am. Anything you say. Ask me anything, and I'll say yes.' Sebastian takes the car along a streetlamp-lit riverside road.

Ahead of him, the Thames winds deep and dark towards Sonning Bridge, its menace only just masked by the expensive pleasure boats moored to its banks.

After a long silence, Constance speaks again. 'Make love to me.'

Sebastian, who has now left the streetlights and the river behind, slams the brakes and the car screeches to a halt in front of a tiny off-licence. The engine stalls.

'Did you just say what I think you just said?'

'Not tonight. But one day. One day, I will ask you and you will have to say yes. And I don't care if you're married with a gazillion kids. You will have to say yes.'

Sebastian doesn't need to think about it. 'Deal,' he says, without a moment's thought for his hypothetically betrayed wife because he assumes she'll never exist.

'Can you drive me home now please?' sniffs Constance, inserting her arms into the sleeves of his coat.

'Yes, ma'am.'

His hands are trembling as he turns the ignition. The car lunges forward into the night with the gentle rustling of tyres on wet asphalt.

Five seconds later, Sebastian's mind is made up. For once in his life, he will share what he truly feels without second-guessing himself.

His eyes riveted to the glistening road, because seeing her would cause him too much emotion, he says, 'Constance. You're not going to believe me, but I think I love you.'

Pulled out of her own thoughts and unsure of what she just heard, she sits up. 'What?'

Harnessing his courage again, Sebastian replies over his shoulder, 'You're not going to believe me, but I think I love you.'

She wipes her face with the cuff of his coat sleeve and leaves behind a small trail of snot. 'You *think* you love me?'

Still eyes-front, Sebastian replies, 'I'm pretty sure. I'm pretty darn sure you've become the most important person in my life, and I have fallen for you.'

'The most important person in your life?' repeats Constance. Her heart swells, but her mind is determined to burst her bubble before it's had time to inflate. 'That's not saying much. Your life is empty.'

Her words spoken, she flinches at how mean they sound.

But Sebastian, empowered by his newfound frankness, is undeterred. 'That's why I'm sure,' he insists. 'It doesn't feel empty now.'

'Hm, okay. Well, thanks I guess,' says Constance, trying for nonchalance.

Considering thirty minutes ago he was begging at her door,

Sebastian is more than satisfied with her apparently tepid response.

His eyes crease. 'What do you say I stick with you for a while? You know. So that I don't miss *the Call*. I wouldn't want to make you wait... What do you say?'

They exchange smiles in the rear-view mirror.

'Shut up,' says Constance. 'We are *not* having sex.'

18

14 FEBRUARY – LANGHAM HOTEL, MARYLEBONE, LONDON, UK

Sebastian's room is a private suite, with a spacious separate bedroom granted an even roomier appearance by the wall-to-wall, floor-to-ceiling mirrored wardrobe.

The lounge is a showroom of sofas and chairs in elegant cream and whites, livened by tasteful moss-green accents and sepia artist photos framed in black.

To Constance, everything still looks hotel-y. Just bigger and shinier, and even more in-your-face expensive.

The outside world is a long-forgotten memory, reserved for those lesser mortals banished to the other side of thick triple-glazed windows.

It is Constance's first time in a suite, and she is as careful pacing the pristine white carpet as she was crossing puddles in her favourite shoes.

For fear of leaving the smear of her lowly presence on this opulent canvas, she curls up in a fawn velvet armchair.

She's wearing the clothes she changed into after their Henley-by-night drive around – a pair of black jeans, an oversized cowl-neck ivory jumper and cute leopard-print ballet pumps.

She's taken so many deep breaths to calm the nervous thrumming in her body that she feels light-headed and everything looks floaty.

She's decided against make-up. Sebastian might have been misled into believing she was pretty by the hint of blush and eyeshadow she wore for their non-date. She cannot in all conscience let that happen again.

He must be allowed to see exactly what he's letting himself in for.

Unbeknown to her, the dark circles under her eyes accentuate their molten chocolate-ness, and the lips she's been biting for the last few hours look invitingly plumped and red.

She entertains fleeting daydreamy thoughts that Sebastian may take her for a Valentine night-out somewhere fabulous.

Although she cringes at the thought of embracing such blatant commercial un-romanticness, her heart flutters every time she thinks of it.

Mostly, she wishes she were safely home with her slightly tatty but comforting cream furnishings. Alone.

She's checking her Instagram messages whenever her phone pings.

> *FitnessPhilly289* @*Myname.sNotConnie* –
> *How did the date go?*
> *Myname.sNotConnie* @*FitnessPhilly289* –
> *Mixed bag, Philly. I'm not going to lie. No sex though, you'd be proud.*
> *FitnessPhilly289* @*Myname.sNotConnie* – *So proud! Lay down the rules now, darlin', men need them. I'm praying for you.*
> *Myname.sNotConnie* @*FitnessPhilly289* –
> *Huh, thanks I guess.*

After long hours talking to the press, Sebastian comes in, sipping from a large bottle of water.

Constance's stomach does a somersault as she takes in his perfectly tousled hair, his casually stylish outfit and the arrestingly handsome face that's doubled sales for the skincare brand he represents.

For the first time, she sees the movie star. Not the man she bundled into Oggie's backseat. Tongue-tied, she can only stare and forgets how to swallow.

'Hey beautiful, how are you doing?' he croaks, his voice long gone.

Their eyes meet briefly, before Constance's composure melts even further and she fixes her gaze on the book open in her lap. 'Just reading,' she squeaks.

'I'm done now,' he says. 'No one had told Tony about my disappearance, so no hissy fit. It was all fine.' When she doesn't look up, he adds, 'I hope you weren't too bored.'

'No, I was okay.' Her frozen demeanour indicates there is more to it.

He crouches in front of her armchair and rests the tips of his fingers on her knees. This is enough to turn her heart into a stampede. 'Why the small voice?' he asks softly.

Constance risks a glance up. At such close range, the movie-star persona recedes into the background and he's just himself again. She finds some words. 'My book's sad.'

He holds her gaze and waits. After admiring the darker flecks in his green eyes for what she is sure was far too long, Constance whispers. 'It's *The Little Prince*. It's about a boy who's really lonely.'

Sebastian swallows and weighs his next words. 'We know about lonely, don't we?'

She nods, her eyes on the pristine alabaster carpet.

With no sudden move, he stands up and holds out his hand.

After a moment's hesitation, she lays trembling fingers into his palms, and he pulls her to her feet.

This time, he smells of spice and leather, a fragrance she does not recognise. Dark spots dance in front of her downcast eyes.

As she is drawn into his strong arms, willing herself to breathe, the swirl of emotions turns into a churn in her stomach, and her panic rises.

She is pressed against a man she's just met. His scent invades her nostrils, the cloth of his jacket scratches her cheek, and as he rests his chin on the crown of her head, the weight of his expectations fall like a yoke across her shoulders.

He's not like the others, she tells herself. *Nothing to fear.* But he is a man, taller, stronger than her. Alien. She lumbers him with the other men who have trespassed on her boundaries. Especially after Philly's stern warning.

His body heat brings nauseating memories of slicks of sweat and flesh pushing against flesh. Her vision blurs, her stomach contracts, and an icy wave washes over her.

Without warning to him or herself, she hunches over and is sick on the inch-thick carpet. As the retching noise wrenches her back to reality, she looks in horror from the small puddle of vomit to his face.

The acrid smell envelops them both in a cloud of shame and distress.

Sebastian has no idea why this just happened, but he can see she's mortified.

After missing only a beat or two, he winks. 'Where's the sick bucket when you need it?' His professional skills enable him to assume an easy-going expression which is belied by his racing heart.

Constance hides her face in her hands and runs to lock

herself in the white marble bathroom, where the wall-length mirror reflects both her pallor and her humiliation.

She wants to flee, call a cab and go home. But her phone is still on the armchair, too far even for voice-activation.

Of course she could lie, blame last night's food or invent an exotic medical condition. Anything to avoid facing up to the fact that a movie star with panty-dropping looks tried to hug her and her only response was to empty her stomach onto his perfectly pressed trousers.

Her cheeks are white hot with self-loathing.

On the other side of the door, Sebastian, more puzzled than disgusted, lifts the hotel telephone and calls Reception. 'Room 800. My girlfriend's been sick. Can you send someone, please?'

He opens the windows as far as they will go. Not far. Suicide risk.

Then he listens at the bathroom door where he hears nothing but silence.

19

14 FEBRUARY – LANGHAM HOTEL, MARYLEBONE, LONDON UK

*C*onstance is still in the bathroom. The maid has come and gone and Sebastian has replaced Constance in the armchair. He is watching the news on his phone. He hears shuffling behind the locked bathroom door.

'Are you ever going to come out, or am I going to have to feed you your Valentine's dinner through the door?' he asks, careful to add a respectful yet humorous tone to his voice.

Silence from Constance.

'Constance? You alive in there? I get it. It's awkward. I tried to kiss you, and you were sick on my feet...'

'Not *on* your feet,' she corrects grumpily.

'Fine, I only got a couple of splashes on my trousers.'

'Shut up!' she hisses from behind the door.

'Don't make a big deal out of it. Happens to me all the time. Stage fright. Buckets of sick!'

Constance can't help a giggle, but she says sternly, 'Just *stop* talking!'

'I'll shut up if you come out,' he croons.

She thinks about it. 'This will never be mentioned again. Ever. Not a word. And don't look in my direction.'

'Yes ma'am, you've got yourself a deal.'

As she comes out of the bathroom looking extremely sheepish, Sebastian pretends not to notice her.

'I'm going back to my room, okay?'

'Are you sure? We shouldn't leave it like this.'

'I'm sure.'

'See you later?'

She nods and lets herself out of his room. Once she's gone, his face falls. 'There goes Valentine's dinner.'

As she walks towards to the lift to her much-less-posh floor, she swears incoherently under her breath. Streams of curses directed mostly at herself.

> ***Myname.sNotConnie*** *@FitnessPhilly289 –*
> *Disaster, he tried to kiss me and I was sick all over him.*
>
> ***FitnessPhilly289*** *@Myname.sNotConnie –*
> *Bless your heart. That'll sure help him remember his manners next time. Try my 'Banana Ginge' to settle upset stomachs. xoxo*

20
15 FEBRUARY – LANGHAM HOTEL, MARYLEBONE, LONDON, UK

Sebastian has waited for almost an hour for the coast to be clear of Tony and his acolytes.

His hand is shaking on the doorknob, as he unlocks Constance's room with his own magnetic pass.

He's holding a Valentine's card in which he's enclosed two tickets to a sold-out Eminem concert. He has wild hopes that she will let him use the second ticket, if he plays his cards right.

Once inside the bright and luxurious room, upholstered in off-whites that remind him of Constance's house, he looks around, puzzled then concerned. He opens the nearest wardrobe and finds it empty.

Puke-gate suddenly takes a different dimension in his mind. Perhaps she was so repelled by his advances she decided to go home.

His throat narrows. 'Constance?' he calls. 'Constance, you here?'

He opens the second set of wardrobes and sees Constance's clothes and bags hanging neatly.

At the same time, Constance calls back. 'I'm in the bath. What were you saying?'

Sebastian leans his forehead against the bathroom door and says quietly, 'I thought you'd gone.'

'Gone where?'

'Away. Without me.'

'Duh! I just tidied a little. I can't have these poor maids going through my stuff. It's not fair on them. Especially after yesterday.'

Sebastian doesn't reply. He's white as a sheet.

Constance says from the bathroom, 'You thought I'd left you without saying goodbye?'

'Yep.'

There is a silence during which Constance builds a close-enough mental image of his expression based on the tone of his voice. She sighs. 'You want to come in? But you can't look, right. I want your eyes shut *at all times*!'

'Deal.' He enters the room eyes shut, sits on the floor with his back to the tub.

'Are you okay? You look a little pale.'

He shakes his head and acknowledges his feelings more honestly than he has in years. 'I was back on my own. I freaked.'

Constance is touched by his distress, but she says brightly, 'I'm still here! Shall I pinch you?'

Without waiting for his reply, she tries to pinch his shoulder through his form-hugging T-shirt but finds no purchase. 'Gawd! There's nothing to pinch. Just muscle and nothing else. You're spoiling my sport!'

'Sorry ma'am.'

'Yes, too right you're sorry,' she says cheerfully. 'You shouldn't be allowed out in public. You just make everyone else feel inadequate! How do you even get so fit? You must spend your life in the gym!'

'I haven't been for a few days.' The thought of getting back on his punishing exercise schedule is too much to bear. He has a vision of Andy, his personal trainer, shouting down at him between the racks of a bench press, and shudders.

'That's why you're all mopey,' chirps Constance, following her own train of thought. 'You make Eeyore look like an advert for anti-depressants.'

Sebastian manages a pained smile. 'I'm just tired.'

As anyone who has ever been clinically depressed will attest, this is standard speak for 'I feel so bad, I can't even put it into words'.

Constance is not fluent in this particular dialect, but she reads his face and accurately assesses the damage.

'You didn't sleep?'

'Not much.'

'Something wrong?'

'Being back here, with everyone, the press, the bodyguards, Regina, Tony... I feel like I'm dragging my own corpse and some undertaker's made me look presentable, after they've removed all my organs.'

'Okaaay... That does *not* sound too good.'

'Nope.'

Constance takes the matter in her own hands. 'Houston, we have a problem,' she declares. 'I'm coming out of the bath. Shut your eyes! I'll know if you're peeking!'

She gets out of the tub, dripping water everywhere, and wraps herself in the hotel bathrobe which is thrice too big for her.

As she twists her hair into one of the hand towels, she says, 'You're super depressed, and exhausted and all around blah, and we need to do something about it.'

Sebastian shrugs. 'Nothing to do, just wait for it to pass.'

'Has it passed before?'

'I've been all right for the last few days.'

Constance pouts. 'You mean since you nearly jumped off a bridge?'

He manages a pained smile. 'I'm okay when I'm around you.'

'But not right now?'

'Right now I feel I'm going to barf.'

Constance watches him with concern, but then decides to make light of it. 'There's a pattern emerging,' she quips.

He can't match her levity. 'When I saw your stuff gone, I thought I was going to pass out.'

'Well, I'm not gone. Check all the cupboards next time before reaching for the sick bucket.'

Sebastian answers glumly, 'I'm making a note of it.'

More gently than her bright demeanour would suggest, she takes Sebastian's hand and makes a futile attempt at pulling him to his feet. 'Right, that's it. This is your hour of need. Come on, on your feet, mister.'

She pulls ineffectively on his arm. 'Sebastian, I can't carry you. Work with me.'

He gets to his feet and shuffles after her to the bedroom.

She leads him to the mahogany and leather bed where she helps him lie down among the perfectly plumped pillows.

She takes a blanket out of the cupboard and stretches it over him tightly, then sits on the bed next to him.

Sebastian has lost all sense of decorum and curls around her while she rubs his back through the blanket.

'There. You're going to feel better in no time,' says Constance in a sing-song nanny voice he finds oddly comforting. 'Don't worry, I'm here.'

Sebastian circles one arm around her waist. One hand still

stroking his back, she rifles through her handbag until she pulls out a small tube of cream.

She carefully rubs some of it on his wrist, and the smell of lavender spreads across the room. 'Give me your other hand.'

Sebastian stretches his arm at an awkward angle but complies without protest. He watches her in silence for a while then shuts his eyes.

Once she's rubbed cream on his other wrist, she rests her hand protectively on his shoulder and picks up the hotel phone.

'Hi, this is room 320, may I please have some chamomile tea with honey on the side? Yes, thank you.'

She rubs gentle circles on Sebastian's back while he lets out a shaky breath. Without leaving his side, she reaches her phone and starts typing one-handed.

A few minutes later, the maid arrives with tea on a tray.

'Could you do me a big favour?' Constance smiles as she proffers a twenty-pound note. 'Give a message to one of your other guests, Regina Havilland, that she-knows-who is with wrong-side-of-pretty.'

The maid frowns and Constance chuckles. 'I know it's cryptic, but it's a joke. Don't worry, she'll understand.'

The maid gone, Constance pours the fragrant infusion into a delicate porcelain cup and stirs in a generous spoonful of honey, before helping him drink.

'I'm so sorry,' he says. 'I feel like I've been chewed up and spat out.'

'What a lovely image. Be quiet and drink your tea, young sir.'

His cup drained, she pushes him back down gently and rearranges the blanket around his curled body.

'Don't be so nice,' says Sebastian.

She turns his face towards her with an already proprietary

hand. 'Not another word about it. I mean it. Ever,' she replies firmly.

He closes his eyes with a pained look.

Constance makes a second phone call. 'Hi, how quickly could you deliver a 41" by 60" in the 12 lbs to the Langham Hotel? It's an emergency. Any pattern. How much to send someone round with it right now? Oxford Circus, I think. Perfect. Can I pay over the phone? Large tip on arrival.'

Constance reads out her details and ends the call.

Sebastian gives her a wan smile. 'Inches and pounds? Who are you? And what have you done with my girl Constance?'

'When in Rome, speak like the Victorians,' she laughs. 'The website was in imperial.'

'What did you order? Drugs?'

'Ha, ha, not funny! You'll like it, I promise.'

'Are you staying with me?'

'Yes, sir,' she replies, copying his Southern mannerisms.

'This may take a while.'

'It'll take the time it takes, baby,' she says.

'I like it when you call me baby.'

She sticks her tongue out at him. 'You're such a soppy thing.'

'I feel my skin's been peeled off. Everything hurts.'

'I know, baby, I know. You're going to be okay though. Just shut your eyes for a few minutes.'

Sebastian complies. Within seconds, he's asleep and snoring lightly. Constance rubs his back and looks out the window, lost in her thoughts.

A while later, there's a sharp knock at the door. Constance jumps in surprise, quickly checking whether Sebastian has woken up but he's still fast asleep.

Constance answers the door to find a crotchety Regina,

dressed in a turquoise tunic and black boot-cut trousers, with an aggressive slash of red lipstick across her mouth.

'Is he still here?' she shouts.

'Keep your voice down,' whispers Constance. 'He's asleep.'

Regina makes to come in, but Constance blocks her way. 'I'm not letting you in.'

Regina opens her mouth for a vigorous retort, but Constance covers it gently but firmly with her fingertips. Regina is so surprised she stops in her tracks.

No louder than a whisper, Constance says, 'You are *not* going to say what you were about to say. I know you have a pretty good idea of what's happening here right now, and I know you remember what happened a few days ago. So, we're going to do things differently today. You are going to trust me. You're going to go away, and the minute he is back on his feet, I promise you will be the first to know.'

Regina opens her mouth again, but Constance takes her hand and squeezes gently. 'Don't worry, Regina. I've got this under control.'

Regina hovers by the door, undecided. She stares at Constance with wide eyes.

'Could you extend our stay by a couple of days maybe?' asks Constance. 'We could all do with a break. Even you. What do you say? You could find an excuse.'

'Tony will breathe fire.'

'I'm sure you can stand up to him.'

Regina rolls her eyes. 'Two days,' she says begrudgingly. 'Two days, not a minute longer. The *Zombie Attack* promo tour is nowhere near finished. I want him in Oslo by Sunday.'

'Thank you, Regina. Thank you very much. That's very kind.'

'Don't get used to it.' Regina turns on her heels and strides down the corridor, swearing under her breath. Constance watches her go with a pensive look on her face before closing the door quietly.

'Is she gone?' asks Sebastian, his face still in the pillow.

'Yes.' Constance wipes her hand clean of Regina's ruby lipstick.

'I feel so stupid,' he says.

'You're just wrung out.' She sits on the bed and squeezes his shoulder. 'Everything's going to be all right, I promise.'

There's another knock at the door. Sebastian lifts himself off the bed. 'She's back, it was too good to—'

'It's not Regina, it's your present.'

Constance goes to the door and receives a large parcel that she struggles to carry. 'See? It's for you. I'll open it.'

She unwraps a blue duvet with teddy bears and laughs at Sebastian's pinched face. 'What twenty-six-year-old guy doesn't like teddy bears?' she chuckles. 'It's not what it looks like.'

Then she removes the blanket and spreads the teddy duvet over Sebastian.

'Holy Moly, it's heavy,' he says.

'It's a weighted blanket. It helps with anxiety and insomnia. It's like a cocoon. It'll make you feel safe. I had one for a while.'

'Feels surprisingly good.'

'Told you you'd like it.'

'Thank you.'

'You're very welcome. Now, go to sleep or I'm calling Regina.'

'That would just be cruel.'

'Shut up, duvet boy.'

***Myname.sNotConnie** @FitnessPhilly289 –*

Smoothie tips for depression plz? Urgent. IRL Celeb having a breakdown.

FitnessPhilly289 *@Myname.sNotConnie – Berry-tastic, see above.*

Myname.sNotConnie *@FitnessPhilly289 – Ur a mean, mean lady. We tried it. Remember? My taste bugs are still on strike!*

FitnessPhilly289 *@Myname.sNotConnie – *eye roll*, try spinach, banana and walnuts, and a good dose of Jesus.*

Myname.sNotConnie *@FitnessPhilly289 – You do know I'm not a Christian?*

FitnessPhilly289 *@Myname.sNotConnie – Yet. xoxo*

21

20 FEBRUARY – THE HOTEL DE CRILLON, PARIS, FRANCE

In the Parisian elegance of the recently reopened Hotel de Crillon, on Place de la Concorde, Constance is sitting at a desk with her pencils and water colours.

She stares out the window at the obelisk that once marked a temple to one of the Rameseses in the ancient Egyptian city of Luxor (or so she read in the hotel brochure).

Sebastian bursts into the room, and a cloud of nervous energy invades the formerly calm setting.

The leather soles of the handmade shoes he's never worn outdoors before are so smooth he slides across the chevron parquet floor.

She stops him from toppling onto the giant white bed. He kisses the top of her head, and she slaps his firm backside quite hard, as a sort of greeting.

He doesn't react; this is routine for them already.

'Hey Miss Kahlo, how's it going?'

'Would you please refrain from insulting my eyebrows. They frame my face.'

'I meant "how's the artist doing?", you ditz.'

'You do know she and I have nothing in common as artists, right? Or is she the only female artist you've heard of?'

Sebastian mimes strangling her, and she lets her head fall to one side with her pink tongue hanging out of her mouth.

He shrugs off the expensive designer leather jacket he's been lent for the interviews, which falls to the floor.

The graceful nonchalance of the move makes her breath hitch.

Why does he have to so damn sexy?

'Will you tell me how you're doing or is it fixin' to be fifty-questions again?' he asks.

'I'm getting by. Admiring the view mostly.' Although this is not the view she's thinking of, she gestures to the Seine and the Palais Bourbon just outside her window.

This is her first time in Paris, and she is charmed by the perfect orchestration of splendid monuments and the trappings of everyday life.

Even through the insulated windows, she can hear the frequent disagreements between Parisian motorists and their pedestrian counterparts.

Sebastian slouches in an elegantly reupholstered Empire armchair and stretches his long legs towards Constance.

His shirt rides up to reveal the obligatory washboard abs he has no choice but to maintain. Constance swallows hard.

'We could go for a walk instead of lunch. Or eat on the go? Have you been for a stroll yet?'

'I walked from the Tuileries to the Louvre and back this morning. It's so varied. You turn the corner and you walk into a different city altogether. One minute all bustle, next minute all quiet. I'm happy to go out again with you though.'

'Great, where would you like to go?'

'Walk along the Seine. See all the bridges. And the Ile de la Cité. What time do you finish?'

'About half past one. Regina's been great at keeping things on track since you put her in her place the other day.'

'She hates me.'

'She respects you.'

'Only because I can shout back imaginative swear words.'

'Don't underestimate yourself. It's not so common a skill, and you ladies take it all the way up to an art form.'

'Shut up, dick sock,' says Constance with a sweet smile.

'See?' He pinches her nose.

'So, is that half past one French time? GMT? Pacific Standard Time?'

'Half past one and ten inches exactly,' teases Sebastian.

'Paris time?'

'Yes, Paris time, Mrs Marco Polo.'

'Miss Amelia Earhart to you, mister! You can laugh all you like, I have adapted wonderfully to your gypsy lifestyle.'

'*Wonderfully*,' mimics Sebastian. 'I'm still amazed you agreed to come on tour with me. I thought you were going to opt for the no-sex long-distance relationship.'

'It's been fine working on the road, actually. Lots of new stuff to see, the museums, the architecture... I've been able to work on my portfolio. On your dime.'

'Oh, not that again,' cringes Sebastian.

'No. Now you've agreed to live at my house when we're in London instead of some crazily expensive hotel, I'm happy.'

'If you're happy, I'm happy,' says Sebastian tenderly.

'Plus, I got you a little present this morning, to say thank you for everything you do for me.'

His eyes light up, and a beatific smile spreads across his face. 'A present? It's been years since I've been given one!'

Constance's heart misses several beats, but she recovers enough to say, 'What about the weighted blanket?'

His grin broadens even further. 'Things with teddy bears don't count!'

In his boyish excitement, he grabs hold of the glossy white gift bag with the delicate uppercase of the black Chanel brand before she has a chance to hand it to him.

'I walked to their Rue Cambon headquarters shop, it's just round the corner,' she explains.

He unwraps the white and black box with the look of a kid on Christmas morning.

'"Pour Monsieur" is a very old fragrance,' she explains. 'It was designed in 1955, but I sampled all their men's fragrances and this was my favourite.'

'So, from now on, I'll be your favourite smell?' he grins. 'Thank you, Constance. I kinda had it with all the little samples my PA Brandie was throwing my way.'

He spritzes himself from head to toe, and the room fills with the elegant fragrance of chypre and bergamot.

He kisses her hair. 'I'll see you for our lunchtime stroll, but now I have to go.'

He bends to grab a bottle of water from the mini-fridge, affording Constance a peek of his well-muscled behind before exiting the room. 'The Prince of Hell is calling.'

She watches him leave with a look of longing then shakes her thoughts out of her head and goes back to her painting.

22

20 FEBRUARY – LEFT BANK OF THE SEINE, PARIS, FRANCE

The bright spring sun dried the cobbled pavement as Sebastian and Constance walked along the Quai des Tuileries and crossed the Seine on the Pont Royal.

They're now on Quai Voltaire, leaning against the green railings and looking across the river to the wounded Gothic magnificence of Notre Dame, its stained-glass rose window and its vertiginous flying buttress.

The weather is cold and Constance's reddened nose peeks out of her giant scarf. She blows on her fingers to warm them.

'You do look exhausted,' she says conversationally. 'You're going to have to wear "street make-up", like a proper celeb!'

'Ha, ha, hilarious as usual,' mock-laughs Sebastian. 'Tony had a burr in his saddle, and I got stuck in a room with him. My ears still ring.'

Constance purses her lips. She hasn't met Tony yet, but his reputation precedes him.

The mere mention of his name is enough to wipe the otherwise permanent smiles of the Californian girls who work for him.

'Just gotta to hold on a couple more days and we can go house-hunting in LA,' adds Sebastian.

'I'm still not sure LA is right for a good Baptist boy like you, baby.'

'I'm a *lapsed* Baptist, and anyway LA is not one place. It's lots of places. Like what you said of Paris. Turn the corner and it's a different environment. It's just much more stretched out. There will be a place that's right for us.'

'I am quite looking forward to seeing it,' admits Constance.

'Looking forward to watching people "sick up" their food on the sidewalks?'

'Stop teasing me! I only said that because I was nervous. How many times?'

Sebastian tries to keep a straight face. 'I also worry about you and these puny, not-quite-long-enough feet and inches.'

Constance grins and her pink nose wrinkles in a way Sebastian finds adorable. 'And my weight is going to start with *one hundred*!' she whines.

But she suddenly becomes upbeat and adds, 'I'm going to set up an online petition to change weight units for American women. To improve the morale of the nation.' She lays out the words with her hands in the air. 'Free! *Lose 100 lbs with one simple signature!*'

'You're going to fit right in!' chuckles Sebastian in a low vibrato that gives Constance goosebumps.

Doing her best to keep her tone casual, she replies, 'I can't believe how easily I've taken to following you around. I suppose we're both good at pretending to be what we're not. Only you get paid for it.'

'But you're not doing that any more, are you? Pretending to be what you're not?'

'Not with you.'

'Good. Because I was able to be myself with you right from the start. When we met, it was the first time in years that what I felt inside showed on the outside.'

'What about with Tony? You've known him for years.'

'Almost ten years.'

'How did you meet?'

'At a gym near Memphis when I was seventeen.'

'A gym? Already making everyone feel inadequate? You started young.'

'Worked. Not worked *out*.' He grins. 'My parents and grandma were already dead, and I sometimes needed the extra cash when my lawn-moving business wasn't doing well. I was just a lanky, shy teenager. My whole family were staunch Evangelicals, and I had always been home-schooled, so I had no friends. They were strong in their faith that dating was an open door for the Devil and pre-marital sex worse than death, so no girlfriends either.'

'Pre-marital sex never did me much good,' says Constance. 'But still better than popping my clogs.'

'Popping your what? Like your cherry?'

'No, my *clogs*. Like wooden shoes. It means dying. Anyway, you were saying they didn't believe in dating.'

'They very much didn't, and "courtship" was reserved for people you wanted to marry, provided all kinds of purity standards were adhered to. My brother Joe had drunk the Baptist Kool-Aid. I wasn't a good-enough Christian for him, and boy did he not let me forget it.'

'Sounds tough.'

'It was. But Tony saw something in me. At first, meeting him was like a ray of sun shining through the clouds. He was this big-shot Hollywood guy, just visiting some family in my town. He noticed me. He encouraged me. He said, "If you look up from your feet long enough, girls will realise what a pretty face you've got."'

Constance grins. 'That worked out well enough.'

'I would go to the gym even when it wasn't my shift hoping to bump into him. He would always smile and slap me on the back. "There's hope for you still, son, don't give up." We took to working out together. He would buy me a drink at the juice bar, and he would ask me about my sad life story. At first, I thought he was gay and trying to seduce me, but he was with a different girl every time, and he obviously wasn't into me that way. When he heard I was a virgin, he surprised me with a visit to this swanky massage parlour that wasn't so swanky they'd never heard of happy endings.'

Constance gives him a sidelong glance and frowns slightly.

Sebastian looks pained for a second then continues his story, if a bit defensively.

'I know why you think it's weird and disgusting, but at the time, I was grateful and elated and I pushed all thoughts on how suspicious it was to the side. When he invited me to come to LA with him to hang out a bit, "have a good time, meet some girls", I left a note for Joe in his letterbox and didn't look back. My brother was livid.'

'What happened when you got to LA?'

'He started drip-feeding me these ideas about doing some headshots and going to auditions "just for a bit of fun". He kept saying I was so handsome, they would sign me there and then. But the more he complimented me and pushed me, the more I was losing what little confidence I had.

'The first time I did go to an audition for a microscopic part in a TV pilot, Tony had to drag me out of the car. I landed in a heap on the sidewalk, people stared and I was so mortified I went into the building just to hide. Someone asked me my name and made me join the line. I looked at my feet the whole time, but at the end of the day they picked me.'

Constance listens intently.

'When I went back to Tony's, he welcomed me like an Oscar winner and threw a party. He was so happy.'

'What show was that? Would I have seen it?'

'No, it never got picked up. It was a Zombie story, like *The Walking Dead*, but not quite as good.'

'So, what happened next?'

'The casting director put me forward for a small part in an action movie he was working on. That was *Judge*. Then they did *Judge II* and the small part got upgraded to a supporting role of the trusty sidekick.

'By that time, I'd taken some acting classes and put in some serious time in the gym. Tony kept saying he had me exactly where he wanted me. He said he was producing an independent sci-fi thriller I would be right for if I could squeeze my way past the audition. They cast me and we made *Highway Man*. No one saw it coming.

'Within the first two weeks of opening, we all knew we were sitting on a pot of gold. That's when Tony went full-blown crazy. He harassed me and threatened me for days until I finally signed a contract with him. It includes a gigantic power of attorney, so now he basically owns me. It's like a return to the star system, when the studios controlled the actors like puppets.'

'That sounds awful.'

'You have no idea.'

'How does Regina get on with Tony?'

'All right I suppose. They argue all the time, but it's mostly for show. I can't even bear to think about the two of them truly pitted against each other.'

'You said Regina wasn't your first agent. You had a

different one before.'

'Yes. Jana was one of Tony's "friends". The Darth Maul to his Sidious.'

'I've no idea what you've just said.'

'I thought you were a *Star Wars* fan.'

'No, I just like C3PO.'

'Anyway. She was Tony's apprentice. His protégé. But at some point, they had a disagreement and I took the opportunity to hire my own agent. Tony was furious, but I'd signed the contract with Regina, and it was too late. He was on my back for weeks after that, berating me in front of everyone.'

'What did Regina make of it?'

'They've known each other for years. She knows exactly what he is and what he does.'

'Do you think he's scared of her?'

'He has nothing but contempt for her. He believes she can't be good at her job because she's fat. He calls her Jabba. Another *Star Wars* reference.'

'So, you have separate contracts: one with Tony, one with Regina.'

'Then I signed another contract with Tony before we started *Fear in the Andes*. He said to keep it on the down low because Regina would want a share but she had no right to it. When she found out, she broke a whole glass cabinet.'

'What a mess. We need a lawyer. Or maybe the Chinese Triads.'

'Or Obi-wan Kenobi…'

Constance hums the theme tune to Star Wars.

'See, you got that geek reference, there's hope for you!'

He cups her chin with a gentle hand and smoothes her hair. A delicious flutter rises from her core.

They smile at each other, a smile that is becoming a pillar of their budding relationship. A smile that says 'you and me against the world', and they both have butterflies in their stomachs when their gazes return to the green waters of the Seine below.

23

2 MARCH – HOTEL ADLON KEMPINSKI, UNTER DEN LINDEN, BERLIN, GERMANY

Constance enters the elegant hotel room with a handful of shopping bags.

Sebastian is lying on the shiny damask sofa, watching the news, after three hours of interviews with the longest queue of journalists he'd ever seen.

He says matter-of-factly, 'We gonna need another room to keep your stuff.'

'It's just one outfit.'

He opens incredulous eyes. 'Like full ski gear?'

'It's a dress for tonight, numbnut.'

'Are we going out?'

'I got a call from Tony earlier, and he asked me to come and see him in his room tonight. I really don't want to meet him, and I figure it's best if neither of us can be found in the hotel. So, to save me from the Californian Ogre, you're taking me out somewhere nice.'

'Good call. Where do you want to go?'

'That's your problem. Call the concierge.'

'Yes ma'am.'

Constance disappears into the bathroom with most of her bags.

Sebastian stirs himself off the sofa only to slump on the bed with the telephone.

He peeks into one of the bags Constance left behind and unwraps a deep burgundy silk dress. He holds it out with an appraising look and ponders what kind of an evening would suit a dress like that. Then folds it back into the layers of tissue paper.

Sebastian's tiredness shows in his tone. 'Concierge? I need two tickets for a classy but wacky cabaret-style show. Tonight. Drag? Fine. And a table for two in a quiet, discreet restaurant afterwards. Any cuisine. Thanks. I owe you, man. Hang on! $200 for you, if you tell absolutely no one where we are.'

'No one?' asks the concierge, who obviously has had experience of dealing with Tony.

'$300.'

'Yes, sir. As you wish.'

24
2 MARCH – POTSDAMER STRASSE, BERLIN, GERMANY

Constance and Sebastian are walking out of the Vaudeville Variety cabaret show at the Berlin Wintergarten theatre.

She is wearing her burgundy dress, a matching shawl and vertiginous heels that cut their height difference in half. She is hanging on to his arm as she negotiates the cobbled surface of the pavement.

His flexing biceps combined with a whiff of 'Pour Monsieur' make her feel lightheaded. He is wearing a baseball cap and a huge scarf over his dark suit.

'That was just so much fun! Such a hoot. I loved it!' Constance gushes.

'I'm happy you're happy.'

'Did you hate it?'

'No, I thought it was very theatrical and entertaining.'

'Where to next?' Constance asks excitedly.

'Dinner. Gastro-pub. Responsibly sourced vegetables.'

'What on earth could that be? Do they talk to them nicely before picking them?'

'We're gonna find out!' he laughs. 'Are you okay in these shoes?'

The wet pavement reflects the stars as well as the street lamps in a perfect nightscape of far and near.

'Absolutely! I don't know what you mean.' Just as she speaks, she trips and spreads her arms to keep her balance.

'Really? I'm practically carrying you,' notes Sebastian.

'I can very well walk on my own, thank-you-very-much!'

'Saved by the bell,' says Sebastian. 'We're here.' As they enter the tiny restaurant, he eyes the rustic decor suspiciously.

They do look out of place in their evening clothes, but Constance doesn't seem to notice. They are led to a minuscule table at the back of the room.

'This is different.' Sebastian comments dubiously. He expects to be recognised in a matter of seconds in such a small place.

'I like it, it's cute!' insists Constance. 'I bet you the food is delicious. This is Berlin, if it wasn't nice, they wouldn't have lasted a month. Don't be such a grouch!'

Sebastian is not in the least reassured, but he can't face going back to the hotel and dealing with Tony, nor does he fancy walking the streets surreptitiously carrying Constance while they search on foot for a more appropriate venue.

As he often does, he decides to indulge her, but not without pointing out the cavalier way in which she mostly addresses him. 'All my fangirls would get heart attacks if they heard how you talk to me.'

Constance's eyes twinkle with mirth. 'Oooh Seb, you're so strong, you're so *hot,* sign my tits!'

He laughs. '*I* would have heart attack if you spoke to me like that!'

Constance cocks her head coquettishly. 'In a good way?'

He chuckles. 'Yes, I think so! But not all the time, mind you.'

'Just like role-play things, between the naughty nurse and the school mistress?'

'I'm starting to like where this conversation is going.'

'Dream on, my friend!' she teases.

The waiter arrives and they order their food, giggling like children and presenting elaborate condolences to their imaginary vegetable dishes.

25

2 MARCH – HOTEL ADLON KEMPINSKI, UNTER DEN LINDEN, BERLIN, GERMANY

Constance is carrying her shoes and walking gingerly as if on broken glass. Sebastian is following behind her, enjoying her discomfort with a cheeky smile on his face.

'I'm going to use the bathroom for a second,' she says.

Sebastian hears the shower and peers through the open door. Constance is sitting on the edge of the large bathtub running cold water on her legs and feet.

He leans against the door frame casually. 'One of the first thing I noticed about you, apart from your breasts peeking through your buttonless shirt, was your little-girl shoes and how you were so careful of them on the wet pavement. It was so sweet. Something simple like that. I was so desperate and so sick of everything, and you were so careful not to get your shoes wet. It warmed my heart.'

Constance does not answer, but she smiles lovingly. 'Do you ever feel desperate like that still?' she asks after a pause. 'Between Zeus and Medusa, none could blame you.'

'When I think about Tony, how he controls me, I still feel trapped and discouraged. But since I've been with you, it's like all the colours have come back into my life.'

'You would tell me if things got bad again, wouldn't you?'

Sebastian nods earnestly.

'You wouldn't have some silly ideas about sparing me to stop me from worrying?'

'You're the strongest person I know. If I'm ever in trouble, I'm coming straight to you,' he lies smoothly, because he doesn't want the argument that will follow if he tells her the truth.

He's been working on a plan to free himself from Tony for days yet has hit nothing but dead ends.

He hasn't yet found a single lawyer prepared to look into his business relationship with his mentor. They're all afraid to rock the boat, a fear that Sebastian can well understand.

Before meeting Constance, he used to feel that fear too.

'Promise?' she asks.

Sebastian nods again gravely.

'Good. Hmm, Sebastian...?'

He pretends to be worried. 'Oh Lord, here we go.'

'Would you rub my feet?' She extends a bare leg towards him and he seizes it without hesitation.

She shivers at his touch, and he wonders whether the thrill that flashes through him will ever disappear.

'I was bracing myself for worse!' he says. 'I'm quaking in my boots when you call me Sebastian.'

'I always call you Sebastian.'

'And I spend my life in constant fear!' he laughs.

He carries her to the bed and starts massaging her left foot, which is bleeding at the toes and heel. 'Is that okay? Not too sore?'

Constance doesn't answer; she is watching him with a serious look on her face.

When he meets her eyes, he tries to read the situation.

Before he can come to any conclusion, she launches herself

at him, grabs his shirt and pulls him onto the bed where he falls half on top of her.

He braces himself not to crush her underneath him, but she pulls him closer. He rests on his forearms on either side of her face. 'I'm not too heavy?'

'I like your weight,' she whispers.

Sebastian grins. 'It does start with a hundred.'

'It's fine, stop worrying.'

Sebastian drops his full weight on her with a smile. She gasps audibly and disappears under him. 'What are you saying down there?' he asks playfully.

Constance can be heard saying 'You're crushing me!' in a muffled voice. He rolls off her with a laugh.

She is looking dishevelled and red-faced. She sits up and huffs. 'Can you undo my dress?'

Sebastian slides down the zip and eases the fabric off her shoulders. She gets up and walks slowly towards the bathroom, hips swaying.

Sebastian folds up his trousers and puts his shirt in the laundry bag with his socks.

There is a knock at the door, and Tony's voice breaks the silence. 'Constance?' he calls far too loud. 'Hey, Connie. Come and play, you British floozy.'

He's slurring his words. Sebastian softly steps towards the door and locks it. 'Come on Seb, sharing is caring!'

Soon, Tony is shouting torrents of insults through the door. Sebastian hopes against all hope that Constance can't hear him from the bathroom.

The room door shakes on its hinges. Then a silence. 'I've got your money, you little piece of shit,' spits Tony through the door.

Sebastian pulls on a T-shirt and forlornly watches the stars out of the window.

26

1 APRIL – SUNSET MARQUIS, WEST HOLLYWOOD, LOS ANGELES, CALIFORNIA, USA

Myname.sNotConnie @FitnessPhilly289 – Just landed in LA! Smoothie heaven. Thinking of you. xx

FitnessPhilly289 @Myname.sNotConnie – How did IRL Celeb recover from nervous exhaustion?

Myname.sNotConnie @FitnessPhilly289 – TLC and smoothies, what else?

FitnessPhilly289 @Myname.sNotConnie – TLC with knickers on I hope…

Myname.sNotConnie @FitnessPhilly289 – Yes, ma'am.

FitnessPhilly289 @Myname.sNotConnie – Praise the Lord! Now, for jet lag u must hydrate, kefir, pear, banana and cherry juice. xoxo

Sebastian chose a two-bedroom villa so Constance could be with him without sharing his bed. He thinks one-bed hotel rooms are still quite far down the line, and his policy is to never rush Constance into premature intimacy.

She is nervous enough about being at such close quarters and dreads the awkwardness of saying goodnight and retiring into her own bedroom.

When they enter the villa, Constance looks around in amazement at the luxurious – if garish – interior.

Royal blue velvet cushions line the mustard yellow sofas, and gold curtains pool onto the blindingly polished mahogany floorboards.

A riot of palm trees in various sizes gives a chic inside-outside twist to the decor, and the sun loungers on their private terrace match the sitting-room sofas.

The room could not look more different from Constance's cream-of-chicken-soup colour palette.

It is an equally far cry from the muted tones of the hotel suites they've been staying in during the last few weeks. London, Copenhagen, Paris, Moscow, Berlin… different cities, same elegant whites and greys everywhere.

Except LA. Here, the decor brings to mind an exotic fruit salad, drenched in sunshine.

Sebastian, who's stayed at the Marquis countless times before, throws himself face down on the bed in the nearest room, leaving Constance free to explore and rummage.

She tracks down the XXXL ultra-white bathrobe and massive matching slippers that she hugs in delight but will obviously never wear.

She peruses the promotional reading material on the desk, with its promises of Disneyland trips, kite-surfing and Hollywood guided tours.

The bed is glorious – medium-hard, memory foam, pristine thick organic cotton sheets, and she christens it with several snow-angel moves.

After perusing the contents of her own brightly coloured bathroom, Constance brushes her teeth.

As she stares at herself in the gigantic mirror, her features stretch into a mischievous expression that would speed up Sebastian's pulse if only he could see it.

Disney leaflets, snow-angels and tiny shampoo bottles have woken up her silly inner child, which in turn has turbo-charged her never-too-far spontaneity.

Affecting distress, she rushes back into his room. 'Ohmygod, ohmygod, Seb! Ohmygod,' she says in one single breath.

Immediately, he forgets how tired he is and lifts himself off the bed. The concern on his face gives her pause, but she is washed away by a wave of giddiness and carries on regardless.

She grabs his arm, and he sits up, encircling her waist between his now trembling hands.

'What? What's wrong?' he stutters.

'I'm pregnant,' she whispers, unable to meet his eyes.

She doesn't see his face crumple, but when he next speaks his voice tells her what she has done.

He sounds like he's speaking from the bottom of a well. 'Is it Mark's?'

She's surprised he even remembers Mark's name, but in dogged pursuit of her 'good joke', she counts to three before declaring, 'April Fool!'

Silence ensues.

Only now does she watch his reaction, a mix of confusion, distress, and anger. Her throat is suddenly too tight to swallow, and her stomach twists.

She freezes the cheerful expression on her face, hoping this will miraculously deflect his anger. She has time to wonder whether he will send her home before he speaks again.

'Well,' he says eventually. 'I'm not sure that was entirely funny. I was just envisaging adopting another man's child.'

Constance already knows him enough to realise she has flounced over a line no well-brought-up Southern Baptist boy likes to see trampled.

Not that many men would find the joke funny, especially given the particular circumstances of their relationship.

Although aware she's been particularly insensitive and crass, she chalks it up to her sense of humour being stuck several time zones behind.

To give Constance credit where it is due, her back-pedalling is as vigorous as it is unacknowledged. It starts with a jolly 'ta-da' accompanied by frantic jazz-hands.

As Sebastian's face is still white and tense, Constance plays her joker and throws herself on top of him, her front to his back, to dispel the unease.

He grunts under her weight.

'Oh, shut up, nitwit. I'm not that heavy!' she trills.

Sebastian huffs into the gigantic pillow, 'Have a hundred pounds land on *your* back, and see how you like it!'

'I'm not a hundred anything,' Constance reminds him coquettishly.

Despite her faked insouciance, Sebastian has clearly received the message that she is super-embarrassed by her faux-pas.

He doesn't have the heart to rub her nose in it, so he swallows his ill-humour and allows the conversation to move on from April Fools and alleged pregnancies.

'So, the petition's already started, is it? Great.' He yawns into the pillow. 'I'm plumb tired.'

Constance has become accustomed to the weird and wonderful expressions that come out of his mouth when he's not in A-lister mode.

She only briefly wonders why a 'plum' should be tired but decides this is not the time to pick holes in his vocabulary.

'I had a decent sleep,' she says. 'You shouldn't have been watching all those movies on the way over.'

'Just checking out the competition. I'm an out-of-work actor now the promo tour is over.'

'No green-light yet on the Canadian log cabin getaway and fox hats for two?'

'They're not even foxes!' he laughs.

'No? So what are they then, mister expert?'

'I dunno, not foxes.'

'We could go on a field trip and check it out.'

'We've just made it here. I'm jet-lagged, I'm not going anywhere. I want to sleep for a hundred years.'

Privately relieved the banter between them has returned to its usual silly groove, she says in a mock Carpathian accent, 'Shall I ready your coffin, my lord?'

'Yes, and send in a few virgins. I need a snack.'

He only means to be funny and expand on her Dracula impression, but despite her residual sheepishness, Constance is a full-time feminist and takes issue with his off-the-cuff remark.

'What is it with men and virgins? You want innocent, pure young girls so that you can turn them into sluts and go deflower the next one?'

Sebastian throws Constance a swift look over his shoulder, gauging her mood.

Having chosen his angle, and because she owes him an offensive remark, he goes for a put-upon look.

'Don't you start feminazi-ing me! It's too early, and I'm tired,' he whines.

'But you have to admit it sets some pretty impossible standards.'

Sebastian bucks up and throws her off. 'Let's talk about impossible standards. Women want a gentleman who helps with the dishes, but also a stud in the bedroom. A sensitive guy who can defend them by throwing punches around.'

'You're getting off lightly,' counters Constance. 'I'm not asking you for any of that.'

Sebastian smirks. 'I'm the luckiest man in the world! Pregnancy jokes? Simply hilarious.'

Instead of apologising, she grins. 'Shut up, sick bucket.'

Sebastian doesn't miss a beat. 'Did you notice there's one in the bathroom?'

Constance's jaw drops before she realises he's joking. She slaps him gently round the back of the head.

'Stop hitting me!' Sebastian rubs his skull and rakes his rusty hair back into place.

'You love it,' says Constance. He rolls his eyes, but she's already busy checking her phone to pull up Philly's jet-lag-busting recipe. Surely, they can get it from room-service.

Just as Constance picks up the peacock blue hotel phone, Regina strides in without knocking. She's wearing a flowing white dress with a short black jacket and a red scarf.

'Talking of Dracula,' says Constance testily.

Sebastian jumps off the bed. 'How do you even have the key to this place?'

Regina straightens her back and drapes herself in her professional dignity. 'It's my job! In case you two lovebirds decide to snort yourselves stupid and I have to mop up the mess.'

'By the way, the sick bucket is in the bathroom,' sniggers Constance for Sebastian's amusement.

He chuckles, and Regina gives him a withering look. 'How old are you? Twelve? I've had more professional child-actors. Right, your press thing is in an hour. If you want to work again in this town, you'll sweet-talk that bitch from the LA Time

Blog crap, she's screwing that producer. You know, the *Bleed you dry* guy.'

'You couldn't make it up if you tried.' Constance, her eyes to the ceiling.

Regina notices. 'Now you're here among the barbarians, you're going to have to look up from your Dickens, *dahling*!' She mimics Constance's posh English accent.

'Oh, you're ready for the Royal Shakespeare Company!' Constance retaliates. 'Look how proper our *liddle* girl talks,' she says to Sebastian.

He steps in between them; he towers over Constance, but in her heels Regina is just as tall as he is. 'Okay, ladies, Jell-O fight's over. Regina, don't burst in on us again or I'll have hotel security take your pass. And you, Constance, don't rile her up.'

'If you're not happy, you can take it up with Tony, you dipshit,' says Regina as she leaves.

Constance says, 'Bite me,' under her breath.

Sebastian rolls his eyes again.

27

1 APRIL – SUNSET MARQUIS, WEST HOLLYWOOD, LOS ANGELES, CALIFORNIA, USA

The sun is setting over LA and dyeing everything a dusty pink.

Sebastian and Constance have just woken from a jet-lag-busting nap. He's in the shower.

Constance is unpacking her case into one of the cupboards while messaging Philly.

> *Myname.sNotConnie @FitnessPhilly289 – Jet lag... gah!*
> *FitnessPhilly289 @Myname.sNotConnie – Bless your heart, keep hydrating, darlin'. Just fruit goodness. Anything that's ever been on a tree branch will do.*

The room door opens slowly. Constance turns expecting to see Regina, but an insult dies on her lips as a man in late middle-age dressed as a twenty-year-old model strides in.

Without speaking, he proffers a hairy-knuckled hand while stepping deep into Constance's English-sized personal space.

She tries to recoil but hits her head on the cupboard shelf. Resigned, she shakes his hand. It is unusually warm.

'I'm Tony,' he declares with the same solemnity he would swear an oath on the Bible to tell nothing but the truth. His voice is high and musical, at odds with his macho-man appearance.

He smells of whisky.

'Hello, Mr Da Ricci,' she manages, hoping to use his surname as a shield against his over-familiarity. It doesn't work. He scrutinises her face with naked curiosity.

'Hm, I'm Constance. Constance Wilkinson,' she adds.

'I know who you are. And I know what you did,' he says.

His eyes narrow and Constance swallows a sudden lump in her throat.

Three seconds too late, he adds a perfunctory smile to his sentence. 'You protected my investment in our fragile young Seb. You did me a good turn.'

He taps the side of his nose. 'You have credit in my ledger, for now.' He takes her chin between his hot fingers. 'And would you look at that? Haven't you got an interesting face?'

She's too stunned to speak and wonders whether he will check her teeth next.

When he leads her by the hips to sit atop the desk, she lets him. 'So tell me about you,' he says, peering into her face.

Hot and cold waves travel up and down her body in erratic patterns, like a freakish weather event, a sandstorm colliding into a blizzard. 'Not much to say,' she mumbles.

'Speak up, I can't hear you.' He cups his ear and brings it so close to her face, she can smell his earwax over the stink of alcohol.

'I'm an illustrator for children's books, and I'm from a little town near London,' she says in the firmest voice she can muster.

'Henley-on-Thames, of Royal Regatta fame.'

Constance's eyes widen in shock. 'Yes, that's right.'

He takes a step back; she lets out a shaky breath. 'But there must be a bit more to you if you've managed to bag a Hollywood star!'

Constance shudders at the compliment-slash-insult and tries to stand her ground. 'No, not really.' With a supreme effort of will, she meets his bloodshot eyes.

In a split second, he's in her space again. 'Oh, but you do have something,' he declares. 'A reticence, a British reserve. Almost a fear. How very appealing.'

He steps back again; she takes a shaky breath.

'You make a beautiful couple, you and Seb. Opposites attract etc.' He bares his top teeth in a masquerade of a smile and brings his face close to hers.

She finally grasps why his back-and-forth footwork is so unsettling. It reminds her of the reeling of a fish.

He lets her dangle on his hook for a few excruciating seconds. 'But don't let it go to your head,' he murmurs. 'My boy is going places.'

His eyes deep in hers, he raps his knuckles on her skull twice, and she uses all her self-control not to recoil.

She reminds herself this man, however repugnant, is key to Sebastian's career, but her temper KO's her better judgement in a single round.

Tony's gauntlet has been flung in her face, and before she can stop herself she picks it up.

She pushes away from the desk where he perched her and stands to her full height.

Although she reaches no further than his solar plexus, she looks him square in the face. 'May I assure you, Mr Da Ricci, I quite understand the situation,' she says in the same tone her mother uses for hired help, flinging her crisp vowels at him like so many daggers of superior breeding.

He pauses to read her face, and a spark of excitement lights his cold eyes.

He opens his mouth to retort but is interrupted by Sebastian coming out of the bathroom with only a towel around his waist.

'Ay, Tony, howz at goin'?' he says, with a larger-than-life Southern twang Constance's never heard before.

For a minute, both men stare at each other. Constance keeps her schoolmarmish expression in place, but her mouth turns dry.

'Heard about your London escapade,' Tony replies eventually.

Sebastian says nothing, but he holds Tony's gaze.

'Oh, you're going try to stare Daddy down to impress the new girl here?' Tony taunts.

'No,' says Sebastian.

'Shame. She needs to know what a spineless little shit she's fucking.'

Constance freezes in place like a deer in the chilly headlight of menace. She wants to rush to Sebastian's defence, but she can't find the words.

For what seems a lifetime, no one speaks. Sebastian stands in front of Tony, silent and motionless.

It is the producer who speaks first. 'I don't want to embarrass you in front of your girlfriend. We'll talk later. Come to my suite at six.'

He turns and before she can stop him kisses Constance on the cheek – not an air kiss, a wet lips one – then leaves without bothering to close the door.

Constance and Sebastian exchange a look. 'Welcome to Hollywood,' he says wryly.

'Goodness, he's a proper Bluebeard,' she exclaims, her voice unsteady. 'How many dead wives does *he* keep in his cellar?'

'Probably couldn't even be bothered to marry them. He's not big on paper trail.'

She does a little jig to shakes off the nefarious impression Tony made on her. It doesn't work.

When she looks to Sebastian for comfort, he is white as a hotel sheet. 'I'm sorry you had to meet him alone. I wasn't there for you,' he says.

She locks her fear and disgust in the mental vault where she keeps her twenty-five years' worth of traumatic incidents and focuses on getting him out of his mood pronto.

'What time is it?' she asks.

'Three p.m., Pacific Time.'

'Three hours until you face "Ronnie Kray" there, whatever his name was again,' Constance says, although she will never forget Tony or his name.

She knows denying people their names helps keep at bay the fear they inspire.

'I won't go,' says Sebastian in a forced casual tone.

'What? Don't you have to?'

'You only need to keep the appointment if it comes through a PA. He'll probably be too busy haranguing someone else by six o'clock to remember I even exist.'

28

1 APRIL – SUNSET MARQUIS, WEST HOLLYWOOD, LOS ANGELES, CALIFORNIA, USA

Tony's toxic aura is still floating in the room, but Sebastian has a range of strategies to deal with his noxious handler. He rings room-service for a bottle of Napa Valley Chardonnay and puts his clothes on.

Constance unfortunately has no such coping mechanisms in her armoury. She did put a brave face on it, but Tony is the embodiment of everything she fears.

His violations of her personal space, unwanted sexual attention, cruel contempt, and the menace in his cold eyes have made her feel more even vulnerable than the throng of press photographers and fans that follow them around the world.

She's still too shocked to even admire Sebastian's sculpted chest, where light brown hair is starting to regrow after a ruthless campaign of waxing for last week's *Vogue* photoshoot.

Constance jumps in the shower to wash off the memory of Tony's hands and lips. She scrubs at her skin until it hurts and sheds furious tears under the rainfall shower. Then she rubs herself dry as if she were sanding a piece of wood, in rough careless motions.

Once her skin is red and raw, she slips into a white dress

embroidered with tiny blue flowers, before joining Sebastian on the private terrace.

They settle on the pristine wooden sun loungers, a glass of perfectly chilled white wine in hand. A few sips later, Constance feels her shoulders relax a fraction, but the dark cloud left behind by Tony is far from dispelled.

The sky is the same royal blue as the velvet cushions in the lounge, and Constance revises her appreciation of the villa's colour scheme.

With its violently green palm trees and the carnival of brightly coloured flowers in hues of pinks, reds and oranges dotting kerbs and gardens, LA does look like a fruit salad.

'This is the life!' she gushes, a little over-enthusiastically to make up for the memory of Tony still hovering between them.

'Pretty cool I get to share it with a pretty cool girl.' Some tightness remains around Sebastian's closed eyelids, and Constance takes the opportunity to check him out.

He's wearing a pair of light blue shorts that reminds Constance of a James Bond movie she went to see once. The waistband stops just below the bottom two of his six-pack.

No need for a photo-finish, Sebastian wears it better.

To manage the fluttering in her stomach, she flexes her toes and makes a mental note to get a pedicure at the first opportunity.

As she chases away thoughts of Sebastian's god-bod, memories of her encounter with Tony flood back.

'So, did you do a good job of sucking up to that blogger?' she asks for something to say.

'I'm a professional,' Sebastian smirks.

Constance is unable to control her jealousy. 'Would she have slept with you, do you think?'

Sebastian is matter-of-fact. 'Probably. I'm a lot better looking than the *Bleed You Dry* guy.'

'I still can't believe that's an actual movie title. Did you want to sleep with her?'

Sebastian turns to look at her. 'No. Now that I've met you, the only person I want to sleep with is you.'

And just like this the weight of the elephant in the room lands on Constance's chest. 'That doesn't make me feel any better,' she huffs.

He sits up to look at her face. 'What makes you feel bad in the first place?'

'You know what,' she whispers. 'The no-sex.'

He strokes the tip of her nose. 'Don't feel bad for me. It's easier for me to hear you say no, than for you to have no choice but to say no.'

'I have a choice, I can say yes.'

He shakes his head. 'You've been down that road; you know where it leads. And I know it too. So, we're not going that way.'

Constance fixes her gaze on the green tangle of palm trees that gives the villa the privacy Sebastian paid extra for.

All of a sudden, the colours do not seem as cheerful and bright as before. 'I'm scared that if we try it will be awful. That would destroy me.'

'It would do me no good either. Hence, we're not having sex.'

'But how long can you wait?'

'As long as it takes.'

'You're just saying that. What if it takes five years?' Constance drops her face into her hands.

'It's not going to take that long.'

'How do you *know*? You can't know that!' Her voice rises

with her anger, and her cheeks flush like a blood stain on cream silk.

'I've been watching you,' says Sebastian. 'I watch you all the time.'

Constance's temper flares. 'And what do you conclude, Doctor?'

'You're growing more comfortable with me every day,' he replies patiently.

'But not in a sex way,' she counters.

'Everything is about sex.' Sebastian says those four words unaware he is opening flood gates he won't be able to close.

Constance slams her hand on the table separating their loungers and knocks her glass over. The liquid gold of the Chardonnay splashes to the floor.

She stands, hands on her hips. 'That's just great,' she shouts. 'So, you've been watching me like a bloody stalker, and thinking about sex all the time!'

Sebastian is going through his shortlist of possible responses, but nothing comes to mind that wouldn't simply fan the flames.

She takes his silence for an acknowledgement of guilt.

He's more like that sleazebag than I thought. I can't be dealing with this!

She turns her anger up a notch. '*Everything is about sex*,' she mocks. 'You've been with Tony too long already! That's exactly the kind of thing he would say!'

These words cut Sebastian deep, but he focuses on Constance's feelings.

Scrambling for words to soothe her, he says, 'Everything is about sex, because sex is not just about sex.'

'How wonderfully cryptic!' shrieks Constance. 'Stop patronising me.'

Because he is young, Sebastian believes he still can talk his way out of the hole he's been digging.

'When we feel comfortable with each other, when we look at each other and smile, when we feel each other's presence without even touching, that's all about sex.'

'What are you going to serve me next? Some tantric crap? I've had enough of this conversation!'

She stomps out of the room, barefoot, in a storm of dark curls.

29

2 APRIL – SUNSET MARQUIS GARDENS, WEST HOLLYWOOD, LOS ANGELES, CALIFORNIA, USA

*C*oncealed behind a jungle of palms and ferns, Constance sits on a white cast-iron bench tucked away from the neat red brick path.

The night is cool; she's trembling in her white dress and her bare feet are turning to ice.

Sobs have given way to hiccups, and the inside of her mouth hurts with tension.

She wonders about calling a taxi and heading straight to the airport, but the tremors won't let her form a single coherent thought. Rivers of tears have washed away her courage.

Now she's met Tony, the dark planet around which Sebastian, Regina and their entourage revolve, she re-evaluates her chances of surviving in this godforsaken galaxy.

How could her small moon not be eventually shattered by the Mephistophelean gravitational forces at play?

She's alone among virtual strangers thousands of miles from home, and she's aching for the warmth and safety of her magnolia and chintz semi-detached.

She misses her favourite blanket as if it were an actual person.

The only saving grace is that she's now in a similar time zone to Philly.

> *Myname.sNotConnie* @FitnessPhilly289 – Met IRL's boss, Lucifer's meaner brother. Plus we had a row. He says our relationship is all about sex.
> *FitnessPhilly289* @Myname.sNotConnie – Walk away.
> *Myname.sNotConnie* @FitnessPhilly289 – Not that easy, stranded in LA with no money.
> *FitnessPhilly289* @Myname.sNotConnie – I don't care if you're too poor to pay attention. Respect yourself. I have a friend in LA who runs a church refuge for young women. I'm calling him. Where are u?
> *Myname.sNotConnie* @FitnessPhilly289 – No need, don't worry, Philly.
> *FitnessPhilly289* @Myname.sNotConnie – I've dialled already. Don't make Wayne trace your phone.
> *Myname.sNotConnie* @FitnessPhilly289 – Who's Wayne?
> *FitnessPhilly289* @Myname.sNotConnie – My husband, he's a police officer. Where R U?!
> *Myname.sNotConnie* @FitnessPhilly289 – Sunshine Marquis hotel or villas something.
> *FitnessPhilly289* @Myname.sNotConnie – Pastor MacKenzie will be at the gate in an hour. You can trust him. We've got you, darlin'. Don't worry. God Bless.

Before Constance realises she's effectively accepted

Philly's offer of the long arm of God, she hears the palm trees rustle and heavy steps draw near.

Tony's sneering face flashes through her brain and as her heart leaps into her throat, she holds her breath. Her lungs soon start burning, but despite the frantic beat of blood against her eardrums, she remains perfectly still.

At least, until she has no choice but to gulp for air and reveals her location. She recoils in expectation of Tony's appearance, but it is Regina's imposing figure that casually intrudes into her private desolation.

She's wearing one of the hotel bathrobes, her face is free of make-up and her hair is wet and sticking out in all different directions.

The agent looks much younger than Constance had given her credit for.

'Trouble in Paradise?' asks Regina.

This is the last thing Constance needs – someone to prod her fresh wounds and make her feel even more naive and foolish than she already does.

She pumps whatever little hostility that still sloshes at the bottom of her tank to shoot Regina a venomous stare.

Then there's nothing left for clever insults. 'Fuck you,' is the best she can manage.

Regina sighs. 'What are you even doing here?'

'None of your business.'

'I mean in LA?'

Constance blows air through her nostrils. 'I was asked, and I said yes. Not that it's any of your business.'

Regina sits heavily on the bench. Constance scoots to the very edge of the cold metal seat and brings her knees to her chin in a vain attempt to redirect some body heat to her core.

'You're no gold-digger. I can see that,' says Regina in a gentler tone. 'I just don't get it.'

'Nobody needs *you* to get it.'

'I've been around a long time—' starts Regina.

'You don't say,' interrupts Constance acidly.

'And I'm pretty good at reading people.'

'But when it comes to "fuck off", you're dyslexic!' Constance is quite pleased with her comeback.

If only she could have delivered it without her teeth chattering like castanets.

Unimpressed, Regina ploughs on with what she came to say. 'It's my job to know what's going on with him. So now it's also my job to know what's going on with you.'

'Well, Dr Ruth, you're absolutely the last person I would ever share anything with, so you're wasting your time.'

Regina's expression remains smooth and professional. 'You're very good for him. He's the happiest I've ever seen him. He's focused, confident, charismatic. If he can keep this up, he's got a future in the industry. He can shed the "hot guy" skin and become a proper actor. A talented one, perhaps.'

'And you know all about shedding skin, you snake.' Despite her combative words, Constance's eyes are shinier than before. 'Get to the point. I haven't got all night.'

'Too busy crying behind palm trees, are you?' snipes Regina. Then she sighs, 'My point is don't throw it away.'

'As if I'm going to listen to a word you say anyway.'

For the first time tonight, Regina shows a hint of irritation. 'Grow up! You're not sixteen any more.'

These simple words, spoken without any particular intent to hurt, sting Constance like a passing jelly fish.

She jumps to her feet as if she's been electrocuted, and barefoot on shaky legs she retreats deeper into the palm-tree jungle.

Regina stares after her and lets out another long sigh.

30

2 APRIL – SANTA MONICA BOULEVARD, LOS ANGELES, CALIFORNIA, USA

For Constance, the fairytale is well and truly over.

As she stands trembling in her sundress in front of the hotel, she feels like Cinderella after the ball. Cold, tired and shoe-less.

Thrust back into drab reality, her anxiety skyrockets, and she is experiencing a spectacular case of second thoughts.

Is she really going to hop into a car with a stranger on the recommendation of another stranger who runs a smoothie recipe account on Instagram?

Constance is suddenly overwhelmed by the sheer number of new people in her life. Normally, she would only ever meet someone new once every few weeks, more often than not clients, and mostly on video-conference while safely ensconced in her upstairs studio at home.

In the last few weeks, she's travelled all around Europe and only landed for her first-ever visit to the US a few hours ago.

She's met more new people than she has in the whole of the previous five years put together. She's fallen in love, she's been verbally abused by near-strangers, met a mega-bully, and was possibly pressured over sex by her new boyfriend.

And now she's waiting for yet another stranger in a car to take her away from the strangers in the hotel.

A long shiver runs down her spine as a massive SUV slows down along the pavement.

She takes a few steps back and flattens herself against the hotel's outside walls. But instantly, she worries she looks like a professional waiting for punters, and half convinces herself the car window will roll down to reveal some seedy stranger offering her money for sex.

Yet the window remains firmly shut and it is the driver's door that opens and a man in jeans unfolds his tall frame.

As he walks round the car towards Constance, she decides he cannot possibly be the priest sent to rescue her.

He wears a buzz cut, horn-rimmed glasses and a well-groomed hipster beard, and looks not a day above forty.

The street is as deserted as a set for a zombie movie, and she pants like a scared rabbit too frozen even to run back into the hotel.

The lanky stranger lollops towards her and extends a hand in her direction.

She bleats in fright.

Unperturbed, he unveils a full semi-circle of blindingly white teeth and speaks in a deep and pleasant voice, with a light yet distinctive Southern drawl.

'Constance? Constance Wilkinson?'

She nods weakly but backs away towards the hotel entrance. Just in case.

'I'm Pastor John MacKenzie, Philly and Wayne's friend.' He offers his long-fingered hand again.

In the space of a second, Constance has to decide how much she trusts Philly and whether that trust does in fact extend to her not-at-all-Pastor-looking friend.

On the spur of the moment, she makes up her mind. She'll

take anyone associated with a kind smoothie enthusiast over the liege man of a greasy sociopath like Tony what's-his-face.

She takes in a quivering breath and gives the Pastor's outstretched hand an awkward shake.

'No bags?' he enquires.

'Maybe I'll get them tomorrow.'

'Good thinking. We can arrange that for you.' He escorts her to the car and holds open the passenger door. 'You look frozen. Nights are still surprisingly chilly.' He catches sight of her bare feet, but makes no comment.

Before resuming his position behind the wheel, Pastor John pulls a plaid blanket from the boot that looks worn but soft. He hands it to Constance without a word, and just like that, secures her trust and fellow feeling.

As she wraps it around herself, she breathes a sigh of deep relief that brings tears to her eyes.

'You'd better call Philly, she's been frantic.'

'I don't have her number, we're only friends on social media.'

'Take my phone. Hers is the number that's been ringing me all evening,' he smiles.

He's younger than she thought, perhaps in his late thirties.

As they turn left onto Santa Monica Boulevard, Constance presses the keys on an ancient Nokia, the same model her mother would let her play with when she was a toddler.

'Hi Philly.'

A shriek at the other end of the line. 'You okay, baby girl?'

Constance's eyes well up because her own mother has never been one percent as pleased to hear her as Philly is, and no one has ever called her 'baby girl' before.

She chokes on her words, 'I'm with your friend. I'm okay.'

At the other end of the line there is a wail of, 'Oh, don't cry, honey. You gonna get me started…'

This is followed by a loud exchange in a deep Southern twang from which Constance only picks out the name Wayne being called out several times.

'Praise the Lord,' says a male voice. 'I'm sure glad you're safe, darlin'.'

Philly wins a sonorous fight and regains control over the receiver. 'Pastor John is gonna take good care of you, sweetie. You don't worry now, that's a good girl. Try and get some sleep, okay, honey? Don't you worry about a thing.'

'Thank you, Philly. Really.'

'Just mind your manners with Pastor John and give him my best, sugar.'

'I will, Philly. Goodnight.'

'Nighty-night, sweetness. God bless.'

'You too,' stammers Constance, unsure of the proper response to 'God bless'.

As she hands the phone back to Pastor John, she's hyper-aware she's not stepped into a church since school, and has never before spoken to an actual 'Pastor'.

'I could do with a coffee,' declares the actual Pastor simply, as he pulls into a Starbucks Drive-thru.

This whole situation reminds Constance so much of the day when she met Sebastian that her voice squeaks when she orders her skinny soy latte with cinnamon.

But the warmth of the bucket-size cup Pastor John places between her hands helps her to relax just enough to find the manners Philly hoped she would mind.

'Thank you so much for coming to get me. I feel very silly. I wasn't in any danger. It was more of a "sticky situation". I think I probably just over-reacted. Panicked even.'

'No one panics for no reason, Miss Wilkinson. It is enough you were uncomfortable and scared. That's all it takes for me to take my man Trevor here', he pats the dashboard, 'out of the garage, and go where God wants me.'

'You've named your car Trevor?'

'A good, trustworthy, dependable name, don't you think?'

She smiles. 'My car's called Oggie. She's a Twingo. You know, the quirky-looking French car. She's older than me.'

'I'd love to tell you Trevor is older than me, but it wouldn't be true! Ninth commandment and all.'

'How long have you been a Pastor?'

'About ten years, since I came out of prison.'

'Like a prison chaplain?'

'No, miss, like an inmate.' His smile is gentle, but Constance's stomach folds in on itself, and she can already imagine her corpse chopped to bits in an empty parking lot.

'No need to be scared. I've accepted Jesus as my Lord and Saviour and turned my back on law-breaking.'

Constance has no beef with Americans' born-again malarkey, but it is not enough to reassure a girl from Henley-on-Thames.

The criminal-turned-man-of-God reads her expression. 'You're just going to have to take a leap of faith, Miss Wilkinson, and trust me.'

She stares at her coffee, un-drunk in her lap. She is quiet while he pulls onto the 101 Freeway.

He bumps her elbow. 'Not easy when no one you cared about was ever trustworthy.'

His attempt at connection rubs her up the wrong way. He assumes he knows her, and she doesn't want to be known by him.

She uses her sternest voice to declare, 'Trusting people is overrated. I've just had a reminder of this.'

He swallows her rebuke, and she immediately feels like

she's just made baby Jesus cry. Fortunately, the night is too dark to betray the pink on her cheeks.

'So, you came over here to stay with a new boyfriend. That's all Philly told me.'

'Not much else to say. He wanted things to go further than I could take them. I warned him, but he didn't listen.'

'Did he hurt you?'

'No, nothing like that. It was more words. Expectations. Nothing that could pass for abuse though. Just a difference of opinion.'

'Being pressured into something you do not want to do can be very subtle. Too subtle sometimes for people to realise what is going on before it's too late.'

'Luckily, it wasn't my first time,' she says with bravado.

'Not your first time? He did it before?'

Constance feels a pinch of guilt. She cannot bring herself to smear Sebastian's reputation any further. 'No, other men. I've built up quite the portfolio over the years.'

He sighs. 'You and thousands of others, young and less young. Male or female. My church receives dozens of victims each month.'

Without meaning to, Constance relaxes her shoulders. 'Somehow it makes it better I'm not alone. I feel a tiny bit less stupid.'

'You have done nothing wrong.'

This echoes what Sebastian said the night he showed up at her door in his rental car. Her heart tears a bit more, and she bites her lip to stop herself from crying.

'You've done the hardest bit,' says Pastor John kindly. 'Things will look a lot better after a good night's sleep.'

'Where are you taking me?'

'Echo Park. The church has a separate building where we house homeless victims, but that's full at the moment, so I will make up my spare room for you. The bed is old, but it's clean and safe. And I've inherited my breakfast pancake recipe from my grandmother. Passed down the generations. You'll love them!'

'Do you live alone?'

'I'm not married if that's what you're asking.'

Constance blushes.

'The spare room door locks from the inside. The Church elders and I are very aware that housing vulnerable young women, who may have been victims of serious assault, alone in a house with an unmarried man is a bit tricky.'

'Sorry,' mouthes Constance.

'You see, that's exactly what I want to change. The victim-shaming. Scared young people apologising for being scared, embarrassed for worrying about their own safety. You're perfectly entitled to ask what arrangements I have made for your overnight accommodation, and to request any alternatives that would make you feel safer.'

'I meant sorry for suspecting you. You've been nothing but friendly.'

'It's time the onus was on men to manage their urges and to discipline themselves, I think. Don't you?'

'I won't be holding my breath.'

'Perhaps best not to,' he smiles. 'Still, we can try to change the world, one heart at a time. With God's grace we can only prevail.'

31

2 APRIL – ECHO PARK, LOS ANGELES, CALIFORNIA, USA

The church is nothing like Constance expected. It looks like the Coliseum reborn: circular, with tall Doric columns and high arched windows.

Despite its scale and architectural pretensions, it is an ugly building, but it could withstand a medieval-style siege, complete with trebuchets and ladders, and Constance feels safer already.

Pastor John's house is an unsightly addition tacked on the back of the church, and the spare room is furnished with garage-sale odds and ends.

Still, it is clean and it comes with its own ensuite, which is far more than Constance ever dared hope for.

As Pastor John indicated, there is a serious-looking lock on the inside of the door that wouldn't be out of place in a diamond wholesale shop.

'I hope you'll be comfortable,' says the Pastor kindly. 'There's coffee, chocolate powder and biscuits in this cupboard, if you fancy a bedtime drink. And I want to hear that lock being used as soon as I'm in the corridor.' He winks. 'And finally a word of caution: turn your phone off. Philly is an early riser and you need a good sleep.'

The clank of the lock makes Constance jump, its echo reverberating as the Pastor's footsteps recede.

She scans the room. It is the ugly sister of the hotel suites she's been living in since leaving home.

The curtains bring back un-fond memories of the body-work on Scooby-Doo's van, and she wonders how she will manage to sleep under that faded orange paisley bedspread,.

She dims the lights, and the car-crash of a decor obligingly retreats into the shadows. Her phone's silent mode was already on, and she has missed thirty-seven calls and twenty-four messages from Sebastian.

As her thumb hovers over the message icon, her gut turns to ice.

It's time for a clean break, you idiot, look at the mess you've made kidding yourself you could have a lovely boyfriend but not have sex with him.

Whatever the Pastor says, this is all your fault, and Seb deserved better. He's normal and you're not. You should be the one begging for forgiveness. Not him.

Man up, do the right thing. Go home and forget about the whole sad affair.

With a supreme effort of will, she ignores Sebastian's entreaties. Instead, she opens her Instagram messages.

> ***FitnessPhilly289*** *@Myname.sNotConnie – Plz sweetheart, tell me u ok!!?*
> ***Myname.sNotConnie*** *@FitnessPhilly289 – Yes, sorry, I'm fine. I'm at the Pastor's house. I'll get myself on a plane home in the morning.*
> ***FitnessPhilly289*** *@Myname.sNotConnie –*

> *Wish I could tan IRL's hide for him! Why don'cha come over our way instead, darlin'. My Wayne and I are just outside Marion, AR, and we'd just love to have u visit.*
>
> ***Myname.sNotConnie*** *@FitnessPhilly289 – That is so kind. I really appreciate it, but I just want to go home. I hope you understand.*
>
> ***FitnessPhilly289*** *@Myname.sNotConnie – I sure do, darlin'. Just message me from the airport. Let me know u R ok.*
>
> ***Myname.sNotConnie*** *@FitnessPhilly289 – I will, Philly, promise.*

Constance spends the next few hours face down on the paisley bedspread, sobbing into Pastor John's mismatched pillows, until exhaustion catches up with her, and it is finally bedtime in Europe.

32

2 APRIL – ECHO PARK, LOS ANGELES, CALIFORNIA, USA

A few hours later, Constance wakes with a pounding headache and dark circles that would not look amiss below the eyes of a serial insomniac.

She smooths the crumpled bedding on which she slept and airs the room. She could swear it smells of her misery.

The shower is hot and the soap blossom-scented, but despite vigorous scrubbing her feet still look grubby.

She turns her panties inside out and dons the summer dress that looked so spring-like and cheerful yesterday when she took it out of her suitcase, but now resembles a trampled cornflower bouquet.

For the first time since childhood, Constance feels the yoke of loneliness across her shoulders. She normally loves being on her own and never wishes for anyone's company. Not so today.

Today, she is crushed by Sebastian's absence, overwhelmed by her own sadness compounded by the sadness she knows he must be feeling.

She only wanted a bit of space. Time to digest the uncomfortable words Sebastian has a habit of speaking.

And now she's in a women's shelter run by a born-again felon, her mind spinning like a top and her heart aching for her supposed abuser.

After another long bout of crying, she shakes her curls and with nothing but her phone in hand, she pads barefoot up the corridor following the niff of cheap coffee.

In the gigantic industrial kitchen that serves as a refectory for the shelter, dozens of women sit in small groups around a conference-room-sized table.

No one pays her any attention and she's grateful, although she suspects this lack of interest is born out of thoughtfulness rather than cold indifference.

Indeed, she couldn't think of anything worse this morning than being put on the spot.

Thankful there aren't any Philly-type personalities in the room, she heads towards the nearest of three coffee machines, stood beneath a sign that reads 'Here, we only use our middle names'.

She serves herself a generous helping of weak coffee, with creamer and brown sugar, and sips her beverage in silence while discreetly observing the women.

All ethnic groups are well represented, but the majority are white.

To Constance's surprise some would not stand out in a 60+ social club, but most are barely out of their teens.

It could have been me a few years ago.

And just like that, Constance the loner feels an uncharacteristic kinship with the other women in the room.

Although they will probably never speak to each other, they have something in common. Something that transcends race and age. All these women would understand what happened to teenage Constance. There would be no cocked heads and platitudes here.

Could *she* relate to what happened to them though? Rapes, beatings, and sexual exploitation are quite outside the realm of her experience. On the vast scale of human cruelty and violence, Constance knows where her own ordeal sits.

But she remembers what the Pastor said the night before, that scared people shouldn't apologise for being scared or for struggling to feel safe.

This must a place for girls like me too. Otherwise, where could they go? Is their trauma not worth addressing just because it isn't as severe as some?

Boosted by this realisation, Constance is working up the courage to approach the group nearest to her chair when Pastor John enters the room and makes a beeline for her.

'Good morning, Miss Constance. Did you sleep well?'

Constance has a sudden attack of shyness because, in the fresh light of the morning, Pastor John appears arrestingly handsome.

Behind his horn-rimmed glasses, his eyes are a piercing baby-blue, and his light blond hair is tousled just right as if by a hair stylist.

He's wearing faded denims and a cobalt blue T-shirt with the words 'God Saves' in a rainbow of fluorescent letters, and he sports the ubiquitous California glow.

As she blinks to recover her thoughts, he pours himself a cup of coffee, and asks, 'What can I call you? It's aliases only here. For privacy. New name, fresh start. Most residents use their middle names, but some come up with interesting alternatives. HelloKitty360 left last week, and not even I know her legal name. Sometimes, returning victims chose a different name the second time. For luck.'

'Returning?' squeaks Constance, having finally found a voice – it isn't one she knew she had; she sounds like Shaun the Sheep.

'You wouldn't believe the proportion of my guests who go back to their abusers in the hope God has finally changed their hearts. I'm dubious myself, but I'm hardly in a position to doubt the power of the Holy Spirit.' He chuckles as if he'd made a joke. 'So, what shall I call you?'

'Constance is fine, I'm not staying.'

'Are you sure? Most women find it healing and inspirational to chat to each other and share their experiences. Perhaps just for a day or two?'

She admits to herself she is tempted, but the thought of another night beneath the paisley bedspread proves too much.

'I'm homesick, I need to get back to England. Be with my things. But I will definitely look out for a support group. I didn't know there could be so many other women like me. With difficult memories.'

'Good plan. I hope you still have time for Grandma MacKenzie's pancakes?'

She nods politely, but her heart sinks. Being in the same room as these women, who have had to flee sexual assault and abuse, brings it home this is not what happened to her with Sebastian. All the contradictory thoughts tumbling round her mind instantly stop and fall into a neat pile.

Whatever anyone thinks, regardless of what happened, there is only one place she wants to be: in the fruit salad villa, with Sebastian.

She has to go back to the hotel. Now. Or even better yesterday. Failing a time machine, she schedules her departure for the second after the last morsel of pancake enters her mouth. Her whole body fizzes with newfound clarity.

As the Pastor busies himself at the stove and turns a pale yellow batter into honey-coloured pancakes, she checks the time on her phone three times. 8.30. 8.33. 8.35…

When presented with her stack, dripping in maple syrup,

Constance has two good reasons to devour them: her last meal was on the flight to LAX, and she can't bear to spend another unnecessary minute away from Sebastian.

Pastor John cleans the countertops and starts one of the dishwashers.

He is talking, but she hardly makes sense of what he says.

'And that's only the tip of the iceberg. We get a lot of college students who say they were one of dozens to have suffered assaults and date rape, but the other girls refuse to come forward.'

This does capture Constance's attention. 'Gosh, that's awful!'

'We have a special system to deal with those. I call it the "Wrath of God envelopes".'

'That's a quite a name,' she comments.

'In the Bible, God often waits until a large quantity of people sin before punishing them in a collective reckoning. Like Sodom and Gomorrah.'

'I'll take your word for it,' says Constance.

He smiles, before continuing. 'When they arrive at the shelter, the victims write a report of the assault, with as many specific details as they can remember, then they undergo a hospital rape exam.'

The fluffy pancakes now feel like lead in Constance's stomach. She knows exactly what her mother would say about the Pastor's poor sense of decorum.

This is not breakfast conversation!

But despite the queasiness in her gut, Constance does her best to listen.

'Then everything is sealed in an envelope with the name of the perpetrator until a certain number of envelopes are received with the same name on it. That number depends on the respective power of the victim and the accused. When it is reached, the envelopes are unsealed and passed on to the police. The victims only officially come forward once they know they can be backed up by another complainant with the same claim. Safety in numbers.'

'But by sealing their envelope, these women condemn others to be raped or assaulted,' says Constance, feeling like she's about to faint.

'Yes, this method makes more victims. But considering most instances are a case of "he said/she said", few court cases would otherwise result in convictions, leaving the perpetrator free to offend again.'

In the lengthening silence, Constance swallows a mouthful of coffee to hide her nervous trembling. 'Does the system work for the general public as well?'

'It also works against corporate offenders,' answers the Pastor. 'If your boss is sexually harassing you, you might relate the events in a letter that will be sealed until one of your colleagues adds credibility to your claim.'

This is the last topic Constance wants to discuss, so far from home and deprived of the sense of security that Sebastian provided.

She looks about to bring up her pancakes at the Pastor's feet.

Finally, he recognises her distress. 'Come,' he says, reaching out to steady her. 'I can see I've upset you. Let's get you on your way home.'

'Yes please,' she manages while the room spins uncontrollably, and the nausea takes over her whole body.

He helps her to the car park and fumbles with his keys, while she struggles to stand straight.

When the car eventually starts, Constance breathes a discreet sigh of relief.

As Trevor merges onto the freeway, the traffic is so dense

it is obvious the journey will take a lot longer than in the middle of the night. Constance's face falls.

'Our meeting was God's will, Miss Constance,' says the Pastor with a reassuring pat on her hand. 'We're both here for a reason. As your C.S. Lewis wrote, "For you will certainly carry out God's purpose however you act, but it makes a difference to you whether you serve like Judas or like John."'

Constance's religious education is seriously lacking, but who hasn't heard of Judas?

The mention of one of the villains in the Bible sends a cold wave of distrust down her spine.

Who exactly am I sitting in a moving car with?

'I don't mean to offend you Pastor, but how exactly did you become involved in women's rescue?'

He catches her eye. 'It would be a good redemption story, but sex wasn't the direct reason I ended up in prison.'

Constance swallows a panicked whimper. 'I'm sorry. I didn't mean—'

He brushes aside her belated remorse. 'Greed was my undoing, Constance. The rat race, the risky accounting practices. All for a bigger house, a flashier car, a bigger diamond for my fiancée. I'm not proud of myself, but at least I didn't traumatise anyone for life.'

'I thought you weren't married.'

'Prison put a halt to my wedding plans.'

'I'm sorry.'

'I'm not.'

In the silence that follows, Constance is left to consider the amount of blind faith it takes to let new people into her life.

She regrets letting her fear of Tony drive a wedge between Sebastian and her.

If she could jump into a car with Pastor John, why can't

she trust the man who has stood by her side during the last few weeks?

As Trevor fights his epic battle against the freeway traffic, Constance feels a physical need to be reunited with Sebastian.

That's going to take the mother of apologies.

33

2 APRIL – SUNSET MARQUIS, WEST HOLLYWOOD, LOS ANGELES, CALIFORNIA, USA

'Trevor' pulls into one of the Sunset Marquis guest parking spaces. It's nearly midday.

Constance's throat is in a tight knot, and Pastor John's pancakes are mosh-pit dancing in her stomach.

He notices her face go grey, and he whispers, 'You okay?'

'I just don't know how he will react.'

'I'm going to come in with you, smooth things out. We'll get your luggage and your passport, then I can take you straight to LAX.'

'I'm not even sure that's what I want to do any more.'

'You'll decide. I'm just there to back you up.'

She nods, careful not to dislodge the tears pooling in her eyes.

As she walks up to reception, the stunning girl behind the counter smiles. 'Miss Wilkinson, good morning. You have a few messages.' She holds a wad of pink slips. Constance doesn't even need to check. She well knows who left them.

'Could I have my key please?'

'Let me announce you first.'

She picks up the receiver and whispers a few words.

'You may go in. Someone will open the door for you. Have a great day!'

Sebastian is waiting in front of the door, looking pale, eyes bloodshot.

'Constance,' he breathes as he claps eyes on her. But when he sees Pastor John, his whole demeanour changes, and an iron curtain of suspicion and anger shutters down his face.

As she steps into the room, 'Pour Monsieur' receives her in its comforting embrace, but Sebastian crosses his arms and stares at her hard.

Paralysed by awkwardness and emotions, she has to dig deep into her reserve of civilised manners, in a way both her mother and Philly – who have strictly nothing else in common– would approve of.

'Pastor, this is Sebastian Anders. Sebastian, this is Pastor John MacKenzie. The Pastor runs a refuge for women victims of sexual assault.'

If the Pastor is surprised to find himself face-to-face with a movie star, he doesn't let on.

On the other hand, Sebastian's face turns even paler. His eyes shine with tears, and he blurts out. 'What? Sexual assault? Did you manipulate her into reporting me to the police?'

'Nobody manipulated me into doing anything,' declares Constance.

'Could we talk inside?' suggests Pastor John, keenly aware that either or both of his companions risk passing out.

There is a long pause during which Sebastian keeps his watery eyes on Constance, and his emotions zigzag from heartbreak to silent accusation to anger and back again.

It robs her of the ability to speak, and she's too ashamed to look him in the face.

As he ushers them into the room, the Pastor is careful to place a comforting hand above (not on) their shoulders.

He's mastered this skill soon after opening the shelter. Most of the people he meets need a gesture of comfort and sympathy, but dislike being touched by strangers, so he's become an expert at supportive but respectful body language.

He leads them to one of the sofas and pours them both a glass of water. Sebastian feels a flash of irritation that this uninvited stranger is playing mother in his hotel room.

'The only reason I'm here, Sebastian,' says the Pastor, 'is to give Constance a lift to the airport. A mutual friend asked me to take Constance to the shelter so she could spend the night on neutral ground,' says Pastor John placatingly.

This is enough for Sebastian's thin control of his roiling emotions to be shattered, and his Tennessee accent to show the tip of its nose.

'It was meetin' my degenerate of a boss that freaked her out so much she ran for the hills. The only thing I said is that sex is not just about sex. It is about bein' comfortable together, feelin' a rapport.'

'Constance felt pressured and scared. She did something about it.'

'Excuse me, Pastor, but with all due respect, I thought you were only here to collect her luggage.'

'I'm also here for moral support.'

Sebastian turns to the Pastor. 'In the two months we've been together, I've been nothing if not respectful. I haven't asked for anything, I haven't touched her. I've never even seen her less than fully dressed. I've been booking suites with two bedrooms so she could have her space and feel safe, and she runs to a rape-victim refuge?'

'No one, least of all Constance, is accusing you of anything more than miscommunication and perhaps some level of insensitivity,' says the Pastor calmly.

This only pours oil on the fire of Sebastian's anger. 'Don't mistake this for what it ain't.' He gestures to the space between him and Constance, his eyes burning holes into the good Pastor's face. 'This is a *courtship*! I've set strict rules of purity for myself when it came to Constance. Nothing was said, Pastor, nothing happened that a chaperone could have objected to.'

The words 'courtship', 'purity' and 'chaperone' are sacred music to Pastor John's ears. His expression mellows and he reaches out with an appeasing hand.

But Sebastian, foolishly, isn't finished. 'If that's harassment, then I'd better go straight to prison because I must have been harassin' hundreds of people.'

Just as Pastor John's face breaks into a friendlier smile, Constance's turns beet red. 'Hundreds of women?' she shouts, suddenly outraged.

'And what if it was? We didn't even know each other!' Sebastian snaps back, not recognising this bright red Constance is in fact green with jealousy.

And before the Pastor can soothe the sting of those words, Constance lets out a wail, grabs her handbag and runs out of the villa, still shoe-less, her green-eyed monster in tow.

Sebastian drops his head into his hands, and Pastor John lays a comforting hand above his shoulder.

'You can't do the job I do, son, without developing a sixth-sense about people. And I can see you mean well. But this courtship will be harder than most. You're effectively living together, so the boundaries are harder to keep, and Constance has had some bad experiences in the past. Arm yourself with patience.'

'It's like walkin' in a mine field, Pastor.'

'Let God heal both your wounds.'

'It's been a while since God has done anything for me.'

'Really?' He scans the room. 'Few would agree with you,

Sebastian. And even if fame and money mean nothing to you, isn't Constance a gift from God?'

When Sebastian sighs wearily, a slow smile spreads across Pastor John's face as he realises his work here is done.

Sebastian is already at to the door when the Pastor calls, 'Don't forget her shoes.'

Too late.

34

2 APRIL – SAL GUARRIELLO VETERANS' MEMORIAL, WEST HOLLYWOOD, LOS ANGELES, CALIFORNIA, USA

It doesn't take Constance long to realise there is simply nowhere to hide in the vicinity of the Sunset Marquis.

The only out-of-the way spot she finds is a tiny park dedicated to war veterans with a couple of seats in the shade.

So, there she sits, wringing her hands and crying her eyes out while going over the events of the previous night and morning.

Now she's alone, without the Pastor babbling in her ear and Sebastian shouting in her face, her mind is clear, and she has retrieved a measure of equilibrium.

Never mind her luggage, she has her handbag which contains her passport and all the little things she loves to carry – her favourite lip balm, her sunglasses that make her feel like Audrey Hepburn, a long-forgotten Milky Way bar, atrociously misshapen but still in date.

She also has found her house keys and Oggie's keys, and she feels a bit more ready to face the next half-hour of hard thinking.

She hides the mess that is her face behind her giant sunglasses and tearfully munches on her chocolate bar.

Okay, you numpty, now you have three options:

Plan A. Go home, never speak to him again. Cry yourself to an early grave and lay dead undiscovered indoors for weeks.

Plan B. Go back to the hotel and unsuccessfully beg for forgiveness, then plan A.

Plan C. Go home and call him when you get there, then probably Plan A.

Plan D. Stalk him for the rest of your – short – life, plus Plan A.

Plan E. Jump in front of a car, just enough to go to hospital, not enough to die. Hope for him to show up, when he doesn't, Plan A.

Plan F. Go back to the hotel, pretend you have had a stroke and have no recollection of even arriving in LA, due to temporary amnesia. If he doesn't buy it, Plan A.

Of course, that's a lot more than three options, but Constance is past caring.

Her heart is telling her to go back to the hotel. Her gut strongly suspects she's massively over-reacted and made a complete tit of herself and hurt Sebastian deeply in the process.

Her mind is going through the short list of attenuating circumstances and possible clever reframing to get herself out of the mess she's made.

What could she possibly say in her own defence?

She wipes her cheeks and leaves behind a streak of melting chocolate.

As she licks her sticky fingers, a shadow falls on her lap.

'Your bodyguard taking a break?'

She looks up to see Sebastian's auburn hair in a halo of light, his face in darkness. His voice is tired.

She clambers to her feet, nearly head butting him in the chin. He has to take a step back, and his face appears out of the shade.

Constance gasps, he looks worse than the day she saved him. His eyes are red, rimmed with purple shadows and a sad smile twists his lips.

'I hope I'm not breaking any restraining orders yet,' he says.

With a poise she didn't know she had, she takes a deep breath to compose herself and declares, 'Obviously I owe you an apology.'

'You think?'

'I clearly over-reacted. I could say it was jet lag or the wine, or that horrid producer of yours, but I think it's fair to chalk this up to my flighty temper.'

'I see.'

'I'm really sorry about this morning. I shouldn't have brought Pastor John into the room.'

'Oh well, I have about another hour of freedom before it's all over the gossip blogs.'

'He's a Pastor! He wouldn't rat you out.'

'Why wouldn't he? He runs a shelter. He's got a good cause. They always need money. A quick phone, a few thousand dollars straight in his pocket. It's not rocket science.'

'I never thought of that.'

'You never thought of anything.'

'That's fair. Although—'

'Although nothing. We've spent two months together, and I've gained zero trust, zero respect from you. You treated me like a sleazy guy you'd met in a bar.'

'I wouldn't have even spoken to a sleazy—'

Constance's apology is not going well.

'I know I'm not perfect, I know you've got trust issues, but that was just so... disappointing. That's what it was, it was just a massive, gigantic letdown with bells on.'

'I'm sorry,' she manages.

'It doesn't matter now.'

'Sebastian...'

'It's okay, Constance, no point wracking your brains for something to say. We can get on with our lives now.'

'But—'

'No need to cry any more chocolate,' he says, wiping the brown smudge on her cheek with a sad smile that rips her heart apart.

Before she can think of any words good enough to make this long nightmare stop, he turns on his heels.

He's about to say, 'You coming?', but Constance gives him no time.

She springs into action. All at once, her sunglasses fall to the ground, her bag spills its contents everywhere, she grabs two handfuls of the back of his baseball jacket, and she yells, 'Nooooooo!'

This stops him in his tracks.

'No! No-no-no-no!' she says again into his back. 'Just no.'

Before he can say, 'We're only going back to the hotel,' she relocates her death grip to the front of his T-shirt. 'No, you can't leave. You just can't!'

He says, 'I'm not leaving,' but she's no longer listening.

'No, no, no,' she stammers like a broken record.

Sebastian's frustration reaches a new height, and his self-control finally breaks. He grabs her by the shoulders. 'It was you who left, not me. Remember?'

'No, no, no,' continues Constance.

'Yes, you did. Tony scared the crap out of you, but instead

of talking to me about it, you pretended everything was fine. You waited until we were having a glass of wine by the pool and I said something you didn't like, and then you just freaked. You were gone all night. I was worried sick. You didn't answer a single message, and the first I heard you were even alive was when the reception desk called me to let you in.'

'I'm sorry. I'm so sorry,' she wails.

'And you arrive with a Pastor neither of us has ever met! Like for some couple counselling crap.'

'I wasn't thinking.'

Sebastian abruptly becomes aware they're making a scene, and the drivers slowing down at the intersection are getting a free show.

LA being LA, they have seconds before someone starts filming them.

He takes his baseball cap out of his back pocket and jams it on his head. Then he picks up her sunglasses and replaces them on her nose to hide her face.

'Can you run in your shoes?' he asks.

'I haven't got—'

'Run!' he says, and he grabs her hand.

Constance would hop, skip and jump anywhere to feel his hand around hers, so she collects her belongings, straps her bag across her body and runs after Sebastian.

35

2 APRIL – SUNSET MARQUIS, WEST HOLLYWOOD, LOS ANGELES, CALIFORNIA, USA

The porters at the front of the hotel are used to protecting famous guests from overly curious passersby.

They don't even blink when Sebastian and Constance pelt up the road with a gaggle of celebrity-hunters on their tails.

The followees are not so sanguine. They don't stop running until the villa door is safely locked behind them and the curtains pulled across the floor-to-ceiling windows.

Only then does Constance collapse in one of the mustard yellow armchairs, her cheeks scarlet and sweat pouring down her back.

By comparison, Sebastian's breathing has not sped up one bit, but his brow furrows. 'You should have said you'd lost your shoes.'

'Didn't have any,' she pants. 'Left without them yesterday.'

As he takes in Constance's near-apoplectic face, he gives her the glass of water Pastor John had poured for her.

She takes a sip that goes down the wrong way, further endangering her breathing.

'Can we talk?' she splutters. 'In a minute… when I can breathe, please can we talk?'

'Is there anything to say?' Sebastian's face is a carefully crafted mask of indifference.

'Yes, lots,' she manages before a coughing fit stops her in her tracks.

He sits heavily on the armchair opposite hers and downs the nearest glass of water.

Eventually, Constance takes a big gulp of air and wipes her eyes.

'I know I've let you down, and I've hurt you. I wish I hadn't, but I did. And I had no good reason. You've never been anything but kind and respectful to me, and I'm not sure why I took what you said so badly. Having a guy like Tony as your mentor is hardly a hallmark of good character, but I should have trusted you more.'

Sebastian nods. 'I appreciate you saying that. But how can we stop it from happening again and again? I can't do drama. My life is complicated enough. I told you what my ex-girlfriend was like. I need someone who can hang on to their sanity even when jet-lagged and stressed.'

'I understand.'

'Do you?'

'Yes, I'm not used to being in a real relationship. I only thought about myself, my feelings. I never thought how my reaction would affect you.'

'It did. It did affect me.'

'I can see that. You look awful.'

'Gee, thanks.'

Constance serves the pièce-de-résistance of her apology. 'If you forgive me, I promise you this will not happen again. Ever.'

Once she's said it, she realises that, with her track-record, this is only the apology equivalent of semolina, not cordon-bleu. She tries to season it with a winning smile. It doesn't work.

'I want to believe you,' says Sebastian unmoved. 'But it's the second time you've run for the door. I can't keep putting myself through that.'

She crinkles her nose the way she's noticed he likes. 'Then who's going to keep you off the ledge with her silly jokes? Who's going to go toe-to-toe with Raving Regina?

'Don't,' he says, trying not to smile.

She stands for extra solemnity. 'Sebastian, you have my word of honour as a lady. I will never run for the door again.'

'Wow, you're bringing the Victorian big guns. You're totally desperate.'

'Yes, I totally am. So, do you forgive me or not?'

'Cross your heart and hope to die?'

'And pinkie swear.'

He stands to peer into her eyes for what seems like an eternity, searching for the key that will unlock their stalemate.

Then he realises what her upturned face, haloed by a tangle of tight curls, reminds him of. A cute, expectant poodle.

He allows himself a private chuckle at her expense and sends up a silent prayer for patience. 'God love you, what am I going to do with you?'

He captures her chin in his cupped hand. She takes it and kisses his knuckles.

His eyes in hers, he stands and pulls her into a hug.

'I love you,' he says against her neck.

'Me too, so much.'

As she hops uneasily from one foot to the other, he remembers she's walked barefoot for the last 24 hours. Indeed, her feet are a mess of dirt, grit and blood.

So, he sits her back in the armchair, wets a flannel and kneels in front of her.

The feel of his hand on her sole sends a wave of awkwardness up and down her body, and she suddenly feels considerably warmer. He repeats the manoeuvre on her other foot, and this time she is braced against the unexpected pleasure of his gentle touch on her skin.

'Is this what you meant by everything is about sex?' she asks.

'Partly.'

'Because it's getting hot in here.' She mimes fanning herself with a droll eye roll.

He tries not to smile, and fails. 'Good.'

He pats her feet dry with one of the blindingly white towels and gets plasters out of the first aid kit he keeps in his suitcase.

36

2 APRIL – SUNSET MARQUIS, WEST HOLLYWOOD, LOS ANGELES, CALIFORNIA, USA

'See what you did to my clothes!' complains Sebastian. His baseball jacket sports two chocolaty hand prints on the back, and his T-shirt is ripped at the collar.

'Didn't suit you anyway,' pouts Constance, poking her head out of her room, in a dusty pink tea dress, half her make-up done. 'You looked like someone out of *Breakfast Club*.'

Sebastian pulls off his torn T-shirt, and the sight of his naked torso is enough to make her vision go blurry.

Damn, girl, calm down!

'*Breakfast Club* is an absolute classic!' he calls from his room.

'Still. You looked like a dweeb in that jacket. Talking about breakfast…'

'I haven't eaten,' he says. 'Have you?'

'The Pastor made me pancakes, but a smoothie would be nice. I don't mind which.'

Freshly showered and changed into slim-fit grey trousers and a mint shirt that hugs his pecs and make his eyes even greener, Sebastian orders one of each smoothie on the room-service menu. Seven to be exact.

'Regina said she'd spoken to you.'

'Did you send her to find me last night?'

'Of course not.' He holds her accusing gaze – one eye lined black, the other not – with no trace of dishonesty.

He's sprawled across the mustard sofa, and his green shirt blends in with the tropical colour scheme.

Shaken to the core by how handsome he is – *I should be used to it by now!* – she lets out a calming breath before speaking.

'It's really important to me that you should not pity me. Seeing me as some pathetic little girl who's been mistreated is robbing me of what's left of my dignity. I rescued you! Not the other way round.'

She dabs on some nude lipstick and frog-marches her curls into a messy bun.

'You did save me,' agrees Sebastian.

Constance joins him on the sofa, her pink dress adding a touch of watermelon to the fruit salad tableau. 'I told you how it had to be. I told you. Right from the start! No sex.'

'You did.'

When he acknowledges the truth of her warning, Constance relaxes and tucks her legs under her.

Until Sebastian's words cut the silence. 'But you wouldn't be here if you didn't want the same things I do.'

Constance knows he is right, but she contradicts him regardless. 'You said it yourself at the Langham, I'm traumatised. And I don't want sex with anybody ever again,' she insists. 'I won't have that hanging over me all the time.'

There is a silence, then Sebastian clears his throat.

Constance realises she's been holding her breath, waiting for his next words. When he still doesn't speak, fear floods her body with adrenaline.

'I warned you,' she says to block the creeping feeling she's being unreasonable.

A silent conversation starts in her mind. *It's my body. I have the right to decide. Yes, but look what happened when you decided. Look at the mess you've made. It's not his fault you're damaged. It's yours. Yours, yours, yours.*

She loses her poise and shifts to hug her legs and hide her burning cheeks in the crook of her elbow.

As Constance's mental chatter gets progressively more abusive, Sebastian remains still and quiet.

Then he sits up and speaks softly. 'There will come a time when you will *want* the world to fall away. You will *want* to forget everything but skin, smell and thrill. You will *want* to get closer and closer, and it will never be close enough. It will be wonderful. And I really want to be there with you when that happens. So I'm just going to love you and wait for the Call.'

The sting of tears on already sore eyelids brings Constance's attention away from her berating of herself.

She's finally ready for some honesty. 'It's so hard being around you. I think about it all the time,' she whispers.

'About what?'

She hesitates for a few seconds before answering. 'I think about a weight on me, and being scared. About the pain, the proper pain, and being so ashamed I'm letting that pain happen to me.'

She tries to hide her face in her knees, but he cups her chin and brings her eyes back into his.

'Talk to me,' he says. 'Really talk. We won't make it otherwise.'

She nods shyly. 'The first time, I realised immediately what I had done could never be undone. He was there, sleeping in my bed with a smile on his face, and I wanted to murder him. Stab him until he bled like I was bleeding. He never realised what he had done. That cut me deep. Being so unseen, like I didn't even exist. Like I was something he'd used and discarded.'

As her words hang in the silence, Sebastian tries to swallow the painful lump in his throat.

He says with an edge of desperation, 'What can I do? Tell me what I can do. I'll do anything. I'll track him down and beat him to a pulp…'

'Don't say that.'

'I'm deadly serious. We could call the police. The man raped you. The Pastor would tell you the same.' He runs both his hands through his hair.

'I would be lying if I said I didn't consent,' Constance continues. 'I did consent, but I didn't realise what that meant. I didn't know I was starting on the path that has landed me here, ten years later. With you, like this.' A single tear makes its way down her cheek.

Sebastian stands. 'He must have known you were too innocent to know what you were letting yourself in for. He could have been kinder, more attentive.' he bites his lip.

'Bad sex isn't a crime,' she retorts with a pained smile.

'Still, I would love to make him pay.'

Trembling, she looks up at him, standing in front of her. 'Sometimes, I look at you. How fit you are, how strong. You've got muscles everywhere. Your arms are just so solid. Part of me thinks "yummy" like every other fangirl on the planet, but another part of me thinks how easily you could pin me down.'

Sebastian pulls at his hair and emits a low growl. He says through his teeth, 'You *know*, you *have* to know, I would never do that. Not to you, not to anyone.'

'I do know, but unless I constantly work to push it out of my mind, I can't help thinking about it.'

He sits down next to her and puts his arm around her shoulders. His added body heat helps her shivering subside.

'Can I ask you a question?' he says eventually. He knows he's taking a risk, but the opportunity might not present itself again.

'About what?'

'About you and Mark.'

She knows what he's going to say, because she's been asking herself that same question on a loop for weeks. 'How come I could do it with him?'

He nods. 'What was going through your mind then?'

'I was working hard at forcing myself, plus physically, he wasn't exactly imposing. Not like you. I could have thrown him off.'

Sebastian recoils. 'I *scare* you?'

Deprived of his heat, Constance shivers again. 'To be 100% honest, you do a little bit.'

'I would never hurt you,' says Sebastian, indignant.

'You could hurt me though, you could hurt me very badly.'

'And so could you.'

'That's no consolation,' says Constance.

Sebastian pulls her closer against him and hopes she doesn't find his contact too upsetting.

In truth, he needs the comfort of her body against his to get through the excruciating conversation he now needs to have with her.

'So, he wasn't physically imposing,' he says slowly. 'Is that the only difference?'

'You don't understand,' replies Constance, tears in her voice. 'I was letting him have sex with me.'

Sebastian swallows hard. 'You were passive? Is that it?'

'No, more like an out-of-body experience. I was going somewhere else in my mind.'

He doesn't trust himself to speak, but without prompting, she continues.

'Then he would go to sleep, and I would have a long shower, get my blanket, sit in the armchair in the corner of my bedroom, and try and put myself back together again, ready for the next day. To make sure he wouldn't suspect anything or think I was weird.'

'Did it work?'

'Not always. Sometimes I couldn't eat for a whole day.'

No matter how upsetting he thought the truth would be, it is worse. He runs his hand through his hair and tries to breathe slowly.

When he lets out a heavy sigh, she smiles at him apologetically. That breaks his heart all over again.

He's never felt for anyone what he feels for her, and the new tender parts of him that she alone has access to are being stabbed and skewered.

Still, he is man enough to forget his pain to focus on hers. 'It's never going to be like that between us, okay? Never.'

She nods, and in the soft light streaming through the curtains she can see his eyes are still sad. 'Hurts like a bitch, doesn't it?'

'A bitch from H E double L,' he says through clenched teeth. It is a testament to his depth of feeling that Constance doesn't smile at the quirky expression.

Before she can reply, a soft knock at the door heralds the arrival of a large tray of multi-coloured smoothies, and they relocate onto the sun loungers to sample them.

The warm sun on her skin cheers Constance up, and it is with a genuine smile that she changes the conversation.

'You know, Regina said some really nice things about you earlier. How focused and talented you are. She sees you becoming a great actor.'

Sebastian shrugs. 'That's her job to say stuff like that. I wouldn't put too much stock in it.'

'I agree with her. For once,' says Constance, her eyes in his.

He chuckles, and her stomach flutters. 'The ultimate unlikely alliance! If you two ever gang up on me, I'll cross the border to Mexico.'

Constance laughs and pinches his cheek lightly. As if by magic his shoulders relax.

'Let's go house-hunting tomorrow,' she says.

'Yes, ma'am.'

37

23 APRIL – SEBASTIAN'S MANSION, PACIFIC PALISADES HILLS, LOS ANGELES, CALIFORNIA, USA

Only three weeks after their hotel heart-to-heart, Sebastian is lying on a sun lounger by a large bean-shaped pool, facing a glorious 180-degree view of the Pacific Ocean.

His taut body is sleek with suntan oil, and his abs and pecs ripple as he moves.

Constance takes in the sights as she walks from the house towards him with two large tumblers of iced tea.

Behind her stretches the pristine five-bedroom/five-baths, 5,000-square-foot mansion Sebastian has just purchased. They moved in a week ago, and Constance still can't believe she lives here.

'Marble and oak everywhere,' she gushed to Philly the day she wheeled her two suitcases past the front door.

She still knows the realtor's description by heart. *Theatre, game room, gym plus sauna, chef's kitchen...* Not forgetting the two separate laundry rooms, which remind her with a twinge of nostalgia of the day a mostly naked Sebastian shoved his soaked-through clothes into her rickety dryer.

Sebastian, more used to the luxury twenty-something

million dollars can buy, draws his eyes away from the ocean view framed in fragrant eucalyptus trees to enjoy the fit of Constance's brand new swimsuit on her slowly tanning hips.

'You're rocking that bikini, baby!' he says with a wink.

'Not too ugly yourself, jerk face,' she replies.

She hands him his drink and sits next to him. These are the exact same sun loungers they had on their terrace at the Sunset Marquis villa. Constance Googled them.

'I can't believe you bought a house and got it furnished and decorated in three weeks!' she gushes. 'Only in LA, darling. Is this not tons better than keeping your stuff in storage?'

'Can't argue with you there,' he smiles.

'I just love this place. The view! The view...' she says, not for the first time.

'You might have mentioned it before.'

'Don't be so grumpy. You love it here.'

'It sure is fixin' to be a pleasant wait before my next job.'

She smiles at the Southern slang he dips in and out of. 'Any news about that read-through?'

'Nope. Nothing.'

'You sound quite blasé about it.'

He turns his brilliant smile towards her; her knees go weak. 'I'm happy,' he says. 'I'm letting Regina do her job. She can worry about my career for now.'

Constance smears sun lotion on her bare midriff before Sebastian's hungry eyes. 'It's not how I imagined it here. I thought it would a long string of parties and celebrities going around in limousines.'

Sebastian tears his eyes away from Constance's shimmering skin. 'Are you disappointed?'

'No, I dreaded it! I'm so glad it's just you and me.' She

smiles a smile Sebastian would describe as tender. 'And it's always so warm and sunny,' she adds.

'You nearly died of hypothermia on your first night here though!' teases Sebastian.

Constance shivers despite the hot sun on her skin, and he notices her mood shift.

Prudently, he steers the conversation onto what he believes will be more solid ground.

'Now we've got this huge house, have you got anybody you would like to invite over? Your parents perhaps?'

She shakes her head and her curls bounce around her face. 'My parents wouldn't want to be in the same airport, let alone in the same house.'

Her tone sounds unconcerned, but Sebastian – who lost both his Mamma and Pop when he was young – is unwilling to believe anyone could feel so indifferent to warring parents.

'How old were you when they divorced?' he asks.

'Fourteen. Within six months my dad had stopped taking advantage of his visitation rights, and by the end of the first year I no longer received phone calls either. He did send a birthday present and a Christmas card with £50 in cash every year, but I don't think I saw him more than three times between the divorce and my move to uni.

'After I got my degree, he took an interest again, because I was all grown up and sensible and no longer spitting angry. But when he tried and failed to persuade me to take up a position as a junior accountant in his friend's firm, our relationship fizzled out again.'

She meets his eyes levelly. 'You know, the usual stuff.'

He swallows the comment he was going to make, and asks instead, 'What about your mom?'

'She's had a long string of boyfriends-slash-fiancés, but I don't think she's ever got over my dad's betrayal. Mummy and

I started growing apart even before the divorce. She had her own struggles and I was a shy, awkward, troubled teenager. No picnic for a mother, I'm sure. Or perhaps I reminded her of what'd gone wrong in her life.

'Nowadays, she takes me being single as a slight against her own powers of seduction. She's never been happier with me than since I've moved here with you. It gives her vicarious kudos.'

'I can see why you thought a girl without a boyfriend was a failure.'

Constance's eyes sparkle. 'Shame I had to trade down after Mark.'

Sebastian nudges her affectionately. The brush of his fingers on her naked shoulder sends hot blood rushing to her face.

'I know you like your men puny,' he grins, 'but it doesn't give you the right to make me feel ashamed about my body. You'll give me body dysmorphia, or something.' His good humour fades when Constance pouts.

'Actually, it's not funny,' she says. 'You're part of an industry that makes everyone else feel inadequate! All these poor women, so thin, so gaunt. Bones and sinews... It's sickening.'

'Someone pass her a bucket,' he jokes, refusing to take her sudden irritation seriously.

'Shut up, Action Man,' gripes Constance.

'What? No "dick sock", no "ass bag"? You're losing your touch, girlfriend. I gotta get Regina over here pronto!'

Finally, Constance smiles. 'She's growing on me, your Regina. She does have an amazing repertoire of put-downs.'

'Told you she wasn't so bad.'

'What about your family? What were they like?'

'Typical Southern family. Third generation living in our

small town, going the extra mile for our neighbours, in church every Sunday. Mamma homeschooling us kids and my Pop working in commercial properties plus volunteering for the fire rescue service. Evenings on the porch and family Thanksgivings with four generations of Anders and a dozen cousins.'

'So, what happened? Are you estranged from them?'

'As you know, Mamma and Pop died when a drunk driver ran their truck off the road. I was nine and my brother Joseph Jr was twelve. My grandma took us in, but she developed dementia and, two years in, we were looking after her more than she was looking after us.

'We still weren't going to school, and Joe was taking out his frustration and grief on me. We limped on like that until I turned fifteen. I set up a lawn-mowing business, because we were poor as church mice, and Joe started working with the local mechanic.

'We never wanted for anything; there was always a homemade pie or a dish of fried chicken for the Anders boys who took care of their grandma like "godly young men".'

'What about the rest of the family? All those people at the Thanksgiving table?' she asks.

'The older ones got older and died, the younger ones got married, had "as many children as the Lord would give them", and my brother and I drifted to the edges of the family.

'Then a few days after my fifteenth birthday, my grandma fell down the stairs and died. My brother, who'd just turned eighteen, got custody of me. In practice, the social worker never bothered to fill in the papers to get me into foster care.

'We lived in my grandma's house until it just about fell around our ears, then my brother decided to sell it. He bought a share of the mechanic's business, married a girl from church and moved into a double-wide.

'Fortunately, one of my lawn-mowing customers offered

me a room above their garage, and I supported myself until I met Tony and he took me to LA. I've never been back to Tennessee since.'

'Gosh, I'm so sorry. I can see why you were reluctant to talk to me about it. And here's me and my poor little rich girl story. Boo hoo, her parents got divorced.'

'So what about inviting your family for Thanksgiving? But you know, not at the same time?'

'Sure, baby. It's really kind of you to offer.'

On impulse, Constance leans across and kisses him on the lips. Sebastian sits up, his heart on fire, and with his broadest grin, he bends towards her.

'Why, miss. I believe you dropped your kiss. May I return it?'

Caught in the full beam of his eyes, Constance blinks. 'Yes,' she whispers.

Sebastian takes his time to kiss her softly. She doesn't pull back, but he doesn't push his luck. As he leans back, he tastes his lips in appreciation. 'Not bad for a first kiss.'

He settles back on the sun lounger, head resting on his folded arms, and closes his eyes.

Constance looks pleased and close to tears at the same time. Her words are at odds with her expression. 'You're such a lame ass.'

'And you are beautiful and taste like heaven.'

'Shut up, we're not —'

'Hush, don't say it,' he grins.

38

24 APRIL – SEBASTIAN'S MANSION, PACIFIC PALISADES HILLS, LOS ANGELES, CALIFORNIA, USA

'Feel the burn!' shouts Constance, as she closes the sauna door behind herself.

She looks like she's lost a fight against an army of strawberries.

Her cheeks are a deep crimson and the parts of her body not covered by her white towel are a marginally lighter shade of red. Her dark curls stick to her shoulders and face like the tentacles of a dozen dead octopuses.

Sebastian is halfway through his tenth mile on the brand new treadmill he ordered yesterday to replace the one on which Constance poured half a litre of vanilla milkshake – allegedly by accident.

He looks dashing in his workout clothes, a loose tank top and matching running shorts. He breathes evenly, hardly a hair out of place.

'Do you want a drink?' Constance offers as she walks past the water dispenser.

'I'm good, thanks.' Sebastian points at the medical-grade rehydration solution he religiously sips every ten minutes.

'You and your electrolytes! I'll have you know milk has

been proven to rehydrate you better than any energy drink… Even better than water.'

'Hear, hear,' says Sebastian without conviction. 'Could you please grab my phone? It's been vibrating and driving me nuts.'

'Gosh, you have thirteen missed calls. All from the same number.'

'Any message?'

Constance keys in his password and listens to his voice-mail. 'Someone named Sanjay Bakshi, from Ellison and White.'

'My accountants. I'm sure it can wait.'

'Apparently, Sanjay doesn't think so.'

'Pass it here.'

Constance throws the phone vaguely in his direction, and he catches it without breaking his steady run.

She downs four paper cups full of ice-cold water, and stops feeling like a steak on a hot grill.

When she returns her attention to Sebastian and the rhythmic rise and fall of his glutes, she notices a sudden rigidity in his back and a hunch of his shoulders. Her stomach tightens in response.

Something's wrong.

Sebastian gives out no clues, as he listens attentively to his caller.

'Yes, I get it.' A long silence. 'How much?'

'What's wrong?' asks Constance, whose virtues do not include patience.

Sebastian shushes her with a finger to his lips. His brow furrows. Constance suddenly feels nauseous.

'Call the lawyers,' says Sebastian into the phone. 'What do you mean, nothing they can do?'

His tone is sharp and business-like, and Constance has

never seen him look so serious. She steps closer to him for reassurance.

'Okay. Yeah. Bye.'

As Sebastian ends the call, Constance all but pounces on him. Her towel drops to the floor to reveal a pink and white bikini. 'What? What's wrong?' she asks.

Sebastian's lips form a tight, straight line, and Constance loses what's left of her composure. 'Tell me. Tell me now.'

'No,' says Sebastian firmly. 'You don't need to know.'

He steps off the treadmill, and meticulously returns all the dials to their original settings. He wipes the machine and takes a long drink from his water bottle.

'Don't you dare,' says Constance, raising her voice. She is struggling to stay calm, but Sebastian's stubborn expression is pressing all the wrong buttons. 'If you're in trouble, you have to tell me.'

'Just money stuff. Don't worry.'

'You're obviously worried about it.'

'I'm not worried.' He manages a carefree smile, but she isn't fooled.

'Angry then. What are you angry about?'

'Enough, Constance. Keep your nose out of my business.'

'Not a chance!' spits Constance, and to underline her determination to hear the truth, she shoves the water cooler so hard it tumbles onto the treadmill and release its contents – all twelve litres – into the motors.

'Not again!' shouts Sebastian, mopping the puddle around the machine with his pristine white towel. 'You've gone and broken this one too.'

Constance opens her mouth to retort, but Sebastian is quicker. 'Mind your own business, ain't nothing you can do about mine.'

He heads for the door, and she stands in his way; as he tries to side-step her, he slides on the wet tiles and lands in a heap against the cross-trainer.

Before he can stand up, Constance is on him, pressing her body weight into him to keep him from rising.

'Either I matter to you and you have to share your troubles with me, or I don't and there's no reason for you not to answer my question. You know you can trust me with any secret. It's not like I'm going to go and tell the press.'

'It's not that I don't trust you. Of course I do. I just want to process what I've just heard without you nagging me.'

'How long before you can tell me?'

'I dunno. A few days.' In an attempt to throw her off his lap, he circles his arms around her bare waist. This is the closest they've ever physically been, but have never felt further apart.

That is until she grabs his face and brings their lips within touching distance. As their eyes meet, a new warmth courses through their veins, and his body reacts to her touch.

If she asked him a question now, he would answer, but she doesn't. Instead she scrambles off him as if she's been burnt.

None of Sebastian's millions of fans would recognise their idol in the distraught stranger staring at Constance.

His breathing is erratic and his mouth twisted in a grimace of pain. His expression reminds her of the moment they met.

Just as she did then, she takes charge and comes to his rescue.

She plants her palms on either side of him. 'You know I'm not going to give up. I want to help you, and I'm worried for you. Just tell me what the accountant said, and let's turn our minds to solutions.'

He sighs. 'Tony has emptied most of my bank accounts.'

She blanches. 'How?'

'Power of attorney.'

'Why?'

He shrugs. 'To keep me in line, I guess.'

'So you have no money?'

He gives a laugh that sounds like a bark. 'Is that a problem for you?'

Constance narrows her eyes. 'Don't even. Have you got any money left, yes or no?'

'No. Just a line of credit the accountants negotiated with the bank and some cash in a couple of savings accounts. They're advising me to get a mortgage on the house, cheaper interest.'

'Surely there are limits to the power of attorney… He needs a reason for such a drastic move.'

'Maybe he heard about my meltdown in London. Danger to myself, not in a fit mental state to retain control over my money, etcetera.'

'That wouldn't stand up in court…'

'He can afford better lawyers.'

'There must be something you can do.'

'Look, Constance, I know how this town works. You don't. Tony saw I was pulling away from him, and he reasserted his power. If I don't do as I'm told, he'll tie my money into so many knots, I'll never see another dime of it.'

Constance sits back on her heels. 'He can't afford a high-profile lawsuit, with a mega-famous actor accusing him of embezzlement.'

'That's not going to be a quick way out of this. Plus, even if I won, I'd never work again after that.'

'Hollywood history is full of wayward actors who had a comeback.'

'The ones who died in poverty for being on some big-shot producer's shit list never make it into "Hollywood History". Had you ever heard of the actresses who got on the wrong side of Weinstein?'

'No,' admits Constance. 'But when the dominoes started to fall, he lost his power and they gained theirs. Tony must have an equally long list of victims.'

'If they never spoke up during the whole #MeToo, when they would have been supported and believed, they're unlikely to do so now.'

'But it's easier to prove he's taken your money than to prove he sexually harassed someone years ago.'

'He won't deny he took the money. He'll claim it's for my own good, because of my fragile mental state. Hard to prove I'm well after I disappeared for three days halfway through a promo tour, nearly killed myself and spent north of twenty million dollars cash on a house not even in Hollywood.'

There is a long silence during which Constance weighs his words in her mind.

'If you can't win, get out of the game. Sell the house. Twenty million dollars is enough for anyone to live on for the rest of their lives. You'll never want for anything. Go start a new life far from here, far from Tony and the likes of him.'

'And let him keep the money I earned? Nope. Not a chance.'

Constance's smile illuminates her face, and Sebastian's heart lurches in his chest.

'Life's about to get interesting,' she says while helping him off the floor. As they walk past the treadmill, she hands him his water bottle.

'Your magic potion,' she grins. 'You're going to need it.'

He grabs the bottle and when he reaches her he pulls the

strings of her bikini top, leaving her struggling to keep the triangles of fabric over her breasts.

'Sexual assault!' she laughs.

'Indecent exposure!' he smiles over his shoulder.

39

25 APRIL – SEBASTIAN'S MANSION, PACIFIC PALISADES HILLS, LOS ANGELES, CALIFORNIA, USA

Constance and Sebastian are dozing on their sun loungers, their fingers intertwined, but not otherwise minding each other. Music is escaping from his headphones, and she's checking her messages on Instagram.

> *Myname.sNotConnie* @*FitnessPhilly289* – *All good now, we had a chat. His boss would make the Godfather run back to his mamma. Bit stressful.*
> *FitnessPhilly289* @*Myname.sNotConnie* – *Tell him if he doesn't behave, Wayne will cancel his birth certificate… Check out my brand new avocado and zucchini 'A to Z' delight.*
> *Myname.sNotConnie* @*FitnessPhilly289* – *For a Christian you're generous with death threats *wink*. You mean IRL or his boss?*
> *FitnessPhilly289* @*Myname.sNotConnie* – BOTH!
> *Myname.sNotConnie* @*FitnessPhilly289* – *I'd*

better do what I'm told and try your alphabetical smoothie, before I make it onto your kill list. xx

The sun is high and the air is still; the soothing sound of crickets is suddenly disrupted by the clickety-clack of expensive heels on the smooth flagstones surrounding the pool.

'Hey, lovebirds! Get out of the sack, I need to talk to you,' hollers Regina. Neither Sebastian nor Constance stirs.

Eventually, a shadow falls on their linked hands, and Regina comes into view wearing a loose, ankle-length, purple tie-dye dress.

Sebastian is the first to open his eyes. 'Hi Regina, would you like a seat?' He gestures to the wrought iron armchair next to his lounger.

Regina grabs Sebastian's square jaw and swivels his face from left to right while air-kissing him loudly.

Sebastian rolls his eyes and takes out his headphones. Regina sits at the foot of Constance's lounger.

'So you're still here?' she says over her shoulder. 'Awesome!'

Regina's expression softens when she turns back to Sebastian. 'I am the bearer of great news!' she booms.

Constance sits up and lets go of Sebastian's hand. He seizes it again.

'All ears, ma'am,' he tells Regina politely.

'I'm bringing you this new screenplay that fell into my lap just this morning. Pure gold. Tough guy with some hidden depths. Just the stuff to transition you into Oscar material. Jerry Blacklock called me this morning with an amazing proposal for you.'

She waits for Sebastian's response, a carefully crafted look of elation on her face.

'I'm listening…'

She takes out of her huge Prada handbag a bound manuscript she shoves into Sebastian's stomach.

'Eric Dravner to direct, *very nice* co-star TBC. And a huge, *huge* budget! Sky's the limit and they just want you! What do you say?!' She doesn't pause for him to answer. 'Shooting's in Hawaii. Three weeks tops, plus two in studio in Burbank. Jehane McCarthy is already signed up, and so is Teddy Booth. Golden opportunity!'

'Sounds awesome,' admits Sebastian. 'Where's the catch?'

'100% no catch. Who do you take me for? And the money is twice what you made last time.'

'When would I start?'

Regina's smile is brighter than the sun. Constance frowns.

'On the first.'

'First of what?' asks Sebastian.

'First of May,' replies Regina without batting an eyelid.

Constance and Sebastian say together, 'Next week?' Then Constance repeats, 'Next week?' even more incredulously, while at the same time Sebastian asks, 'Who dropped out?'

'Bruce Willis,' replies Regina.

Sebastian's jaw drops. 'Bruce Willis?' he stammers.

Constance speaks over Sebastian. 'But he's fifty!'

'Try sixty,' he says.

Regina fails to keep the irritation out of her voice. 'All right, they're desperate. And I've managed to shoehorn you into an audition tomorrow. So, you're going to make yourself look pretty, learn your lines, get your butt over there two hours early and wait nicely in the corridor until they're ready for you! *Capisce*?'

'But really, Regina, next week! Come on,' says Sebastian.

'Next month, next week, tomorrow, today… what does it

matter?' says Regina. 'This is perfect for you. I had to beg them to give you a shot!'

Sebastian rubs his face, takes the script, and walks slowly back towards the house.

'Really?' shouts Constance, squaring up to Regina. 'You're telling him today for next week? He's knackered, he needs to rest. We've just got back from a round-the-world promotion tour. He's got a lot on his mind. He can't start Monday. No bloody surprise you drove him to suicide!'

'Oh, shut your mouth, doll face. Drawing ducklings has never got anyone a mansion in Hollywood.'

'This is Pacific Palisades, not bloody Hollywood! And it worked for Walt Disney, you shit-for-brains! I'd forgotten what kind of slave-driver you are!'

'You're so fucking pampered, you can't even realise that, right now, there are at least forty – four-zero – other agents scrambling over each other to claw that opportunity for their guys! How do you think this business works? Han Solo is going to audition for that part!'

'You mean Harrison Ford?'

'Yes, Brunette Barbie, I mean Harrison fucking Ford *and* Samuel L. and every other fucker within thirty years of the right age group and vaguely the same colour! But my guy – my guy, he has the face of a fucking angel and abs that don't need three months in the gym. He's ready to go and he's hard-working, and he doesn't bitch about his co-stars! That's the kind of dedication that gets you somewhere in this business. And I, missy, am gonna get him somewhere! Whether *you* like it or not!'

Constance listens to the whole tirade open-mouthed.

'I've been singing his praises in four octaves all morning for this,' Regina continues. 'You don't know how this town works. I'm his agent, do you understand what that means? I fight for him, day and night, to bring him what he needs to make a career. When they say, "He's a nobody," I say, "He looks like a Greek god!" When they say, "He thinks Method acting is a cleaning product," I say, "Look at that slab of abs! Those are not spray-painted on!" When they say, "We like the sound of Brian Balfour," I say, "Seb can start Monday!" That's how this works. He knows it. That's what he's got to do. So, spare us your whining, little girl!'

'You are one of two worst individuals I have ever met,' retorts Constance.

'Well, you haven't been in LA very long, *darling*!' Regina snorts. 'What are you still doing here anyway?'

'I live here,' says Constance acidly.

'Give me a fucking break!'

Alerted by the raised voices, Sebastian returns to police the poolside. 'Hey, ladies. Calm down. I'm gonna read this now and I'll let you know by six.'

'I've already said yes on your behalf,' Regina points out.

'Let's just hope I like the script.'

'It's eight million fucking dollars. You'll do it, or I quit.'

'What does Tony say?'

'How do you think I was talking to Sam Woodhouse in the first fucking place, asshole? He's a fucking Academy Award Winner, he wouldn't even be talking to me if Tony wasn't twisting his dick!'

'Okay, I get it. Verbal agreement only though. Give me until six o'clock tonight.'

'Sure, boss man,' Regina sneers before stalking away in a gunfight of heels on stone.

'Gawd!' Constance exclaims, appalled. 'That is no way to treat a client.'

'I'm not her client, I'm more like her meal-ticket,' quips Sebastian.

His light tone smooths Constance's furrowed brow. She lets out a big sigh. 'Hawaii, eh? Not so bad.'

'Yes, not so bad,' agrees Sebastian, a bit too keenly.

40

26 APRIL – SEBASTIAN'S MANSION, PACIFIC PALISADES HILLS, LOS ANGELES, CALIFORNIA, USA

Sebastian and Constance lounge in their enormous sofa, eating salad from plates balanced on their laps while watching a TV show. It's the advert break.

She's wearing shorts and a vest top, her hair piled on top of her head in a precarious messy bun.

He's sporting slightly too large sweatpants and a slightly too small T-shirt. His hair is wet from the shower and sticks out in all possible directions.

'So how many days are you actually going to shoot in Hawaii? Regina is no friend of details.'

He chuckles. 'Schedule says three weeks, but first one week in San Francisco to shoot scenes inside a twelve-foot sailing boat. Then Burbank for eight weeks and after that Hawaii.'

'That's only four weeks away from home. Not too bad.'
'Not too bad' is her new catchphrase, as she insists on putting a positive spin on what is by any standard not an ideal situation.

'We'll still have to be in a hotel while shooting in Burbank. Can't afford to waste the travelling time.'

'What? What do you mean? You're going to stay in a hotel an hour away from your house?'

'I'm going to work eighteen hours a day, I can't go home every night. By the time my head hit the pillow, I'd have to get up again. Also, it's nice to be in the same hotel as the rest of the crew. You bond, you get more stuff done.'

'But what about me?' asks Constance in a tiny voice.

'You can be there with me when you want to and here when you don't.'

'I can't just sit in your hotel room for eighteen hours a day.'

'Then find something to do.'

'Are you saying you want me to go home?'

'To London? No.'

'What am I going to do without you here?'

'Do the same stuff you would be doing in London. Working, making friends, sightseeing? I dunno.'

Constance gives her salad a murderous look. Sebastian is watching her closely through his eyelashes while still eating.

After a long silence, he says, 'It's the sex scenes, right?'

Constance straightens as if she's been tasered. 'Course not, that's ridiculous! The whole thing is ridiculous! Aphasic Afghanistan veteran turns surfer pro and finds a treasure under the sea with the help of busty damsel-in-distress. It's basically the plot of *Nemo*!'

Sebastian can't see the connection. 'The fish thing?' he asks, incredulous.

But Constance is too busy ranting. 'They've only got one bloody plot. Every story is the same.'

'All about orphan fish,' deadpans Sebastian. 'I'm playing a human Nemo. Wish the director told me that. It's really going to help me with my prep!'

'Shut up, you know what I mean.'

'I know what you *mean*, but I can't understand two words of what you're *saying*.'

Constance changes tack. 'Shush, I'm watching TV. It's not all about you, you know,' she frowns.

'Obviously not,' he jokes. 'It's all about Nemo.'

'Shut up! I can't hear a thing.'

'It's *Biggest Celebrity Hoarder*, you don't need to hear it.'

'You *said* you were happy to watch it.'

'Hang on.' He pushes her plate away, and sits on the coffee table in front of her. He leans his forehead toward hers. She has no choice but to look him in the eyes.

'It's a job,' he says softly. 'With an *actress*. We're not really having sex. We're not even going to be fully naked.'

'It's shit enough when your boyfriend gets paid to suck face with an underwear model, but it gets a whole lot shittier when he does things with her he doesn't do with you.'

They both look down at the floor and there's a long silence. Constance is on the verge of tears.

'How about we pretend we're both actors and we're doing a love scene?'

'W—what?'

'We script it. We arrange the setting...'

Constance panics, 'You want to film me—?'

'No, not film. We decide exactly what we're going to do. Who's putting their hand where, who's leaning which way, who's kissing who and how. Everything gets worked out in advance. Like a shoot.'

'I don't know. That sounds pretty weird.'

'Let me tell you it would be a lot less weird than with a film crew,' he laughs.

She thinks about it. 'You're not making it sound very romantic.'

'That's my whole point. It's *not* romantic at all when

you're acting. It's awkward and sweaty. Those lamps are like sitting in an oven. And you have those ridiculous strips of fabric to cover your junk, and the girls have duct tape across their nipples and you're both wearing make-up everywhere. It's embarrassing and gross.'

'It sounds pretty much like my sex life so far,' she pouts.

Sebastian arches an eyebrow but lets it go. 'What do you say? Let's give it a shot.'

'You're not selling it to me. It sounds far too kinky.'

'One, you will see what I'm doing out there with these girls, it's nothing like what I would do with you. Two, you will see I too have some experience with pretending I'm enjoying sex. Three, if it really sucks, we can console ourselves that it wasn't for real.'

'Four, you get to paw me everywhere, you man-slut.'

'No ma'am, I only get to paw you where you agreed. Them's the rules.'

'I don't know. I'm embarrassed just thinking about it. But it definitely makes me feel better about you doing the beast with two backs with that girl.'

'Strictly doggy-style, it's in her contract.'

Constance's jaw drops, she looks at him with panicked incredulity.

'Something to do with her boob job scars,' he adds.

'You are pulling my leg!'

Sebastian grins with all his white teeth. 'Yes, ma'am.'

Constance kicks him in the leg.

'Ouch! That hurt! You gonna be a proper little dominatrix, once we get you started!'

'Shut up!'

Sebastian mimicking her, says, '*We are not having S.E.X!* Gotcha.' He gets up and walks towards the stairs. 'But we're doing a sex tape!'

'We are *not* doing a sex tape!' shouts Constance.

Once he's out of sight, her indignation is replaced by awkwardness. She puts her hands to her burning cheeks and stares at the floor.

41

26 APRIL – SEBASTIAN'S MANSION, PACIFIC PALISADES HILLS, LOS ANGELES, CALIFORNIA, USA

Constance is perched on a chrome and leather bar stool with her knees propping up her chin. She's hugging her legs.

Sebastian is sitting on the white granite bar with his legs on either side of her.

He's wearing swimming trunks, his skin perfectly smooth and tanned, but covered in coloured stickers.

She's wearing leggings and an off-the-shoulder yoga top. She has masking tape down her arms and neck with words and numbers scribbled on them.

'I told you it would be more comfortable on my bed,' says Sebastian. 'Or on the sofa. Have you seen many sex scenes in kitchens before?! It's just too dadgum uncomfortable!'

'I don't want to do that in a bed!' insists Constance. 'I've got enough traumatic memories, thank-you-very-much. This is shaping up to be a cringe-fest! I'm not doing that in my bed. I've got to sleep there tonight!'

'I said *on my* bed, not in yours.'

'N-O, no!' shouts Constance.

Sebastian looks heavenward and prays for patience. 'Let's

recap. First, I take your right arm here, near the elbow. Then you put your left hand on my right shoulder, where it says "Hand #1". Have you got this?'

'Yes,' she hesitates.

'Then, I grab you by the waist, here and there.' He points to the stickie notes on either side of her yoga top.'

'Okay.'

'Then what do you do?'

Constance frowns in deep concentration. 'I put both my hands on your chest, where it says "Hand #2" and "Hand #3", which is ridiculous, because I haven't got three hands!'

Sebastian releases a calming breath. 'Great, that's it. What next?'

'You tilt me towards the microwave and kiss me on the neck.'

Sebastian nods. 'While you press both your hands on my shoulders blades—'

'With my fourth and fifth hands. I get it!'

'The whole point is for you to know exactly what's going to happen, before it happens, so that you don't freak out.'

'And you can get another notch on your bedpost,' she pouts.

'There are no notches on my bedpost, as you well know, since we've not been apart for months,' Sebastian corrects patiently.

'I'm sorry. I'm just feeling so silly. This is not working for me.'

'At least you're getting the measure of how romantic or arousing it is *not* to shoot a love scene for a movie.'

Constance blows air out of her mouth to shift the heavy lock of hair that covers half her face. To no avail.

Sebastian delicately tucks it behind her ear. They exchange a meaningful look as she leans her face into his hand.

'This is a stupid idea,' she says.

Sebastian winks. 'I was just starting to have fun.'

'Sex pest.'

Sebastian smiles. 'Prude.'

Constance gives him a bashful look that stops his heart. On impulse, he grabs her shoulders and bring his face within kissing distance of hers. 'I love you,' he says.

Overwhelmed by the scent of chypre and bergamot, Constance only just manages to hold his gaze. 'I heard you the first time. And the second time.'

Sebastian lets her go, but they stay close and stare at each other.

'You remember when I said everything was about sex, because sex wasn't just about sex?'

'How could I forget?' replies Constance with gentle sarcasm.

'When you call me "jerktard" or "dick sock", what I'm really hearing is "I love you".'

'That explains a lot,' says Constance under her breath, but her soft expression is unchanged.

Sebastian ignores the interruption. 'That's about sex. Because it's not the words or the actions, it's the feelings. The feelings between us, they've been there right from the start. The sexual attraction, the rapport, it's getting us through all the other shit. Some people may have a "normal" sex life, kids together, but when you don't have that connection, you're just turning up in the final five minutes of the game, just in time to read the scoreboard and go home. You've missed all the anticipation, the joy, the fear, the despair, the redemption... You've missed it all.'

Constance nods in agreement. 'What are we going to do?'

'We're going to keep loving each other, and we're going to be patient. We'll get there.'

She peels off a strip of masking tape from his pecs and takes hair away with it. He grimaces. She leans in and kisses the sore skin.

He holds her arm out and removes the tape that runs along the inside of it and kisses a trail from her wrist to the crook of her elbow. Her cheeks go pink, but he avoids her eyes and turns to put the tape in the bin.

They continue to rid themselves of stickers in silence.

42

10 MAY – HOTEL IN BURBANK, LOS ANGELES, CALIFORNIA, USA

Constance and Sebastian have been living in a grubby hotel room for the last ten days.

Their room boasts two double beds, usually left unmade by the maids until the evening sun stains the sheets a dirty yellow.

The brown carpet is sticky from too many chemical cleaning treatments, and patches of intense wear are visible at the foot of the beds.

The shortest distance from the beds to the bathroom has been mapped out by thousands of feet, leaving an imprint the size of the Grand Canyon.

The bathroom itself – which they have to share – is a milky-coffee-coloured shrine to the '90s, complete with patterned wall tiles framed in browning grout, and the sucker-punch smell of disinfectant.

The only redeeming feature is that the shower is suitably powerful and hot, and Constance spends half an hour every morning, eyes shut, under the warm jets. It is without fail the best moment of her day.

Sebastian does not have the luxury of long showers. He has to make do with five minutes before his 5 a.m.

rendezvous with Maggie, the make-up artist tasked with making him look the right kind of tired and depressed. Or to be precise a more attractive and manly version of the tired and depressed look that he's been sporting ever since arriving in Burbank.

His week in San Francisco was hell. Twenty hours a day immersed in water gave him eczema all over his body and chronically bloodshot eyes.

He'd stopped eating and, with his cheekbones threatening to break through his skin, Constance hardly recognised him when he came home for an overnight stay before joining the rest of the crew in Burbank. She insisted on going with him, but she is at her wits' end trying to cheer him up.

She has visited every art gallery, cinema, and museum in the town, and she's even cycled the Ballona Creek circuit twice.

She is in no mood to shop for clothes; such a frivolous pursuit would be too much at odds with Sebastian's pain-filled days. So, she does what she can to keep herself from sinking into despondency by drawing.

She's sitting at the fake oak veneered desk, surrounded by the strewn contents of her art box, and she doesn't turn around when Sebastian enters.

Sadness fills the room.

He lowers himself onto one of the beds with grunts of pain.

For a long time, they don't speak or move. Eventually, Constance comes to sit by his side. She sighs. 'Shoulder rub?'

Sebastian has his face in the pillow. 'Hurts everywhere.'

'I can't believe it's all going so slowly, it's been over a week and they still can't get all the harnessing right.' She lifts the hem of his shirt. 'Is that another bruise? It's the size of my hand.'

'I freaking hate these freaking scenes!' moans Sebastian.

'And the lighting is still shit. The 3rd AD is gonna get it now, finally.'

'We could leave. Just go away, change our names.'

'I need the cash, if you remember.'

'No, you don't. By most people's standards, you're filthy rich and set up for life.'

'Not after Tony sues me for breach of contract and takes the rest of my money.'

'Have you heard anything from the accountants?'

'I told them to lay low.'

'You did what?'

'I told them to pretend nothing had happened. I'm not gonna to waste my cartridges.'

'But now he thinks he got away with it. He must be rubbing his hands in glee.'

'If I know him at all, me not doing anything is unnerving him more than if I went on some hopeless legal rampage.'

Constance can only cross her fingers he is right. Her hatred for Tony has grown exponentially in the days since the crew settled at the grotty end of Burbank.

Between her morning hot shower and Sebastian's return late at night, she has ample time to daydream about all the ways she would like to rip apart Academy Award Winner Tony da Ricci PGA.

She has visions of his life imploding like the Death Star at the end of *Star Wars*. One small, determined fighter, hitting the secret weak spot at the heart of the war machine.

Yes, that could work.

'Regina is spitting furious,' says Constance to change the subject. 'She called the lawyers in front of me earlier.'

'Rich pickings?'

'Relatively modest – "cocksplurt" and my personal favourite, "nutsack grooming"…'

Sebastian gives a tired chuckle and Constance continues. 'Apparently, that's what the lawyers have been doing while you're getting bashed around instead of checking the Health and Safety clause in your contract.'

Sebastian doesn't reply.

Constance tries to cheer him up. 'I was sitting there, minding my own business, drawing naughty little bunnies who won't brush their teeth, and listening to this volcanic eruption of anger and X-rated swearing. Made me feel quite dirty.'

'I can't wait to go home and sleep for weeks, then have sex for weeks, then sleep again,' he says with feeling.

She grins. 'You thought I wouldn't notice you slotting S.E.X. into that sentence?'

'A man can dream,' he winks. 'That thought is the only thing keeping me going at the moment.'

She frowns.

'Mind you,' he continues. 'I do also get excited about the position of the bread rolls in Da Vinci's "Last Supper". Apparently, if you see them as musical notes and read them from right to left, they sound like a requiem.'

'W—what?' stammers Constance, successfully distracted from talk of sex.

'True story. Look it up.'

'You're such a muppet,' she says with a dramatic eye roll.

Sebastian falls silent.

She leans over him, holding her hair away from his face, and listens close to his cheek to hear if he's sleeping. She drapes the comforter over him and curls up next to him with an arm over his shoulder.

'What a nightmare,' she says to herself.

43

10 MAY – HOTEL IN BURBANK, LOS ANGELES, CALIFORNIA, USA

*B*oth Sebastian and Constance are sleeping when Regina lets herself in.

She's wearing a black skirt suit, and the tail of her burgundy silk shirt is hanging loose on one side. She taps Sebastian on the shoulder.

Even her whisper sounds tired. 'Eric wants you for a close-up on Set 3.'

He stirs awake, rising up on his forearms. He does a double-take noticing Constance's sleeping form beside him.

It's the first time she's fallen asleep so close. Reluctantly, he rolls off the bed, trying not to wake her, and he disappears into the bathroom.

Constance opens her eyes.

'What a nightmare,' Regina says to her.

'You're doing all you can,' Constance says earnestly.

'I know I'm a temperamental, loud-mouthed pain in the ass, but I look after my clients. My job is to keep them away from douche-baggy, incompetent, asswad directors who can't get their shit together. You know what I mean?'

'With you all the way. What's Tony up to?'

'Pawing the leading lady. What else? He likes them stick-thin and preferably frightened.'

'He's such a shit.'

'Says anybody with a vagina in the Northern Hemisphere. Nothing new. What bugs me most is not what we're going through right now... This *Towering Inferno* of flaming shit they're shooting is going to be out there at-a-screen-near-you with *his* name on it.' She indicates the bathroom with her thumb. 'For. Ever.'

Constance deadpans, 'I'm thinking Outer Hebrides...'

'Save me a seat,' says Regina.

'Or a witness protection programme; we could have aliases.' Constance is feeling brave and adds cheekily, 'You could be Mrs Moreno, our housekeeper.'

Regina chortles. 'I've already cleaned up enough shit for you two. You would be my manicurist and he my pool boy, Arnie.'

Emboldened by Regina joining the game, Constance continues. 'Or we could travel the world as a mime trio act. You'd rock the beret and the stripy top.'

'What's that?' asks Sebastian from the bathroom.

Constance and Regina answer together, 'Shut up, Arnie!' They smile as they catch each other's eye, giggling like naughty schoolgirls.

Constance stands and hugs Sebastian briefly as he leaves with Regina in tow. She stares at the space where he was with a look of intense longing.

At least, he has Regina with him.

44

8 JUNE – HOTEL IN BURBANK, LOS ANGELES, CALIFORNIA, USA

*A*month later, in the same hotel, Constance and Sebastian are standing on either side of their bedroom threshold.

Inside, Constance is trying to shut the door on herself, while Sebastian struggles to keep it open.

The timer-activated overhead lights decide they've spent long enough in the corridor and plunge them into a near-darkness interrupted only by the red emergency exit signs.

Constance is crying and letting loose an uninterrupted flow of lamentations. 'I can't believe you cheated on me! I'm such an idiot. Of course, you cheated. Four months we were together.' She lowers her voice to a furious whisper. 'No sex. You're not a monk! But I can't believe—! I can't believe you went and had a *baby*!'

Sebastian tries to stay calm, but mostly fails. 'I didn't,' he growls. 'She's *lying!* It's not my child. And I know that for certain because I've never had sex with her. I didn't cheat.' He too is lowering his voice to a fervent whisper. 'I was *waiting*. I *am* waiting for you.' He says louder, 'Let me *in*!'

Constance has tears dripping from her wobbly chin. 'Go away! Everyone can see you!'

'I don't care! I don't *fucking* care if the whole hotel can hear me. Baby, none of it is true. If you only knew what these women are like. It's not the first time this has happened.'

Sebastian takes advantage of Constance's surprise to gain access to the room. He closes the door behind him.

In the dimly lit room, the beds are still unmade, and the remnants of Constance's breakfast clutter the desk at which she normally works.

Today, she has done nothing but cry. Ever since that text hit her phone halfway through her daily banana and kale smoothie. She wasn't prepared for what she saw when she distractedly opened the link under a laconic message entitled 'thought u should c this'.

She wished she had kept to her rule never to open anything with bad spelling. 'Randy Anders' announced the headline. 'I'm keeping my baby,' said the article. A quote from a blonde with two inches of make-up on her face and boobs fit for flotation, if not lactation.

Most of the West Coast would have seen the article by now, the cherry on top of a trashy celeb-obsessed personal blog, compulsively read by everyone and their yoga instructor in Twinkle Town.

'Not the first time it happened?' she shouts. 'Not the first time? How many kids have you got then? I can't believe it!'

'You can't believe it because *it's not true*! I haven't had sex with her. I've never had sex without protection. Ever.'

Constance counters a tad over-dramatically. 'Oh, I might be naive but I've heard all about women fiddling with condoms to steal men's sperm!'

'I'm sure you're an expert, babe,' says Sebastian, trying

and failing to lighten the mood, 'but I wouldn't be that careless as to leave *anything* behind.'

'Gross!' Constance says grumpily.

'Let's sit down. Talk to me.' He tries to lead her to the stripy green and red sofa squeezed between the twin wardrobes. He has a hold of her hand and for a minute he thinks she's calmed down.

'No, I need a break.' She pulls her hand out of his grip with so much force that it hits her in the stomach. Undistracted, she continues. 'I just need to be on my own.'

Sebastian grabs two handfuls of his hair. Maggie in Hair and Make-up will have a fit. 'Okay listen,' he says.

'I don't want to hear it.'

'She's not the first one. She's just a cynical girl, hungry for a bit of attention and mischief. She believes I sleep with so many girls I couldn't be sure whether she was lying. Maybe she's ashamed to be pregnant, or she's trying to make herself interesting, trying to garner some support. I don't know. What I do know is I remember all the girls I've slept with, and she isn't one of them. Her baby cannot possibly be mine.'

He takes a swift breath and she doesn't seize the opportunity to start shouting again. His stomach relaxes. 'I've not been with another woman since I've met you. We've been together all the time. I've been working or I've been with you. When am I supposed to have fathered a child?'

'I want to believe you. It's just that I could so well understand if you wanted to have a bit of sex on the side. I'm being so rubbish and making no progress. There's just no end in sight. I can't imagine how discouraged you must feel.'

Sebastian is exasperated. 'God! Why is it so hard for you to understand? I want a future with you. I want to spend the rest of my life with you. So, I'm waiting. What's six months? What's a year when I can be with the only girl I've ever loved?

I'm so in love with you. I'm not interested in anyone else. You fill all the space. I look at you and I see no one else.'

Constance pouts, 'You must admit celibacy is a strain for you.'

'It's not easy, but where I come from lots of people still wait to be married to have sex.'

'Arranged marriages and religious nuts!'

'Or maybe some men just wait for their girls to be ready.'

'You've been watching too many Hallmark movies! Life isn't like that. This is all bullshit. I can't go through this every time a bimbo wants her minute in the spotlight. I've got to look after myself.'

'I'll look after you,' promises Sebastian.

'You're not in a position to do that. Your life is too public. I'm too private. I just want to crawl under a rock right now.' Constance manoeuvres him back through the door.

'Don't do it, baby,' begs Sebastian. 'You promised you'd never leave again.'

'It's you who's leaving,' says Constance, as she pushes him out and shuts the door on him.

She expects a knock or some words whispered through the wood panel, but nothing comes. Instead she hears the soft rub of his trainers on the hallway carpet as he walks back to the set.

Now she's alone, she crumbles in a heap.

45

8 JUNE – MOTEL IN SHERMAN VILLAGE, LOS ANGELES, CALIFORNIA, USA

Constance commits the capital mistake of choosing the Interstate 5 South instead of Highway 101 when she drives off the hotel parking lot in Sebastian's brand new Audi.

To be fair, she is crying her eyes out and probably shouldn't be behind the wheel in the first place.

Now she is stuck in the LA traffic, which reminds her of London and makes her miss Oggie the Twingo so badly her stomach aches.

She'd love to go home to Henley for a while, but for obvious reasons – there is after all a whole continent plus an ocean between her and her own front door – she will have to settle for Pacific Palisades.

She's somewhere in Sherman Village when it strikes her. She doesn't have the keys to Sebastian's mansion, and there is no way she's turning around to go and ask him.

Girl, you need to calm down first. Think through what Sebastian said.

Her hands are shaking, as she flicks the indicator and swings into a motel parking lot. 'Miko Hotel' announces the neon sign. 'Vacancies available.'

The building looks uninviting, cream and squat with long-suffering palm trees standing guard in front of each tired-looking room door. But she needs somewhere to regroup, and this will do just as well as the next crummy motel.

She is sure the bored teen at the reception already knows that Sebastian cheated on her with a freshly pregnant bimbo. Notwithstanding girl code, she secretly agrees with him for preferring someone who actually likes sex to a nothing-special frigid illustrator from the Home Counties.

Once the story breaks, and it will, she believes 100% of men will side with Sebastian, and the majority of women too. When you have a chance to share a bed with a sex symbol like Sebastian Anders, you get over yourself and you stake your claim, before the next busty blonde has a chance to.

You snooze, you lose.

Despite insisting she only needs a single room, she is handed the key to a family room with two double beds and a sofa bed, plus a foldable cot in the closet.

This underscores what she will never have, and fresh tears pour down her face before she's even had a chance to close the door.

She's packed haphazardly but manages to retrieve a linen dress from her suitcase that still smells faintly of 'Pour Monsieur' and looks like she's slept in it.

She hangs the dress in the bathroom while she showers in the dim hope steam and gravity will de-crease the fabric. When she finally comes out of the shower, her skin wrinkled and raw, she steps into a humid cloud that brings sweat back to every single pore of her skin.

She cries while she rubs her body dry and slithers into the dress, which immediately sticks to her skin like a wet paper towel.

Staring at her open suitcase, she realises she's forgotten her toiletry bag, and the motel doesn't provide deodorant. She's also left her hairbrush behind. She will look like an '80's hard rock lead singer for the foreseeable future.

The room is too quiet, and she turns on the TV. The local news comes on and explains the massive traffic jam in which she was stuck is due to an overturned milk truck. The freeway will be blocked for hours and the anchor-woman advises all motorists to make alternative arrangements.

If this is anything like London, the whole area will be gridlocked, and any route – no matter how convoluted – will keep her stuck in Sebastian's car for hours.

She doesn't think she can actually sit in the car that smells of him, with his Starbucks reusable coffee cup still in the driver's retractable cup-holder. Nothing she can do right now, except wait for the traffic to clear.

She's trying hard not to think at all. But the fight she had with Sebastian replays on a loop in her mind. His distraught face, his pleading eyes, his muscles bulging with the effort he made to keep their bedroom door open.

I was waiting, he said. *Don't leave, you promised.*

She can't blame him for having needs. Was she really expecting him to stay celibate just for her? That wasn't fair. She shouldn't have asked him that. She set him up for failure.

This is all my fault. My own stupid fault.

She tries his number. Straight to voicemail. She throws herself onto one of the beds, the right one, the one she always slept in when they were hotel-hopping round the world, and she dissolves into sobs.

46

10 JUNE – PARADISE BAY RESORT, O'AHU ISLAND, HAWAII, USA

Sebastian's new hotel room is a far cry from the dump they stayed in in Burbank.

It is light and clean, with open views on a sea of palm trees. The turquoise ocean beyond reminds him of their house in Pacific Palisades.

Except he is alone. So alone he can't enjoy the chatter of tropical birds gallivanting outside his private terrace, nor the multi-coloured fruit salad that magically appears twice daily on his coffee table, nor the cheerfully named smoothies he orders for his lunch as a memento of Constance.

To date, he's tried Mango Mambo, Pineapple Paso Doble, and Kiwi Quickstep, but he feels not at all cheered up.

Quite the contrary.

He looks even more exhausted than he was before the fight with Constance, and his right shoulder hangs at an unnatural angle. He's been told it's not dislocated, but he's not so sure. The shot the crew doctor gave him has dissolved the pain into a tepid cloud of sedation.

He throws himself on the bed and pulls out his phone and makes a call.

'Constance?...' A pause. 'Baby, it's me again. Did you get my messages?' A pause. 'I've just finished an eighteen-hour stretch, including nightshift. I'm beat... just lying there on my bed. Wishing you were here. You know, like when you used to lie on my back... and I would complain about your weight. We would joke about pounds and stones and that petition of yours... I miss you, baby. I miss you so much. I would give anything to feel your weight on top of me. Without you, I'm floating. Like a boat in a storm. Call me baby, please. Just... call me. Please.'

He finishes the call, his eyes closing already. He falls asleep. An hour later, he jerks awake, sitting up abruptly. He makes another phone call.

'Constance, it's me again. Bad enough I've had to fly out here without you, I can't understand why you're not answering my messages. What's happening? Are you really breaking up with me? Don't you believe me? Don't give me the silent treatment, you promised not to leave me ever again. Please call me. Please.'

Sebastian lies awake for a while, checking his phone several times. Eventually, he drifts off back to sleep.

Some time later, there's a knock on the door, followed by Tony marching into the room like Louis XIV entering the Versailles Hall of Mirrors.

'Get your ass to Set 2,' he declares without preamble, the smell of bourbon travelling on his breath. Alarm bells start ringing in Sebastian's mind. It is still early for the stink to be so strong.

'Some douchebag fucked up. The shots are unusable. They want to redo the scene. Go to make-up first.'

Sebastian raises his head, and his eyes meet Tony's. 'I've been told to go on a break.'

'Sorry, I can't find the fuck I'm supposed to give. They

need your face in front of the camera and your feet on that mark in twenty minutes. Get your ass off the bed.'

'You guys have been riding me too hard, man. I'm hanging by a thread. The way I feel... People aren't meant to feel this way. If this goes on any longer, I won't have to do anything dramatic. I won't even have to make a decision. Just lay there and die.'

Tony's expression changes into a rare display of concern. He sits next to Sebastian on the bed. 'Hey buddy, what's up? Is it because of that girl?'

Sebastian remains silent while he stares at his blistered feet.

'She's not worth it, man. If you'd tapped that, you wouldn't be pining for her now. Bitch 101. Gives you blue balls.'

Sebastian still doesn't speak.

'I know she didn't put out,' continues Tony softly, 'and that is so fucking infuriating, believe me I know. I feel for you, but you have to pull yourself together. The movie needs you. This is a great opportunity for you, I need you at the top of your game. You can get all the pussy you can handle when we get back to LA.'

'I don't know if I will last that long. I'm falling to pieces, Tone.'

There is a long silence during which Sebastian stretches out on the bed. He closes his eyes. In his mind, he's back in his new home with Constance in her red bikini.

When the blow lands, he doubles up over the pain in his gut.

As he opens his eyes, he sees Tony, his face a mask of rage, his fist raised, ready for a second punch. 'Any more of your "I'm gonna die" shit, and I'll have you committed, you psycho! Fly over a cuckoo's nest. Straightjacket…The whole fucking nine yards!'

Because Sebastian is young and fit he manages to roll off the bed quicker than Tony can hit him again, and takes refuge on the terrace. He just has time to slide the patio door shut before Tony spits on the glass and unleashes a torrent of insults.

'Get your ass over here, you pathetic motherfucker. Fuck your teenage angst and go to work before I break your fucking face! Then I'll eat it and spew it up. You hear me?'

On his side of the reinforced glass panels, Sebastian, his biceps straining to stop Tony from opening the door, can only stare into a pair of bloodshot eyes.

'You are being paid millions for this!' shouts Tony. 'For three months of your pathetic life, you're being paid more than 99.99% of people will ever make in their lives. You are beyond fucking lucky, you're blessed. And I have to stand here and watch you cry in your pillow because you're tired and some girl gave you the boot? You make me sick!' Tony's fist slams into the doorframe.

Sebastian is suddenly afraid of what he might have to do to Tony to avoid being thrown off a fifth-floor balcony. Being charged with assault is the last thing he needs right now.

As the window rattles, Sebastian's heart is beating like a drum, and his muscles tense in preparation for a physical assault.

'Go to work, your motherfucking man-whore!' Tony screams from inside the room. 'What do you think the crew is doing? Don't you think *they*'re tired? Do you think they want to see you moan and cry and feel sorry for yourself? *Ooh, I'm earning millions, pity me!* They're doing the same hours as you and for the fucking minimum wage. You disgust me. If they knew what a limp dick you are, they would spit in your face and go home! You're so fucking weak, you make me puke. I'm going to barf all over your fucking face.'

When he temporarily runs out of insults, Tony goes silent. He's staring missiles at Sebastian.

This is the moment Sebastian was waiting for. 'Step back and I'll come out,' he says as calmly as he can manage. He was right; perhaps he didn't need to do anything to die. Maybe Tony would take care of that too for him.

Like a pantomime clown, Tony's face goes from furious to conciliatory. 'That's all I'm asking, man. For you to do your job.'

With clammy hands, Sebastian slides the patio door open, and Tony steps aside to let him back into the room.

'I know, Tone. I know,' he says.

Tony clasps Sebastian's shoulder. 'Come on, son. It'll be all right.'

'Constance was right about at least one thing.'

'What's that?'

'Californians do have a thing about puking.'

47
11 JUNE – HE'EIA STATE PARK, O'AHU ISLAND, HAWAII, USA

On the open-air film set, the temperature is unbearable. It is midday, and the mercury has already reached 43 degrees Celsius, which is unseasonably high.

The dark volcanic ground reflects the heat, and the mountainside on which the cameras are rigged has turned into an oven that the ocean breeze has no chance to cool down.

The sun blazes and the crew members all wear sweat-stained caps. Except Sebastian who can't afford to mess up his hair.

They're shooting an action scene where Sebastian is supposed to take a swan dive into a waterfall that will be digitally added in post-production.

He is strapped to a crane high above the ground with not a scrap of shade to protect him. He's been there for seventy-three minutes, and one of the director's assistants is keeping an eye on her chronometer because the maximum allowed in Sebastian's contract for full exposure to the sun is seventy-five minutes.

Sebastian has found staring at the ocean tricks his brain

into thinking he is cooler than he actually is. It's a small consolation but better than none.

Finally, the second assistant-director is informed the seventy-five minutes have been reached, and he shouts, 'Cut. Take 10.'

Sebastian is lowered back onto the ground by a pulley system that cuts into his shoulders, but he is so relieved to come down from his personal Calvary, he doesn't even mention it to the technical crew in charge of the crane.

As he walks unsteadily to the shaded area designated for his breaks, he is given a two-litre bottle of mineral water and pours half of it into his mouth without taking a breath. Then he hauls himself onto a wood and fabric director's chair with 'Sebastian Anders' written across the backrest.

Overhead, the tarpaulin has trapped the heat from the ground and although he is now out of the sun, the temperature is even higher than it was at the top of the crane.

Sebastian is drenched in sweat and an assistant helps him change his shirt for an identical dry one, complete with fake blood stain and artfully positioned tears.

'I heard it's not supposed to be this hot at this time of year,' she says, scrambling for something to distract him from his exhaustion.

He attempts a smile. 'I'm dreaming of Canadian winters and fox hats right now.' The assistant's stomach flutters, and she laughs awkwardly. 'Only another week, and we go home,' he says. This has been his mantra since he arrived in this green, black and turquoise furnace.

'Tony is now talking about two weeks,' corrects the assistant shyly.

Sebastian exhales slowly. The hairdressing assistant dries his sweaty hair and attempts to recreate the exact tousled style that Sebastian has sported in every single take so far.

He gulps down another swig from his bottle and pushes down his exhaustion and his heartbreak. *I'm a professional. I can do this,* he tells himself on a loop.

Until he is called back to his position in front of the cameras, and his mind goes blank, ready to shoot the scene. Again.

Minutes later, a thunderclap tears the silence of the set, followed by anxious shouts. The crane to which Sebastian was strapped has just collapsed, and he lies sprawled on the ground among the broken rigging.

48
11 JUNE – ADVENTIST HEALTH CASTLE HOSPITAL, KAILUA, O'AHU, HAWAII, USA

During the drive between the film set and the hospital, Regina's composure has had ample time to melt.

The ambulance's siren and the top-speed driving have shredded her nerves, and she hangs on to Sebastian's limp hand with a toxic mix of fear and fury that bodes ill for anyone who will stand in her path.

Her normally explosive temper has been dialled up to volcanic, and according to her FitBit, her heart beats at 138 beats per minute.

When the ambulance doors open, she's so light-headed one of the EMTs has to help her out, and she has to run to catch up with the stretcher.

Under the corridor neon lights, Sebastian's face looks like a corpse's, blood is coming out of his nose and mouth, and bruises are forming on his shoulder and forehead.

The only signs of consciousness are his blinking eyelids every time the stretcher passes through a set of doors.

That and his bloodless lips mouthing 'Constance' on repeat.

Regina, who is one of America's rare atheists, is chanting 'Oh my God, oh my God' under her breath and does her best to keep up with the paramedics.

Then a nurse in a cheerful Hawaiian-style uniform, with hibiscus flower and palm tree print, stops her at the entrance of the operating theatre.

Regina can't stop saying 'Oh God... Please, God'. She braces herself, both hands on her knees, and bursts into tears.

No one has come to support her. The crew started rebuilding the rigging and repairing the crane before Sebastian was even in the ambulance. They're going to reshoot the scene with Sebastian's body double, and tweak it with CGI.

The poor guy is paid just enough to put food on the table, and raised no objection when the AD gave him his orders.

A kindly nurse with dainty cornrow braids silently leads Regina to the family waiting room. Based on the expression on the agent's livid face, she assumes Regina is Sebastian's mother. She presses a plastic cup of water into her hands and squeezes her shoulder gently.

'Don't worry, honey. We've got a fantastic spinal team here. He couldn't get better care, even on the mainland. Can I call someone to keep you company? The surgery will take a few hours.'

'No,' stutters Regina. 'There's no one.' Tears start streaming. 'He's got no one, and neither have I.'

'If you need anything, just ask for Haunani,' she points at her name badge. 'My shift doesn't end until midnight.'

'Thank you,' hiccups Regina.

Three hours later, she hasn't left her seat. She's wrapped in a blanket Haunani gave her, because the shock was making her teeth chatter.

She absent-mindedly sips on a cup of the green tea one of the nurses had brought from home for herself but donated to

Regina because she cuts such a pitiful figure, alone in the family room.

A strident ring tears the silence – Regina's phone ringer is always turned up to the max. This time, it makes her jump, and she nearly pours the tea all over her lap.

She doesn't recognise the number, but bets it's someone from the shoot calling for news.

It isn't.

The unmistakable British accent causes Regina's hackles to rise, but before she has a chance to speak, a torrent of words bursts out of the phone.

'Regina, it's me, Constance. What's happened? Just seen a video on my Twitter feed. Is he all right? How is he? Is he in hospital? Are you with him? Regina, can you hear me? Regina?'

Regina has no time for Constance's outpouring of concern and guilt. 'What the fuck are you calling me for? Haven't you done enough damage dangling him on your hook for days?'

'What do you mean? I haven't heard—'

'He was at breaking point because of you!' Regina interrupts, and spit flies out of her mouth onto her phone screen. 'He's been calling you night and day.'

'I haven't—'

'I tried everything to keep him going, but he wanted to die because of you—'

'Did he jump?' squeaks Constance, trying to stop her stomach from roiling.

'What do you care, you bitch!'

The thought Sebastian might have tried to kill himself again sobers Constance up. Her voice is controlled when she speaks again.

'Regina, shut up for one second and answer my bloody questions! I've been trying to call him for days. His phone goes straight to voicemail. I've left millions of messages. And I definitely didn't make him fall off a bloody crane! How is he? Is he going to be ok?'

'I've no clue what you're playing at, little girl. But it sure would be better if you were here if he wakes up.'

'*If*? What do you mean if he wakes up?'

'He's been in surgery for three hours, and they haven't told me a thing.' Regina's voice breaks. 'But judging by the height of the crane, he's in pieces right now.'

A wave of unnatural calm descends on Constance. She knows what she has to do. 'I'm leaving now,' she says to Regina. 'Just hold on, I'll be on the next plane out of LAX.'

She grabs her passport and slams the door of the Miko Hotel family room, where she's been holed up for three days, and drives out of the parking lot in Sebastian's Audi.

As the tyres screech onto the 101, she books a LAX to Honolulu flight from her phone and puts her foot down the accelerator.

He can't die. I love him. He has to know. Please God.

49

12 JUNE – ADVENTIST HEALTH CASTLE HOSPITAL, KAILUA, O'AHU, HAWAII, USA

The sun is setting on O'ahu when Constance's taxi pulls up to the hospital in Kailua.

She bursts through the automatic entrance doors like an Olympic runner, and as she reads the signs for the Surgery Block, she bumps into Regina.

The agent is exiting the main lobby gift shop with a cushion she's purchased to save her bottom from another ten hours on the hard seats of the family waiting room.

Hanging to Regina's arm for dear life, Constance stammers, 'Did they say anything?'

The recriminations and put-downs Regina has prepared for this very moment die on her lips as she takes in Constance's bloodless face, her eyes lined with crimson, and the pained twist of her mouth.

For once, Regina accesses the considerable vat of kindness she keeps well-hidden in her generous bosom. 'No, but he was still somewhat conscious when he came in and he was asking for you non-stop. It was heartbreaking.'

'Somewhat conscious?' stutters Constance.

'He could see me. Just about.' Regina swallows hard at the memory of the pain in Sebastian's eyes and his rigid jaw.

'What happened?'

'Faulty crane, underpaid stunt guys. Ass wipes! I'll make them eat their own dicks.' Regina manages before bursting into fresh tears. Constance hugs her tight.

'How far did he fall?'

'The fucking thing was *thirty* feet!' Regina sobs.

'Twelve metres,' says Constance in a trance.

'What?'

'Nothing. Life's just so messed up. At least they have a specialist spine centre here. I looked it up in the taxi.'

Regina pulls herself together. 'Nothing like Cedars-Sinai. I'll have him transferred as soon as.'

'Let's get a coffee. We're in shock.' Constance pushes Regina in the direction of a tiny coffee shop area, hidden behind a row of the ubiquitous palm trees.

As they sit amongst the painted sunsets and exotic birds, Constance, who didn't know she could switch her phone on during the flight, messages Philly while Regina orders for them both.

> ***Myname.sNotConnie*** *@FitnessPhilly289 – IRL was in accident. In hospital in Hawaii now.*
> ***FitnessPhilly289*** *@Myname.sNotConnie – How bad?*
> ***Myname.sNotConnie*** *@FitnessPhilly289 – Fell off a crane.*
> ***FitnessPhilly289*** *@Myname.sNotConnie – Where are you?*
> ***Myname.sNotConnie*** *@FitnessPhilly289 – Kahlua or somewhere like that. Pray for us.*

Half of Constance's coffee goes overboard when Regina's shaky hand fails to slow its landing.

'So, how come you're even here?' asks Regina. 'I thought you dumped him.'

Constance shrinks under Regina's accusing gaze. 'This girl claimed he is the father of her baby,' she starts to explain.

'And you believe that? You're even dumber than I thought. Comes with the territory.'

'How can you be sure he isn't the father?'

'If you need me to tell you that, then you have nothing to do here.' Regina's lips clamp into a mask of reprobation, and Constance feels her cheeks turn pink.

'How can you be so sure?'

'How far along is the expectant bimbo?'

'She didn't say.'

'Did she *look* pregnant? I take it there was a picture.'

'Are you seriously saying you didn't see the article?'

'If I did, I don't remember it. So did she?'

'Look pregnant? No, not really, perhaps a hint of a tummy.'

'You're such an idiot,' concludes Regina.

For the first time in four days, Constance's shoulders relax.

That is until she remembers Sebastian is still in surgery.

50

12 JUNE – ADVENTIST HEALTH CASTLE HOSPITAL, KAILUA, O'AHU, HAWAII, USA

A few hours later, Constance's feelings of guilt have spread through her system like venom.

I should have believed him. This is all my fault. If only I'd been there with him.

She and Regina have not been able to get any news of Sebastian, except the semi-reassuring facts that he survived surgery and that the surgeons have finished resetting his bones.

On his general health or prospects of recovery no doctor has ventured more than a non-committal shrug and the same exact words. 'It's too early to say.'

Regina has raided the gift shop and is fighting her fears with box after box of chocolate, washed down with litres of coffee. Her breath now smells like the bins behind the counter at Starbucks, and discarded wrappers surround the two seats she's appropriated in the family waiting room.

Constance's reaction to stress could not be more different. She's made herself small by tucking her knees under her chin and can only manage a few sips of water at irregular intervals.

She's also chewing on a lock of her hair. This is a bad habit her mother thought she'd successfully stamped out by brushing bitter leave-on conditioner on her daughter's hair every morning before school between Year 1 and Year 4.

Constance has kept it up regardless, only when no one is watching her. Except today. Today, that simple rule no longer applies, and she bites her split ends as if Sebastian's life depends on it.

Regina and Constance have run out of things to say to each other hours ago, but a newfound kinship makes their silence more comfortable than the whispered anxious chatter the other family in the room is keeping up.

They're an elderly lady and her middle-aged daughter waiting for news of their husband and father. Constance was able to piece together the scattered information they gave the nurses, and it appears the patient fell while putting a jumper over his head at the same time as he walked down the stairs.

'I always tell him, "With your arthritis, you have to wear your cardigan, Fred." Don't I, darling?'

'Yes you do, mom. You do. None of this is your fault.'

'Is he going to be all right?' asks the older lady for the thirtieth time.

And for the thirtieth time, her daughter replies patiently, 'He's a tough nut. He'll be alright.'

'Yes, he is a tough nut, isn't he?'

'The toughest.'

And on and on it goes. They've been there with Regina and Constance for hours, their bodies almost melted into each other, hands clasped between them.

They take turns at rubbing each other's knuckles, and the daughter has already brought two sets of coffee in styrofoam cups that reminded Constance of the greasy-spoon coffee shop on the Great West Road.

She can't help but steal frequent glances at the picture of love and fear mother and daughter form, and she can almost see a Fred-shaped hole behind them, his arms extended to hug both women.

She wishes she could sketch them and reunite them at least on paper, but she abandoned her art supplies in the back of Sebastian's Audi in the LAX Quik Park.

Constance wonders what her life would have been like if she and her mother had ever been that close. She's noticed Regina also stares at times, and she would give good money to know what the agent is thinking when she does.

Constance has never really felt close to anyone. She's used to being alone. She's even more used to *feeling* alone. Her disconnectedness was just the background of her life, like the sky above and the ground below. Something that didn't need to be noticed. Something that kept the world the right way up.

Meeting Sebastian changed all that. Being with someone whose company she can bear for hours at a time loosened the grip of loneliness on her life.

And when she was alone again, at the Miko Hotel, the sky crashed down, and the ground rose up to swallow her.

A pain settled in her chest no amount of Tylenol could kill. Reality faded away. She didn't eat. She slept a lot but woke to the same nightmare and her sanity slipped away a tear at a time.

The first time she called Sebastian she hoped to at least hear his voice on the recorded message, but there was nothing. Just a beep, then silence. He'd deleted his voicemail greeting. Why? To punish her for breaking her promise?

You had one chance at happiness and you blew it, you idiot.

Now the only way she could ever hear his voice again was on YouTube.

She'd left message after message. Two or three an hour the first day, then less, then none. The last day of her confinement at the Miko hotel was spent staring at the wall and eating her hair. In the same clothes – in the same underwear! – she had arrived in.

The same she is wearing now.

A sudden wave of self-disgust lifts the veil of anxiety that had clouded her thoughts.

'I need to have a shower and change my clothes,' she declares to Regina.

'I was wondering what the smell was,' says Regina half-heartedly. 'They have showers in the restroom on Level 2, Haunani said.'

Constance is gone before Regina can hand her the bag of mini-toiletries she always keeps in her capacious Prada.

The agent returns to stealing glances at Fred's wife and daughter under her eyelashes. Regina misses her late mother very much.

51
12 JUNE – ADVENTIST HEALTH CASTLE HOSPITAL, KAILUA, O'AHU, HAWAII, USA

Constance is wearing what can only be described as a garden's worth of hibiscus flowers masquerading as a summer dress. That's all she could find in the gift shop.

They did also sell sensible white cotton knickers, but they didn't have her size. As droopy drawers are exactly what she does not need at the moment, she had to go for the 'Visit Hawaii' hot pants.

After a short shower, she has wrestled her hair into a top bun of which Madame de Pompadour would have been jealous, and the mascara and lipstick she found at the bottom of her handbag, plus a few squirts of jojoba suntan oil, have restored her to a semblance of self-respect.

She knows Sebastian is still unconscious in recovery, but she has butterflies at the simple thought of being in the same room as him.

Haunani pretended to believe Regina was Sebastian's mother and Constance his sister and neither disabused her.

Constance's breath catches with anticipation when she is led her into the intensive care unit, holiest of holies from which she had hitherto been banned.

The first thing she notices are the machines surrounding Sebastian's narrow bed. Here is the full complement of life-support equipment, beeping and jingling like amateur bell-ringers.

Nothing she's ever seen on *Grey's Anatomy* has prepared her for the shock of seeing this beloved's body festooned with tubes and surgical tape.

Behind her, Regina takes a sharp breath. There is a moment of suspended silence, before she says to Haunani, 'We're going to need a private room. With a view. Preferably at the end of a corridor. Can't have gawkers! And make sure we get two comfortable chairs. We're both staying until he wakes up.'

'Of course, ma'am,' replies Haunani placatingly.

She's dealt with relatives in all shapes and sizes and she has rightly pegged Regina as a repressed, kind-hearted control-freak. She will agree with whatever Regina cares to ask and will deliver what she can.

This is just another day at the office for her. But she never loses sight of the fact that for the patients' families a stay in hospital is a rare occurrence, possibly even a first.

That's what makes Haunani so good at her job. That's why she gets the thank-you cards, the chocolates, and the hand-drawn stickmen families in neat decreasing order under the blue crayon sky.

Not quite as welcome as a pay rise, but still much better than nothing.

As she hurries to discuss Regina's demands with the charge nurse, she hopes the poor young man on whose behalf they are made will live to see them granted.

While Regina texts Tony to tell him Sebastian is finally out of surgery, Constance approaches the bed with as much reticence as she would a wild beast.

An animal fear has replaced her anxiety. Her legs struggle to support her, and her dry mouth makes it impossible to swallow. Too frightened to disturb the network of IV and oxygen tubes, she bends near Sebastian's ear.

He doesn't smell like himself. The stench of Betadine and day-old sweat masks the comforting fragrance she was expecting.

'I'm here,' she whispers. 'I don't care you if don't want to talk to me. I'm here until you tell me to go. I'm sorry for everything. So sorry.'

Sebastian shows no sign of having heard any of it. His face, rendered expressionless by the sedatives, is a poor caricature of his handsome features.

At this moment, although he is right there, close enough she can touch him, she misses him so much she can't breathe.

Across the bed, Regina is stroking Sebastian's hair in gentle, slow strokes. Witnessing such an intimate interaction makes Constance feel like a voyeur, and she lowers her gaze to the ground.

Later, she is grateful when Sebastian opens his eyes just after Regina has gone to the restroom. She wouldn't have wanted Regina to intrude on her own moment with him.

When Sebastian returns from the fog of anaesthesia, his pupils darken as he registers Constance's presence by his bed. He blinks and the promise of a smile forms around his mouth.

'Hey, dick sock,' says Constance tearfully.

52

13 JUNE – ADVENTIST HEALTH CASTLE HOSPITAL, KAILUA, O'AHU, HAWAII, USA

Night falls so fast on this side of the island, it is light when Sebastian is wheeled into his private room – with a view! – and dark by the time the nurses finish transferring him into bed.

After Constance and Regina's raid on the gift shop, his bedside table is covered in flowers and locally-made chocolate bars.

Regina follows Haunani out of the room to issue further orders. Namely instruct hospital staff to kowtow to Tony when he finally shows up and direct him to Sebastian's room with the obsequiousness due to his rank.

The nurses will have a good giggle about it several hours later when they finally have time for a quick coffee break.

Sebastian is now lying, half-awake, pale against the fold-marked baby-blue sheets. The lacerations on his face have been stitched up, and his neck is in a brace. He still has an IV in one arm and a collection of tubes linking him to a variety of machines.

Constance, in her hibiscus camouflage, is sitting in one of the two chairs, her forehead resting on his limp hand.

The regular beeping of the instruments is like the chirruping of ocean birds. It is the music of life, and they both find it soothing.

Sebastian's awakening has had the same effect on Constance's face as a luxury facial. All the worry wrinkles look like they've been Botoxed. She can't stop smiling.

'Regina told me what happened,' she says, not even trying to find words to convey the depth of her emotion. 'The crane wasn't anchored properly. Next time you want to try a twelve-metre fall, make sure there's at least some water at the bottom.'

Sebastian's throat is still sore from the intubation and his lips move ineffectively. In the end, he just rolls his eyes.

'Some good came out of it,' Constance smiles. 'Regina has not dropped a single F-bomb in several hours. In fact, she's hardly spoken. So, silver lining and everything.'

The grin on her face makes Sebastian feel instantly better, but he still can't speak so she continues, effortlessly bridging the chasm between banter and romantic fervour.

'I was so worried, baby. You weren't answering my messages. When I saw that video on my news feed, it was like I'd dropped from a great height.'

Sebastian frowns.

'Sorry, wrong choice of words,' she blushes. 'Actually, no. That is exactly how I felt, like I was falling with you.' She brushes the hair off his sweaty forehead. 'You must have been so scared. You must have thought you were dying.'

He nods his head weakly.

'I can't do without you, okay?' Constance whispered in his ear. 'I need you to be alive. I wouldn't want to live in a world where you aren't.'

'I love you,' croaks Sebastian. Every words spoken feels like a hammer blow to the head. But it's worth it.

Now he's said what was important. She can fill in the blanks, as he is sure she will.

'Oh, sweetheart, I love you too. So, so much. I can't see any future without you. You cannot leave me now. Okay?'

Sebastian can't face talking again, his head is still pounding from his last utterance. So, he does his best to smile.

'Are you laughing at me?' Constance asks, suddenly anxious. 'Do you think I'm a fool? Are you going to dump me the minute you've had your way with me? Am I reading this all wrong?'

Sebastian squeezes her hand weakly and makes a poor attempt at head shaking.

'No, you don't think I'm a fool? You're not going to dump me?'

Her face has crumpled in on itself. She leaves him no choice. Sebastian speaks so quietly Constance has to lean in to hear.

'If it makes you sad, it's a no,' he says. 'If it makes you happy, it's a yes.'

Constance's eyes well up, and she wipes away tears. Then she sits up with a brighter expression on her face. 'Let's have a code: blink once for "more chocolate" and twice for "scratch my nose".'

'Kiss me,' mouthes Sebastian.

'That can be three blinks.'

Sebastian blinks three times.

Constance pretends to be helpful, 'Have you got something in your eye?'

He rolls his eyes, and she kisses him softly on his dry lips. She dabs at her wet eyes with a corner of the bedsheet before kissing him again. They look at each other in silence.

'I feel like we're married,' she whispers eventually. 'It

doesn't matter if we haven't signed the papers. In my heart, we're like this.'

She interlinks the fingers of their hands and kisses them. He looks at her and nods.

53

14 JUNE – ADVENTIST HEALTH CASTLE HOSPITAL, KAILUA, O'AHU, HAWAII, USA

Constance is curled up in the chair closest to Sebastian's bed. She's blowing bubbles out of a pink plastic wand, and he blows them away when they drift past his face.

'Not much bubble juice left, I'm warning you,' says Constance, shaking the bottle.

'You'll have to find something else to entertain me.'

She winks. 'I'm thinking belly dancing.'

He tries hard not to smile because it hurts. 'That would work.'

'Or C3PO impressions.'

'I gotta admit you're real good at them.'

'So, why is it that I didn't receive a single one of your calls?' she asks. 'Or any of your messages?'

'Beats me. You can check my phone if you don't believe me.'

'I believe you, but it's just so strange.'

She dials her number from his phone. The phone on her lap doesn't ring.

'It's not on silent or anything. I don't understand.'

She fiddles with Sebastian's phone, turning it on and off, then checking the recent calls list.

'I can see you've tried to ring me sixty-four times.'

'I told you…'

'Hang on, that's not my number.'

'What do you mean?'

'It says "Constance" but the number isn't mine.'

'I rang you lots of times on that number before, and it was working.'

'Did someone prank you?'

'That would be a crappy prank. I can't think who... Wait. Where did all my messages go? To someone else?'

Sebastian looks even paler than before. He stares at Constance in wide-eyed horror. 'Those were very personal. Private.'

'Wait a second,' she says. 'What about my phone? I couldn't call you either.'

Constance checks her own phone and turns the screen towards Sebastian.

'Is that your number?'

'No, that's not it. What the f—?'

Constance stares at the screen. The colour drains off her face.

'It's the same number you were trying to call. We were both ringing that same number and leaving messages. Oh my God.'

Sebastian tries to sit up; Constance pushes him back down with a firm hand on his shoulder, her eyes never leaving his.

'Who could have done that?' he asks.

'And why?'

Constance rubs her eyes, hoping to wake up.

Sebastian is quiet for a moment, then he says, 'Blackmail or celebrity gossip columns or both.'

Constance mouths 'bloody hell', her face blank. 'That's like spy stuff. The lengths they go to.'

'But who could have had access to both our phones? Who would know when we were going to be apart and trying to call each other?'

'A stalker? One of your fangirls?'

'Motive perhaps. No opportunity.'

'One of your people?' she suggests.

'Why would they do that? Money?'

Constance frowns. 'My messages can't have been that interesting. I never said any more than "Sebastian, I know you're busy, but please call me". Not much to print in the gossip rags.'

'I said a lot of things I wouldn't want printed, or heard by anyone but you.' Sebastian feels violated, but he doesn't want Constance to suspect the depth of his distress.

'But nothing's come out yet, has it? Your press people would have told you. They couldn't have missed it.'

'Perhaps someone wants something to hold over me.'

The truth comes out of nowhere and hits them both in the face at the same time.

'Tony,' says Sebastian. 'Trying to keep me in line, as usual.'

'Or trying to get rid of me,' adds Constance.

'Same thing. Two birds, one stone. I bet he planted that pregnancy story to split us up, then changed the numbers to stop us reconciling. Just his style.'

Sebastian and Constance hold each other's gaze for a long while. A silent conversation happens between them. Their body language becomes cautious. Sebastian pulls Constance closer to him and hooks his arm around her neck.

He speaks in her ear. 'Go and get us two new pre-paid phones. Check no one follows you.'

Constance nods and exits the room calmly. A few minutes after she's gone, he makes a phone call. Constance's phone on the bedside table does not ring.

Sebastian speaks into his phone, sounding annoyed. 'Honestly, Constance. Turn your phone on! Am I supposed to send smoke signals? Call me later. Love you.'

He then uses Constance's phone to call the number labelled 'Sebastian' and lets it ring for a while but leaves no message.

He looks at the lock screen on his phone where Constance, haloed by an explosion of her dark curls, is immortalised mid-C3PO impression.

Outside the sky is a perfect Hawaiian blue. He wishes he could enjoy its beauty, but the revelation of Tony's new treachery has turned his internal weather back to grey and rainy.

54
14 JUNE – ADVENTIST HEALTH CASTLE HOSPITAL, KAILUA, O'AHU, HAWAII, USA

Myname.sNotConnie @*FitnessPhilly289* – *Hi Philly! IRL's doing better. Doctors think he will walk again. Thank you for your prayers.*

FitnessPhilly289 – *Thank the Lord. How are you doing? Don't forget to eat.*

Myname.sNotConnie @*Fitnessphilly289* – *Hospital food is awful, but tropical fruit everywhere. You'd be in heaven!*

FitnessPhilly289 @*Myname.sNotConnie* – *I'll be in heaven when the Lord calls me home and not a moment earlier…*

Myname.sNotConnie @*Fitnessphilly289* – *Figure of speech Philly, Gawd! Oh, and someone messed with our phones and recorded our messages to each other. Super stressful.*

FitnessPhilly289 @*Myname.sNotConnie* – *Creeps! Don't forget to eat, sweetheart.*

Myname.sNotConnie *@Fitnessphilly289 – You said that already!*
FitnessPhilly289 *@Myname.sNotConnie – And hydrate. Not just coffee. Actual H2O.*
Myname.sNotConnie *@Fitnessphilly289 – Isn't that the gas that makes you talk funny?*
FitnessPhilly289 *@Myname.sNotConnie – *eye roll* I wonder how you're still alive…*
Myname.sNotConnie *@Fitnessphilly289 – Probably smoothies *wink**

A nurse enters Sebastian's room, throwing Constance a side glance full of disgust. She is followed by Tony, who unashamedly stares at her tropically-clad behind.

'So, how's our action hero?' he asks jovially.

Sebastian shudders awake, and Constance grabs his hand.

'Nurses making you happy?' winks Tony.

Constance and Sebastian both cringe. They don't dare look at each other.

'Spinal cord is intact,' says Sebastian laconically. 'But I feel like I've been through a meat grinder.'

'Yep, I've spoken to the spine guy. A complete loser, but he eventually showed me the X-rays, and everything looks fine. You're in one piece. I've lined up an exclusive interview for you. It's important you say it wasn't the studio's fault. You know, "no one could have known... highest standards of professionalism…"'

'Regina is going to rip you a new one when she hears you've organised an interview without her.'

'The fat bitch will just have to get used to it. I'm the boss round here.'

'I'll talk to her,' offers Sebastian. 'She'll be cool with it if she thinks it's coming from me. She can't let me have it while I'm all hooked up on IVs.'

'Yes, you do that. You owe me.'

'I owe you?'

'Who do you think has been smoothing it out with the studios, hey, limp dick? They wanted to fire your ass after that fall. You're lucky they're pussies, and I was able to talk them down. They're going to dock your pay though. Tough break.'

Sebastian opens his mouth to retort but thinks better of it. He says instead, 'Uh, Tony, do you think you could sort that salary thing for me as well please?'

'You're such a no-nut wonder. You always need Daddy to sort out your messes.'

'It's just I need the money. The new house, you know.'

'You shouldn't have gone and bought something so out of your league... You think you're DiCaprio or something? You're just a kid from Tennessee. Without me, you're nothing. You should have checked with me before letting this lovely little piece of ass get ideas above her station.' He winks at Constance.

She clears her throat.

'Too late now,' says Sebastian. 'House is bought and furnished.'

To steer the conversation away from the quicksands of their financial dealings, Constance asks Tony in a carefully controlled voice, 'Did you find out what happened? On the shoot, I mean.'

'Crane guy fucked up, stunt guy fucked up, AD fucked up. All fired. Ball ache, we'll have to reshoot the scene.'

Constance's self-control snaps like an old rubber band. 'What reshoot?' she shouts. 'He's not reshooting anything.'

Bringing the smell of stale whisky into her personal space,

Tony uses his bulk to corner Constance in her chair. 'And what are you going to do about it?' he asks.

She doesn't back down. 'And what are *you* going to do about it if we get twenty doctor's certificates saying he can't stand up?'

'I will sue his ass into Judgment Day, and you, missy, might get a night visit from a friend of mine or two,' Tony whispers.

Sebastian, still attached to his IV tubes, struggles to get out of his bed. The machines beep an alarm.

With a flourish and rapacious smile, Tony whips an envelope out of his suit pocket. 'By the way kid, here's your hospital bill. Your little stunt is going to cost you $150,000.'

'You know I haven't got the money, Tony.'

'Nothing to do with me. Your spine. Your bill.'

'Give me my money back and I'll be happy to take care of it.'

'Talking of which, here's a document I want you to sign. So, save us both the hassle, and just sign it.'

'What's it about?' asks Constance.

'Nothing to do with you, sweet cheeks.'

Sebastian skim-reads the document, his frown deepening. 'I can't sign this. This would exonerate you from all responsibility for emptying my accounts with your power of attorney.'

'It's like giving him permission to rob you!' interjects Constance.

'Not asking you, boy. I'm telling you. Sign it or I will have the lawyers here in two hours. You know how convincing they can be.'

Sebastian pales further. His jaw twitches. 'I'm not signing this. Not now. Not ever.'

'Signature under duress is not valid anyway,' says Constance.

'Look who's been reading the dictionary.'

'Fine,' says Sebastian. 'Send the lawyers. I'll get my own.'

'With what money?' smiles Tony.

'We'll go to the press,' Constance warns, her voice wavering. Behind her, Sebastian moans a warning.

'Have you ever read anything about me in the press?' asks Tony.

She stares.

'It's no coincidence.' He leans in and whispers, his lips pressed to her earlobe. 'Do you think you're the first little girl who wants to rebel against Daddy? Watch your step, you little cunt.'

Constance blinks as shame floods her body. Her humiliation is so complete, she can't find in herself an ounce of anger with which to retaliate. She focuses her efforts on not crying.

'Leave her alone, Tony,' Sebastian says, in a voice slurred by painkillers.

Tony stares into Constance's eyes mercilessly as she dissolves in a pool of self-loathing. His face is inches from hers, and all she can see are the open pores on his sunburnt nose. His sozzled breath is warm on her face.

Eventually, she winces.

'Yeah, that's better. Good girl,' he drawls. Then he deliberately he places an open palm on her left breast and leaves it there.

Constance's breathing becomes erratic, and she stands frozen in disgust and fear. But something wakes inside her. Something hard, strong, unyielding. All the fear and shame she felt are replaced by a preternatural calm.

She meets Tony's eyes and holds his gaze then, as deliberately as he seized her breast, she takes his nose in between her thumb and index. She doesn't squeeze, just keeps her fingers there while staring him down.

It is Tony's turn to blink in surprise.

'You're holding my boob, I'm holding your nose. Now what?'

Behind her, Sebastian drags himself out of bed, but Constance maintains her laser focus on Tony.

Eventually, the producer swats her hand away. 'Now we see, little girl.'

'Now we all see,' says Sebastian, hooking his arm around Constance's shoulders, for support as much as protection.

Without another word, Tony turns and exits the room like a Shakespearian actor with more awards than talent.

His departure propels Constance back to reality, and she helps Sebastian back into bed.

'I'm going to destroy him,' he says in a hard voice Constance has never heard him use before.

'And I'll help you.'

55
15 JUNE – ADVENTIST HEALTH CASTLE HOSPITAL, KAILUA, O'AHU, HAWAII, USA

Constance pulls a brand new phone out of her beach bag, courtesy of the hospital shop.

Sebastian winces as he tries to speak. 'You put in your real number?' he asks.

His excursion out of bed has left him with pains all over his body. The purple bruise on his cheekbone turns the green of his eyes the same colour as the palm trees outside the window.

When she presents the phone, still in its plastic wrapper, he whispers, 'Hide it in the drawer.' Constance can barely hear him over the rhythmic beat of his heart-rate machine.

His pain combined with this reminder of the absurd situation in which they find themselves ties her stomach into a series of nautical knots.

Sebastian swallows hard. 'I have to get away from this man.'

She finds a place among the cuts and scrapes where she can touch his arm without hurting him. 'Where is your contract? I'll find you a lawyer.'

'Tony never gave me a copy.'

'A lawyer can request it.'

He shakes his head weakly. 'You heard him. He probably has half the California bar in his pocket. The way he talks, he's got half the world on a leash and the other half under his boot.'

'We need someone who can play his game.'

He buzzes the nurse. 'Haunani, could you please find Regina for me?'

They're all on first-name terms by now, and the whole ward has a duly signed autograph by Sebastian Anders.

'Your mom?' asks the nurse. 'Sure thing, honey.'

'She's not my mom, she's my agent.'

'I saw her face when they brought you in. She may not be your mom, but she didn't get the memo,' she smiles.

As Haunani glides out of the room with butterfly grace, Constance resumes her seat next to Sebastian's bed.

She brings her face so close to his, she could count the shades of indigo in his bruises. 'How are you feeling?'

'Like I've just woken up with a scorpion on my pillow.'

'We know something he doesn't,' she whispers into his ear. Sebastian discovers her warm breath is a pretty decent painkiller and wishes he could bottle it for later.

'We know what he did with the phones. We have the advantage,' she continues, wholly unaware of her analgesic powers.

He signals for her to bring her ear closer to his mouth. She smells of suntan oil and holidays, and for an instant he forgets where he is and why.

'I told him I needed money to pay for the new house,' he murmurs into her ear.

Her head snaps back. 'I thought you bought it outright,' she says out loud.

'Shush.' He pinches her T-shirt and pulls her closer. 'I did. But if he thinks I'm broke, he will think I'm not as dangerous.'

They're nose to nose, so close they could kiss, and the world doesn't seem such a bad place after all. 'Oh, devious. We need to beat him at his game.'

'Why do you think I asked for Regina?'

Constance sits up, forgetting all about discretion. A 'V' of concentration appears between her eyebrows. 'We need to prepare in secret and hit him under the cover of night.'

Sebastian frowns. 'This isn't some crappy war movie, Constance.'

'It's a fight, baby. We hit first, and we hit so hard that we don't have to hit again.' Constance has never hit anyone in her life; she's never even seen an actual fight. She's pretty sure this *is* a line from a movie.

'I keep thinking about where to go from here. There's no escape, every way I think to turn, he's barricaded the door. I'm so screwed.'

'You're going be fine,' says Constance in her sing-song nanny voice that worked so well the day of the teddy bear blanket. Indeed, under the hospital gown his shoulders relax. 'You're going to get out of the hospital, finish the film and go on the promo tour.'

She runs her fingers through his silky hair, and his eyes close. 'Once your handsome mug is on every magazine and millions of people are listening to your every word, you'll have the upper hand.'

His eyes meet hers, mint and chocolate. 'Look at you,' he smiles. 'All cold and calculating.'

Constance whispers her response into his ear. 'I just feel very protective of you.'

A shiver runs down his spine. *If only I could bottle that too.* 'Isn't that a line from that *Twilight* movie?'

'Sue me,' she pouts. 'It's a good line.'

Sebastian chuckles, and with the movement of his battered

chest all his aches and pains return at once. But he doesn't allow himself to grimace until Constance becomes distracted by the soft ping of her phone.

> ***FitnessPhilly289*** *@Myname.sNotConnie – U eating?*
>
> ***Myname.sNotConnie*** *@Fitnessphilly289 – Poop's hit the fan, Phil. Producer I told you about. Recorded our messages to blackmail IRL, plus embezzlement, threats, all sorts. Got a smoothie recipe for that?*

56

15 JUNE – ADVENTIST HEALTH CASTLE HOSPITAL, KAILUA, O'AHU, HAWAII, USA

The smell of lunch trays comes in from the corridor as Regina clickety-clacks into Sebastian's room.

It is only 11 a.m. but it will take the nurses two hours to serve the meals. Their gentle chitchat will do for the soul what the overcooked beef patty and undercooked potatoes will do for the body.

Regina has slept at the hotel overnight and looks almost back to her normal self. Her colourful outfit, a garish peach silk dress worn with a magenta short-sleeve jacket, is testament to her return to strength, but a softness around the eyes betrays the seismic shift of her heart when she heard the crane fall.

Her brusque tone – an ersatz replica of her usual military cadence – does little to hide how worried she is about Sebastian. 'Not out of bed yet? You'll get bedsores! I read—'

'There's something you need to know,' interrupts Sebastian, his face tense with the effort he makes to speak.

'Sit,' says Constance, offering Regina her chair, the one closest to the bed.

Regina waves her away with an impatient flick of her

hand, sending ripples of chocolatey perfume across the room, but she bends towards Sebastian.

'It's about Tony,' he starts.

Regina could take on a teenager in an eye-rolling competition, and she gives a fair display of her skills. 'Oh there we go again. He's a scumbag. He's pinched the butt of every single nurse on this ward. Tell me something I don't know.'

'He's embezzled fifteen million dollars of my money.'

Under her self-tanning tinted moisturiser, Regina's face pales two skin tones. 'What?' she croaks.

'My earnings for *Fear in the Andes*, *Slow Motion*, and *Zombie Attack*.'

Regina's mouth hangs open as if on freeze-frame.

'Everything but what I got from the skincare line and the Abercrombie money.'

Eventually, the agent catches on. 'But you haven't paid me for those movies yet…'

Sebastian nods. 'That accountant told you about that tax loophole? It was a scam.'

'How long have you known?' stammers Regina, whose purse area is even more tender than her well-guarded heart.

'He admitted it to us this morning.'

'He's not even ashamed,' Constance chimes in.

'Have you met the guy?' snipes Regina. 'He must be so proud! He thinks he's untouchable, above the law. I'm going to kick him so hard in the balls he'll snort out sperm.'

While Constance take a private moment to enjoy the imagery, Sebastian says, 'How?'

'Dunno yet. But that's one point five million of my hard-earned money, shovelling shit for the likes of you.'

'Thanks,' says Sebastian, unruffled.

Regina's face heats up, her cheeks matching her magenta jacket. 'I know where the bodies are buried,' she mutters to herself. 'Every single he-grabbed-my-crotch settlement. Every aspiring actress robbed of her career.'

She drops her head into her hands, and a wave of caramel and vanilla spreads around her.

Constance tenses. 'Why didn't you go to the police then?'

'Do you really still not understand how this works, you dimwit?' Regina snarls. She counts on her fingers. 'One, a climate of fear. Two, iron-clad non-disclosure agreements. Three, isolation of the victim with everyone looking the other way. Four, if the victim persists, heavies with a foreign accent. Five, a gagging out-of-court settlement in exchange for more money than you've ever dreamt of. Works every single fucking time. Over twenty years' experience.'

'You seem very well informed,' says Constance, her upper-class vowels cutting through the air like an icy wind.

Regina straightens up. 'In this business, you toughen up or you get out. I wasn't always fat and middle-aged. I've been the one cornered between the bed and the bathroom. It didn't break me.'

'It obviously broke your bloody conscience!'

'And a good thing too,' admits Regina. 'Having a conscience did me absolutely no good. But I survived. And if some snowflake bleeding hearts find it objectionable, they can eat me!' She stares Constance down, the tendons in her neck ready to snap.

'That's not getting us anywhere,' Sebastian intervenes weakly. 'You want your money. I want out of my contract. Let's work together to bring the bastard down.'

'What about me?' asks Constance, her voice wobbling.

'You stay as far away from him as you can,' replies Sebastian.

'We don't need you yapping at our ankles,' adds Regina.

While the other two hold each other's gaze, Constance

experiences a surge of anger the likes of which she has never felt. Not even when dealing with her mum. Not even after those awful nights of one-sided sex. Not even when Tony grabbed her breast.

As evidenced by her regular exchanges with the agent, her anger normally burns white hot. But Sebastian and Regina's rejection has doused the flames.

An icy calm descends on her, and she plasters a bored expression onto her face.

'Knock yourselves out, guys. Not a party I want to attend.'

Sebastian turns to her with narrowed eyes, but she sits down placidly and gobbles a piece of chocolate.

'This is a one-time thing, Seb,' warns Regina, oblivious to the subtle sea change in the room. 'I help you get your money, I take my cut. Preferably without Tony going nuclear on us. I'm not going to kamikaze my career over a bunch of #MeToo grunts who couldn't take the heat.'

'Roger that, Reggie,' says Sebastian, forcing a smile.

'First I have to speak to Malcolm Malone. He too had business dealings with Tony and his vampire accountant, but he bought a mansion in Beverly Hills last year though he hasn't worked in years.'

'I knew there was a reason I put up with you, Regina,' says Sebastian.

'Yep, honey plum. Unlike you, I'm not just a pretty face.'

As she exits the room, leaving behind her a fragrant trail of Thierry Mugler's 'Angel', Constance and Sebastian glance at each other.

She looks away first, keenly aware he's noticed how quickly she accepted being sidelined.

He sees the fear etched in the little lines around her eyes and curses Tony for bringing back so many of her worst memories.

Myname.sNotConnie *@FitnessPhilly289 – So sick of these people, Phil. Hollywood's rotten to the core.*

FitnessPhilly289 *@Myname.sNotConnie – Not news to me, darlin'. My cousin's daughter went there to do some auditions, came back with a shaved head and drug tracks all over her arms. These are bad people. Stay away.*

Myname.sNotConnie *@FitnessPhilly289 – But IRL is stuck there, and I can't leave without him.*

57

16 JUNE – ADVENTIST HEALTH CASTLE HOSPITAL, KAILUA, O'AHU, HAWAII, USA

This is Sebastian's fifth day in hospital, and Regina has flown back to LA to squeeze some truths out of poor Malcolm Malone ('Mal-Mal' to his fans).

Sebastian is off morphine and his pain is now managed with lower grade painkillers.

Leah, the cute physiotherapist with her perky blonde ponytail, is pleased with his progress. But she hopes to prolong his treatment until she finds the courage to ask him for an autograph.

She's even tried to take a surreptitious photo on her phone while pretending to disconnect a call, but the ever-present Constance has eagle eyes and put her hand between the camera and a sleeping Sebastian before Leah had a chance to press the button.

Despite Leah's best efforts, Sebastian has not yet been able to walk more than a couple of steps.

Constance has spent the last forty hours in the same ill-fitting clothes, kept on her feet by gallons of sweet coffee and the canteen's rebarbative fare.

She is too exhausted to read anything, so she has been

doodling stick-figure Sebastians on the travel brochures she's found in the hospital's shop.

Cartoon Sebastian is having a much nicer time in Hawaii than the real one, checking out the sights and swimming under waterfalls.

Now Constance has run out of margin space, little Seb's adventures have come to a premature end.

Nose blind to the harsh hospital smells and eyes glued to a tiny triangle of blue sky, she curls and uncurls the same strand of her unwashed hair around her index finger.

So much could still go wrong.

The press could discover where he is being treated and descend on the small hospital like a swarm of locusts. Regina could turn on them and cut a deal with Tony. Worst of all, Sebastian could end up having to sell the first home that's truly been his since his parents died.

And then, there's the plan Constance is working on. Because she'd rather die than sit on the sidelines while Sebastian plots Tony's comeuppance alone.

Constance knows about men like Tony. Sebastian and Regina think she's naive, but they are the ones who fail to understand.

Tony and his cronies are the cancer devouring women's power and sense of safety. How could women ever achieve equality while being assaulted, victimised, and blackmailed at every turn?

Don't be too good, don't be too clever, don't dare to achieve your dreams.

All because some ill-adjusted man somewhere will notice your efforts and do his damnedest to bring you down with the semi-reluctant help of women like Regina. Those who tried and failed and who feel vindicated when they watch yet another woman fall off the greasy pole.

Constance is ashamed of the years she has spent hidden in her childhood home, in the bedroom where she was assaulted, thinking herself safe, when in fact she was just stuck. A prisoner of the trauma inflicted on her by men who were never taught to see women as equals.

Her rumination is disturbed by Haunani's colleague Iris.

Haunani has cut corners to make Sebastian's stay easier, turning a blind eye to non-family visits, arranging beds and chairs for Constance and Regina, and protecting his privacy like a hawk.

Iris, however, has done her job and no more. When she comes into the room, her pinched face alerts Constance to some new irregularity that's challenged the nurse's definition of patient care.

'Your *parents* are here to see you,' she tells Constance. 'They refuse to stay in the waiting room. They ask if you could join them in the coffee shop.'

Constance's jaw drops. Her parents? All she needed to complete her ordeal.

How do they even know where she is? Her father knows nothing of Sebastian's existence, and her mother is in Hong Kong holidaying with Rupert, her latest rich boyfriend.

With a gasp, Constance realises Hawaii is nearer to Hong Kong than London, and she wonders whether her mother had her followed. As to why her mother might want to travel with her father she is stumped. Unless Rupert is pretending to be her dad.

Yuck!

In shock, she staggers down the various corridors that separate Sebastian's VIP room and the general public's zone, smoothing her greasy hair compulsively and assessing her chances of smelling of BO.

Her stomach churns as she approaches the coffee shop. She

hasn't seen her parents breathe the same air since her father slammed the door of the Henley house, over ten years ago.

If only she'd had time to change her clothes and brush her hair, she wouldn't feel so nauseous.

No doubt her mother will say she stinks and looks like she's the one who fell off a crane.

As for her father, she hasn't seen him in years, so there's no telling what his reunion words will be.

58

16 JUNE – ADVENTIST HEALTH CASTLE HOSPITAL, KAILUA, O'AHU, HAWAII, USA

As Constance steps into the diminutive coffee shop – a portion of corridor cordoned off by a row of potted palm trees – she is greeted by an overwhelming smell of cheap coffee and by two overweight strangers in matching red Arkansas Razorbacks T-shirts.

Both immediately step into her personal space.

'Constance, is that you darlin'?' says the woman.

'Huh, yes,' replies a stunned Constance. 'May I ask—?'

'It's me, Philly. And that's my Wayne. We're the Johnsons…' The woman enfolds Constance into a cushiony hug that smells of hand soap and laundry powder.

'Pretty neat to finally meet you, honey…' says Wayne with a friendly clap on Constance's shoulder.

'We couldn't let you go through all this alone, you poor sweet gal…'

'We had some air miles left over from my cousin Josiah's weddin'…' adds Wayne, as if that explains it all.

'And we couldn't bear to think of you, all alone here, with your poor broken IRL Celeb…'

Neither of them is good at concluding sentences, but both

excel at taking over from the other without missing a beat. Constance still hasn't been able to get a word in edgeways.

'How is he?' asks Wayne. 'Philly's been so worried…'

'I've been prayin' for you every day, and then the Lord said, "Why don'cha go see for yourself, Philly…" so I said to Wayne, "We have those air miles from Josiah's weddin'…"'

'And it's real quiet at the Sheriff's Office in June, so I said to Philly, "It sure would be neat to take a vacation in Hawaii…" and she packed the bags so fast, she almost forgot my best shorts…'

'He's had them twenty years… full of holes, they are. You can almost see his religion, if ya know what I mean, honey… "Wayne," I said, "this poor sweet gal is havin' a real hard time, she doesn't need to see you in your rags…" But would he listen? No, ma'am…'

'And the rest, as they say, is history…' concludes Wayne philosophically.

Between the hugs and the strange speech patterns, Constance's brain has ground to a halt.

Philly gently guides her to one of the tiny tables and sends Wayne to buy coffees.

'I just can't believe it, Philly,' stutters Constance. 'You're here. For me.'

She struggles to reconcile the plump, late-middle-aged woman in front of her with the gym-bunny she had in mind. But the eyes carry the same kindness and gentle humour pervading Philly's messages, and her strange dialect is certainly familiar.

'Of course, darlin'… I thought you could use a friend.'

'How did you know?'

'Who asks for smoothie recipes at any hour of the night, honey…?' says Philly quietly.

'That's just so nice of you, thank you.'

'You bet, sweetheart…'

Wayne returns, carrying the largest coffees available on the premises, accompanied by a tray of pink iced doughnuts that make Constance's teeth hurt.

He wedges himself between one of the potted palm trees and the table, one meaty arm around Philly's shoulders.

Constance is distracted by how much he looks like a cop, all salt-and-pepper buzzcut, and military bearing belied by a paunch she assumes is full of iced doughnuts.

'So how's the patient…?' he asks through his first mouthful.

'Better than could have been expected,' replies Constance with a tired smile that goes straight to Philly's heart. 'He's no longer on morphine, so he feels a bit more like himself.'

'Bless his heart. Is he in any pain…?' asks Philly.

'His body is stiff from lying in bed for a week, and he's still recovering from his surgery, plus of course he's broken three ribs and is covered in bruises.'

'But his spine is okay, is it…?' asks Wayne.

'Once the swelling has gone down, he should be able to walk again.'

'Praise the Lord…' says Philly.

'Amen…' says Wayne.

'So where are you two staying?' asks Constance.

'Here in Kailua…'

'There was room at the inn…' winks Wayne. 'And real neat it is too. With one of those round pools with bubbles…'

'How did you find me?'

'You said "Kahlua", but that's an alcoholic beverage… I checked on Google…'

'Then we looked up hospitals in Hawaii, and it wasn't hard to find the right one…' explains Wayne, tapping his temple knowingly. 'Not when you're in law enforcement. The hardest was to convince Nurse Iris to let us see you...'

'Yes, that was the hardest...' agrees Philly. 'She might have got the idea we were your parents... Not sure how... not the brightest bulb on the Christmas tree...' she winks.

'So how're ya feelin', darlin'...?' says Wayne.

Constance has just taken a nibble of the least diabetes-inducing doughnut, so Philly answers instead. 'Exhausted... Look at her, Wayne... The poor thing is dead on her feet...'

'Whad'cha say we take you back to our hotel for a few hours, so you can rest? Your boyfriend isn't goin' anywhere, is he now...?' says Wayne.

'Or I could stay and keep him company, if you want, darlin'...' offers Philly.

Everything is going too fast for Constance, but she thinks about Philly's warm and fragrant embrace and that's exactly what she needs at the moment. Well-intentioned hugs from someone who cares enough to have come several thousand miles to support her.

So yes, Philly and Wayne are strangers, but who else is there?

'Perhaps a small nap, then, if you don't mind?'

'Yes, a small nap... Can't hurt...' says Philly, catching Wayne's eye.

'Exactly. The rental is out front...'

'I just need to tell Sebastian. So he won't worry.'

'Sebastian? What a sweet name,' comments Philly, hands clasped under her soft chins. 'Like my—'

Wayne doesn't wait to hear the rest. 'I'll bring the truck to the main entrance, darlin'. We'll wait for ya.'

When Constance returns to Sebastian's room, he's fast asleep, and she doesn't dare wake him. She feels awful abandoning him, but she needs what Philly can give, so she leaves a note by his bedside and kisses his forehead.

Just a couple of hours.

As she slips out the room, Constance realises the Johnsons still have no idea who Sebastian is, and they didn't even ask her.

59

22 JUNE – "LONG ACRES", MARION, ARKANSAS, USA

A couple of hours turn into a week, and after Sebastian is discharged, he and Constance fly back to the Johnsons' farm near Marion, Arkansas.

'Hush your mouth…' says Philly when Sebastian tries to argue, and she sounds so much like his mamma with her Southern drawl and no-nonsense caring that he agrees to everything.

They sneak out of the hospital in Wayne's rental truck, right under the noses of a contingent of journalists and paparazzi.

On the plane back to Arkansas, Philly and Wayne sit on either side of Constance and Sebastian who feel like children travelling with their parents. For the orphan and the estranged daughter, it fills a part of their hearts that hasn't been reached in far too long.

Philly and Wayne have lived in Marion all their lives. 'Population, 12,345!' Wayne jokes at least three times during the journey, proud as if his own wit should be credited for this lucky numerical coincidence.

Philly has her own catchphrase, 'We too live in LA. Long Acres!' – and it has had a few reruns too.

The Johnsons' farmhouse – twice the size of Sebastian's Pacific Palisades mansion – is just outside town, down a tree-lined dirt road that has definitely seen smoother days.

The property has been in Philly's family for three generations, and it is her childhood home. When her brothers and sisters left to start their own lives in town, Philly couldn't bear for the house to be sold, and she refused Wayne's marriage proposal until he promised to one day buy it off her parents.

Long Acres boasts five bedrooms, each complete with massive ensuite and roomy walk-in closet, and the barn could easily accommodate Constance's Henley house.

While they were still praying the Lord to bless them with enough children to fill their humongous home, Wayne and Philly had the upstairs remodelled in preparation, strong in their faith the Lord had called them to marriage and procreation and could not now deny them the keenest wish of their hearts.

Sadly, the years passed, and their hopes faded along with the pink and blue wallpapers in the empty rooms neither of them could bear to enter.

Wayne and Philly's entire families live within twenty miles of Long Acres – bar cousin Josiah, of course, who moved to Washington DC to become an Evangelical lobbyist. So, the guest room is used as a junk room and Philly has been meaning to update the decor for the last ten years.

As Wayne insists no unmarried couple should share a room in his house, Constance and Sebastian have taken up residence in the pink and blue rooms respectively. There, they have found the clean, cosy comfort of yesteryear, with immaculate white bedding that smells of lavender and quilts Philly inherited from her Grams.

Despite generous helpings of Philly's kefir, pear, banana and cherry juice smoothie, it has taken the four of them a couple of days to sleep off the jet lag. But on a bright Arkansas morning, they eventually congregate in the massive kitchen, where a table for twelve looks lost in the middle of the room.

Philly, in her 'I love Jesus' apron, serves jet black coffee with crispy bacon and perfectly fluffy pancakes. Pastor John and Grandma MacKenzie, eat your hearts out! Sebastian can't find it in his heart to come clean about his gluten-free diet.

God only knows if he still has a career now Tony's no longer on his side, so he might as well eat and be polite to his kind hostess.

The ever-present TV is on mute, and the conversation flies back and forth from the history of Long Acres to the minutiae of the Johnsons' genealogy.

Ten days into their acquaintance with Philly and Wayne, Constance and Sebastian have got used to nodding and smiling without attempting any further contribution to the dialogue between the Johnsons. The system works flawlessly.

'After breakfast, you two men must take a walk around the farm...' says Philly.

'The Good Lord's sunshine and fresh air is all you need!' adds Wayne.

'Miss Leah said you must walk two miles every day...'

'Or hobble at least...' winks Wayne.

As Constance pours herself yet another cup of the delicious coffee she likes almost as much as the smoothies, Philly exclaims, pointing to the TV screen with her fork. 'Isn't that the movie you're in, sugah...?'

Wayne turns the sound on, and the four of them watch, mouths open, until the news item ends and the ad break starts.

After a beat, Philly asks, aghast, 'What just happened...?' She can't believe what she heard.

Sebastian's lips are pressed together into a tight line, so it is Constance who answers. 'It appears Sebastian's been replaced by another actor. They're reshooting all his scenes so Sebastian can be edited out of the movie he nearly lost his life for.'

'Can they do that…?' squeaks Philly.

Sebastian replies, 'They can do anything they like.'

'But that's not fair…' says Philly.

'No it isn't, but that's Hollywood for you.'

'After all they did to these poor actresses… I shouldn't be surprised…' comments Philly.

'Did you know any of them…?' asks Wayne. 'The poor gals…'

'It's not just the actresses,' interjects Sebastian.

Wayne's eyes widen. 'The guys as well…?'

'The actors, the crews, the agents, everyone,' answers Sebastian, his face a storm cloud. 'Anyone they can get away with bullying and harassing.'

'Such wickedness…' comments Philly.

'Oh man, California…' says Wayne, pushing his hands into the pockets of his jeans, a sure sign of his profound disagreement. 'Why you left Tennessee, Seb, I'll never know…'

'Too many sad memories,' says Sebastian.

'I hear ya, but California…?'

'It's Sodom and Gomorrah all over again…' wails Philly.

'It's not just California, it's everywhere,' interjects Constance. 'I'm from London, and we have scumbags there too!'

'Language, young lady!…' snaps Philly.

'But she's right, honey,' says Wayne. '"In his arrogance the wicked man hunts down the weak, who are caught in the schemes he devises."'

'Psalm 10:2…' says Philly, who cannot bear to let a Bible verse go unreferenced.

'Yep, that's me,' sighs Sebastian. 'Now I've got to get myself out of those schemes, and it ain't gonna be easy.'

60

23 JUNE – "LONG ACRES", MARION, ARKANSAS, USA

*C*onstance has fallen in love with Philly and Wayne, but if she has to spend another day with them and their Bible quotes, she is likely to go berserk.

Sebastian, on the other hand, has adapted to their quiet routine in a way he never thought possible after years of travelling the world in plush hotels.

If he's honest with himself, Long Acres feels more like home than his own house in Pacific Palisades. Still, he can see Constance going quietly mad and decides to take action before the inevitable clash happens and feelings on both sides are hurt.

Sebastian wakes early and joins Wayne for his morning walk around the property. The grass is dry and rustles beneath their heavy boots as they step perfectly in sync. Sebastian's hobbling days are finally over.

'Sir,' he starts, 'I wanted to tell you how much Constance and I have appreciated all your help. We are so thankful for you and Philly and everything you've done for us.'

'Y'all are such nice young people. It would'na felt right to leave y'all to face your troubles on your own. The way this

Tony character has treated ya over the years would make a preacher cuss…'

Sebastian smiles; it's the expression his grandma used when she was angry.

'People like that,' continues Wayne, 'they need stompin' on, like a snake under your boot. You hit first and you hit hard!'

'That's exactly what Constance says.'

'She's brave, that gal. So, if you don't want her gettin' into a fight for ya, ya gotta do the stompin'…'

Wayne stops in his favourite spot by a hundred-year-old oak tree and looks down the gently rolling hill towards the pond just beyond the property fence.

Sebastian stands next to him, his eyes on the swirling clouds, pure white against the turquoise sky.

'Problem is he's protected by dirty lawyers and probably some cops too.'

'Hang on, I don't like hearin' idle gossip about the force, but if that's the case – there are bad apples everywhere – you must use what ya got.'

'What have I got?'

'Ya've got the good Lord on your side.'

'He's not been much help so far.'

'Watch your mouth, boy.'

'Sorry, sir.'

'As I said, you've got the good Lord on your side, and you have a good reputation and an honest face. People are realisin' what's happenin' in the new Babylon. They know how rotten it is. If you speak up, who's gonna believe him over ya?'

'He can pay any number of newspapers to discredit me.'

'Newspapers are fake news! Everyone knows it. Ya can write your truth on the Facebook. Look, I know your daddy died when ya were little and now ya think of this guy like he's your Pop. But he's not. He's not even your friend. Ya don't owe him anythin'. Whatever he did for ya, it was for money. He didn't help ya on your path; he took ya away from it. So now ya've got to break the spell. He's not invincible…'

With Wayne's heavy paw on his shoulder, Sebastian whispers, 'He threatened to have me locked up in a psych ward if I speak up. Because I tried to kill myself…'

Having finally spoken his biggest fear, the one he's kept from everyone, even from Constance, he looks up at Wayne expectantly.

The older man frowns. 'Well, that wasn't very smart, was it?' Then his police training kicks in. 'Have ya got scars?'

Sebastian shakes his head.

'Were ya standin' on a ledge with the police and the EMTs below?'

'No, I was about to climb over the side of a bridge when Constance found me.'

'Well, she sure isn't gonna run her mouth. The queen protects her king. That Tony guy can't prove anything. It's all speculation.'

This strikes Sebastian as a revelation. He releases the breath he's been holding. Tony may be a master of threats, but what can he actually do?

'So ya gotta step up now, ya hear me?' continues Wayne. 'Ya gotta step up and be a man.'

'Yes, sir.'

'Do the right thing, whatever the cost. Ya can't go wrong doin' the right thing.'

'No, sir.'

The matter settled to his satisfaction, Wayne starts walking the perimeter of the fence again. 'Now, what are your intentions about our sweet Constance?'

'Huh, I'm going to marry her…?'

Wayne's eyes narrow. 'Is that a question, boy?'

Sebastian meets his steady gaze. 'No, sir. I'm going to marry her. I've been wanting to marry her since the day we met.'

Wayne's face split into a wide grin. 'Ain't that the berries! When ya find the one, ya don't wait around, turnin' your hat in your hands. Ya go and ask her daddy for permission to court her. None of this travellin' around together, stayin' in the same hotel and Lord knows what else…'

Sebastian, who doesn't get offended easily, is irked at Wayne's casual words about his relationship with Constance.

'With all due respect, sir, Constance's father abandoned her, so I won't be asking him any permission. And I've always treated Constance like my mamma would have expected. There's been nothing improper.'

'I'm sure glad, son, but she needs a good man. Not a nice boy.'

'I hear you, Wayne.'

'Now, do y'all need money? I've got a little stacked away…'

'That's real kind, but I have some money too, money Tony doesn't know about, and I intend to use it well.'

'That's my boy…' chuckles Wayne, as he knocks the wind out of Sebastian with a paternal slap between the shoulder blades.

While the men are on their man-to-man walkabout, Philly and Constance sit elbow-to-elbow on the shaded front porch, surrounded by caladiums unfurling their hot pink leaves and impatiens in a riot of purples and reds.

Both women are cradling gigantic smoothies that threaten to spill over with the rocking of the swing seat.

This is a new recipe Philly concocted when she heard June was the official 'National Fresh Fruit and Vegetables' month. It contains strawberries, apricots, lettuce, lime and yams, and Philly affectionately named it 'Miss Sally's Smoothie'.

Fifty percent of her brain is busy making small adjustments to her recipe *–perhaps lemon instead of lime…?* She needn't even change the name. The other half frets about Constance's quiet demeanour.

'So, who licked the red off your candy?…' Philly asks.

The colloquialism doesn't even raise a smile.

'I'm fine,' lies Constance.

'No ya ain't. Whatcha hidin'?'

'Golly, you're far too suspicious, Phil.'

'Ya're not the kind of gal to leave your man fight his battles alone… Ya're plannin' some kind of righteous vengeance. Whatcha got in mind?'

Constance sighs. 'Tony's has stolen millions of dollars from Sebastian to make him toe the line. It's like blackmail. And now that stuff about being edited out of the movie.'

'I know. That is wicked.'

'And you don't know the half of it, Philly. Tony grabbed my breast the other day, under Sebastian's nose, as he lay in his hospital bed. Just to show he could…'

'Bless your poor little heart… and when y'all've been *waitin'* and everything… Disgustin'!'

'So I'm thinking that man needs taking down.'

'I agree, honey! What's the plan? Tar and feathers? Boilin' oil? Snake pit…?'

'I like your thinking, Phil, but I'm more inclined to hit him in the money bags.'

'Is that a euphemism?' Philly smiles.

'No, I want to destroy the fortune Tony's so proud of and he's been using to abuse people and shut them up.'

'What about Seb's contract with him?' she asks.

'Step one, free Sebastian from his legal obligations. Step

two, bring Tony his comeuppance,' explains Constance. 'I want to be the one to sucker punch him in his ugly moobs.'

'Sounds dangerous. Are ya sure ya don't want to speak to Pastor John, sweetheart? He could help…'

'Do you think he'll condone murder?'

'"Do not repay evil with evil." Peter 3:9…'

Constance resists the impulse to roll her eyes, but her face betrays what she thinks of Philly's advice.

Philly nestles Constance's hand between her own. 'Don't try to beat wicked men at their games. There must be another way you can right this wrong.' she says softly.

'I wish it were so.'

When Philly gives her the third-degree for details, Constance clamps her mouth shut and no matter how soapy Philly smells or how warm her hands, she refuses to divulge the rest of her plan.

61

24 JUNE – "LONG ACRES", MARION, ARKANSAS, USA

On his return from his walk with Wayne, Sebastian had a spring in his step and a strange light in his eyes.

He announced without preamble that he had a surprise for Constance and they would be leaving at the end of the week.

When Philly started crying, Wayne shushed her with a meaningful look that stopped her in her tracks.

On their last morning in Long Acres, Sebastian and Constance feel like toddlers embarking on their first day at school. They hold hands under the table for moral support.

After the loving care lavished on them by the Johnsons, the real world will be a rude awakening.

Constance clears her throat and struggles to swallow the extra-delicious breakfast Philly got up at dawn to prepare. She sips on a yet-unnamed smoothie and bits of raspberries get stuck in her teeth.

Sebastian is more composed and devours the pancakes, bacon, homemade hash browns, sausage and eggs like a man who's never heard of juice cleansing.

Philly finds something to wash in the sink every time her emotions get the better of her.

Wayne, sitting at the head of the table, is the only one who seems unperturbed by the imminent goodbyes. His eyes do glisten though when he slides towards his young guests two rectangular parcels wrapped in brown paper and tied with twine.

'Wayne, we don't have anything for you both,' cries Constance.

'Hush your mouth, just open it…'

Constance's expression changes to amusement when she unwraps what looks like a pink torch with a wrist strap. 'Thank you, super useful to keep in the car.'

'It's a taser, ya silly gal,' Wayne smiles. 'For personal protection. And it's got a whistle. Now, ya must promise to keep it in your purse, okay? I don't like the idea of ya travellin' the world all defenceless…'

'That is very thoughtful,' she says, her eyes down to stop the tears from falling. 'I must remember to put it in my suitcase when we get to the airport. Wherever it is we're going on Sebastian's "surprise trip", I doubt the airline will appreciate a weapon on board!'

'Your turn,' Philly urges Sebastian, pushing his parcel into his hands.

From the wrapper, he unfolds a 'Born in Tennessee' black T-shirt.

'Not as good as Arkansas, but pretty darn close,' comments Wayne.

Sebastian pulls his new shirt over his clothes. 'Thank you, sir.' And he stands to give Wayne a bear hug, from which both emerge shiny-eyed, a fact the women pretend not to notice.

62

30 JUNE – VICTORIA STATION, LONDON, UK

It is only two hours since they landed at London Heathrow airport, and the taxi ride into London took a lifetime.

As they cross the concourse at Victoria Station, sampling the Eau de Sweaty Carriage emanating from the throng of commuters, both achieve the delicate feat of inhaling through their mouths while panting for breath.

Sebastian has a vice hold on Constance's hand and pulls her through the rush-hour commuter crowd.

'Gawd! Only a Yank would go from Heathrow to Henley via Victoria Station!' she complains. 'We need to get to Paddington!'

'I'm not a Yankee, and we're not going to Paddington,' Sebastian says over his shoulder.

His hair has grown since the hair artist last tended it. Constance watches the movement of his rusty locks as he turns back to face the crowd, and she almost forgets what she thinks of his journey planning.

After a minute, she rallies. 'All the trains from London to Henley leave from Paddington!'

'We're not going to Henley.'

'If only you told me where we're going on this "surprise trip" of yours, it would be tons easier,' she pouts.

'Nope.'

'Paris then? You do know the Eurostar goes from St Pancras station, don't you?'

'I am not illiterate!'

'Are you going to tell me or not?' She stamps her foot.

'Not. I thought I made that clear when I said it was a surprise. This way, please.'

As they wind their way through the grand entrance hall with their small cases in tow, Constance struggles to keep up with Sebastian's longer strides. He lets go of her hand and grabs her case before blazing a trail across the sea of commuters, like Moses parting the Red Sea.

Finally, they arrive on their platform, tucked away at the far end of the station. All is revealed, and the scales fall from Constance's eyes. She gasps in delight.

'Oh my gosh, oh-my-golly-gosh! The Belmond British Pullman! That's the one that connects to the Orient Express! How did you even? It's booked years in advance!'

'Not if you're a recently injured movie star apparently.'

Her blissful expression morphs into a frown. 'But the paparazzi, they're going to be all over you. No way to escape. We'll be like prisoners.'

'Stop worrying! The staff are very accommodating. They have plenty of famous people travelling with them, it's all very discreet.'

Sebastian hands their suitcases to an attendant and hauls Constance up the metal steps. In wide-eyed wonder, she caresses the wood panelling along the narrow corridor, bordered on one side by plush cabins and on the other by old-fashioned pull up windows.

'I've always wanted—' she whispers.

'I know.'

'That's just the best surprise!'

'I'm glad. Just wait until you see our suite on the Orient Express.'

Constance's lips form the word 'suite' and her feet hardly touch the floor as she floats behind Sebastian towards their appointed seats.

63

30 JUNE – ORIENT EXPRESS, FRANCE

*A*fter a short coach ride through the Channel Tunnel, Constance and Sebastian finally climb onto the Orient Express.

Theirs are interconnected cabins in pure 1920s style, with inlaid wood surfaces polished to perfection, beautifully crafted nightstands and luxurious patterned upholstery a certain Mr William Morris would have been proud of.

Constance's eyes widen further when she takes in the soft monogrammed blanket rolled at the foot of her bed. In a second of weakness, she wonders whether it would fit in her small suitcase. Fortunately, it clearly wouldn't, thus relieving her of any thievery temptation.

'And I'll be over here.' Sebastian guides her through the small partition to his side of their suite, an exact match for hers.

'This is so gorgeous, I just have no words,' she says.

'Long may it last! If you start plotting alternative itineraries to the restaurant car, I might have to strangle you,' he smiles.

She takes his hand and kisses his knuckles. 'You may surprise me again any time you like.'

Her gaze still riveted to the bygone marvels of their cabin, she misses his knowing smile.

Later, at dinner, Constance and Sebastian lounge in the deep Brunswick green velvet armchairs of the 'Etoile du Nord' restaurant car.

Her midnight blue halter-neck dress is a fortunate match with the decor, and Sebastian looks red-carpet handsome with his Hawaii/Arkansas tan, offset by a pristine white shirt and light grey jacket.

The conversations are muted, and the tinkling of crystal, porcelain and silverware creates a pleasant counterpoint for the steady rumbling of the train.

After the waiter takes their order – champagne and lobster – Sebastian presents her with a gift, beautifully wrapped in thick flowery paper and pink ribbon. She opens it to discover a guide book to Venice and a copy of Agatha Christie's *Murder on the Orient Express*.

She clasps her hands to her chest. 'Have you booked a murder as well? How thoughtful of you.' She lowers her voice. 'I hope it's Tony.'

His low laugh puts a funny feeling in her stomach. She reaches her hand across the table to take his, but he stands up.

'No murder, but I've got another gift for you.'

'My goodness, yet another! You are spoiling me rotten. I'm so sorry I didn't get you anything.'

'Just wait, you can give me the best present ever in a second.'

Sebastian whips a small red velvety box out of his trouser pocket and goes down on one knee in the middle of the aisle.

Constance brings both her hands to her face to hide the reddest cheeks she's ever had.

'Will you marry me?'

She emits a strangled cry. 'Are you sure?'

'Yes, I'm sure.'

'Me?' she stammers.

'Who else?'

'But you know, I may never be able to—'

He cups her chin and closes her mouth. 'I want you to be my wife.'

'Are you sure?'

He smiles patiently. 'I'm asking the question here, Constance. So, what do you say?'

She bats her eyelashes before answering, 'Yes, definitely yes.'

As he stands up, the other diners give him a discreet round of applause, and he thanks them with a smile. Not a single camera phone is brandished, and attention politely returns to their meals and their conversations.

Sebastian holds Constance's hand as if it was a scared baby bird and slips the ring onto her finger. He breathes a discreet sigh of relief when he finds it fits perfectly.

Once he's back in his seat, he beams. 'You see, you've given me the best present I've ever received. I've never wanted something as much as I want to be your husband.'

'My husband…' repeats Constance dreamily.

They kiss over the table, and Constance finally notices the ring that's been under her nose the whole time. It's a traditionally cut solitaire in a platinum setting. It fits her small finger perfectly.

'Crumbs! It's the size of a small egg,' she giggles. 'I thought you were broke!'

'Glad to hear you're not marrying me for my money.'

But, never distinguished for her attention span, she's already moved on. 'Look,' she says of the curly pattern bordering the crockery. 'It's like Hercule Poirot's moustache.'

'You are such a ditz,' laments Sebastian.

64

30 JUNE – ORIENT EXPRESS, FRANCE

'We've just got engaged! I insist.'

'But Constance, we said we would wait.'

Sebastian closes the door of the cabin suite. It locks with a soft noise imprisoning the cloud of 'Pour Monsieur' that follows him everywhere.

Constance shakes her dark curls to emphasise her argument. 'We can't just go to our separate beds like nothing's happened! I'm going to be your wife!'

She turns to him. 'You sure? Are you still sure?"

'Of what?'

'That you want to marry me.'

'I asked you only an hour ago. Yes, I'm sure.'

'We must at least get to third base.'

Undeterred by Sebastian's frown, she underlines her declaration with rapid hand gestures. Then doubt crosses her face. 'Wait! Remind me. What's third base? I can never remember... you know, some heavy petting. At least.'

'Third base? Heavy petting? We're not doing anything before marriage.'

'How backward is that? Very Tennessee,' she snaps.

Due to his years of experience not rising to Tony's baits, Sebastian keeps his voice calm. 'Do you think you owe me sex because I proposed to you?'

Constance's hands still. 'I don't know. It just wouldn't feel right otherwise. A normal girl—'

'Just stop talking,' he interrupts. That's it. Just close your mouth.' He holds her lips shut, but she nods like a toy dog at the back of a car. 'How much have you drunk?' he asks suspiciously.

'It's not that—' she starts, before he puts his palm across her mouth.

'Hush now,' he says.

She nods obediently.

'Yes or no answers. Do you want to sleep in my bed tonight?'

Another nod.

'Naked?'

'Yassh,' she mumbles through his hand.

'And do stuff?'

The nod comes more slowly.

'See! You're just not ready,' he says. 'Plus, you're tipsy on champagne.'

She pulls his hand away from her mouth. 'No, I'm not. Just giddy with excitement. Because I'm engaged to you. Me!' she squeals.

'Calm down! You're going to make me regret it,' he says in a mock-grumble.

Her face falls.

'Of course not, you silly mule,' he smiles. 'You can sleep in my bed, but that's it. I'm not made of stone. I haven't got supernatural self-control.'

The bed in question is narrow but inviting with its thick white sheets with heavy woollen blankets.

Constance gingerly strips to her silk camisole and tights while stealing looks at Sebastian, naked but for his boxer shorts.

It's been a while since she's seen him undressed. Since the hotel in Burbank, in fact. Various bruises and scars he acquired in Hawaii are still visible on his otherwise smooth and tanned skin.

By the look on his face, it appears Sebastian has also missed seeing her without her clothes, and he swallows when she reaches for his bruised torso.

'Where does it hurt?' she asks, unable to tear her eyes away.

'Don't worry about me,' he says, feeling more vulnerable under her gaze than in a room full of film crew.

'I'm nervous. I'm going to do it all wrong.'

'Did you not hear me? We are not doing *anything*.'

'Just a smallish cuddle.'

He climbs into the bed first, careful not to box her against the wall, as he is sure she is going to change her mind about the smallish cuddle as soon as the bedcovers are pulled over them.

Constance stretches next to him and even her curls tremble. 'Are we going to have a code word?' she asks in a breathy voice.

'A code word? For the things we are *not* going to be doing?' He slides an arm under her neck.

'You never know, I might—'

'Constance, we are not having sex!'

'That's my line,' she pouts.

Sebastian chuckles. 'We could kiss.'

'Yes, naked kissing in bed. That's good. What base is that?'

'Base number 9 and 3/4.'

'Now, you're just being silly.'

'That makes two of us.'

'Are you kissing me or not, then?'

Tentatively, he presses his lips to hers. They're soft and yielding. In his mind, he's giving himself a stern talking-to.

Step up. You can do it. Just a kiss.

When her lips part open and her arm snakes around his shoulders, she revels in his delicious scent, but he has a moment of panic.

What's happening? Don't! Not now!

He pulls away. 'Okay?' he asks to hide the fact that he's the one who chickened out.

'If it's too much, I'll just say "stop". That's the code word.'

'Stop? That's your code word? Do you even know what a code word is?'

'I don't care right now, kiss me again.'

'Just once and then you sleep, right?'

'Yes, yes. Gawd, you'd think you don't want to have sex with me!'

'That's exactly what I've been saying. I don't want to have sex with you. It's too soon. We're waiting.'

'Just another kiss.'

He complies with more reticence than the first time. His self-control is hanging by a thread. It's hard to stop when she's so soft and warm against him, with her hair scattered like a dark sunrise around her face. And she keeps saying yes to everything, in a way that's messing with his mind.

Once the kiss ends, too soon for Constance's taste, Sebastian changes tack to distract her and himself. 'Don't you want to take your tights off?' he asks.

'Okay.' Constance sits up abruptly and start rolling them down from the waist.

Sebastian stops her, his hand on hers. 'Was that a yes okay, or a I-don't-really-want-to okay?'

'It was an I'm-not-sure-what-I-want okay.'

He stops her with a gentle hand, and lies on his propped up elbow, his eyes on her. She's cringing under his gaze.

'Since I ended up dripping onto your backseat,' he says, 'I've got pretty good at reading you. But when it comes to sex, you're going to have to talk to me. Say some yeses that mean yes and some noes that mean no. Can you do that?'

'My thoughts are all jumbled up, and I *don't know* whether it is in a good or a bad way.'

He sits up and climbs across her body to stand in the narrow space between the bed and the wardrobe. He offers her his hand to help her stand.

'I'm sorry for starting things I can't finish,' she says in a small voice. 'I don't want you to think I'm a tease.'

'With Tony assaulting you less than two weeks ago, you were brave to give it a try. It still makes me sick just thinking about it. I can't imagine how you feel.' He drapes the monogrammed blanket across her shoulders.

He supports her arm while she shimmies out of her tights.

'Even I could tell it wasn't about sex,' she says. 'He tried to take control by breaking through my boundaries. But after all I've been through, if he thinks he's going to push me around like this, he's got another very long think coming.'

'Don't worry. He's got more than a think coming his way.'

She searches his face, but he grabs her in his arms and carries her to the adjacent cabin.

'That's where you're sleeping tonight!' he says, dropping her into the bed, which bounces softly under her weight. 'I don't want to drag you through Venice tomorrow half-awake and in the bad mood of the century.'

65

1 JULY – ORIENT EXPRESS, ITALY

The next morning, in their cabin, Constance and Sebastian savour a cup of Darjeeling with home-made all-butter shortbread.

He's been daydreaming as the landscape rushes past, while she's devouring the last few pages of *Murder on the Orient Express*.

She closes the book with a clap. 'Do you know how they brought down this incredibly horrid man in this book?'

'They all took turns stabbing him.'

'Oh good, you've read it. That's what we need. For everybody who's ever been hurt by Tony to come together in one place.'

'Death by a thousand cuts.'

'The Wrath of God,' she declares with a strange look in her eyes.

Sebastian wonders if Constance has spent too long with Philly and Wayne and opens his mouth to ask what she means, but she shushes him loudly.

'It's a secret. Anyway, we're almost in Venice. Let's not talk about that toad Tony any more. Think about lovely Venice and the Bridge of Sighs, the Grand Canal, St Mark's Square, the Doge's Palace…'

'Are you sure you've been reading a murder mystery? Sounds like you've learnt the tourist guide by heart.'

'No harm in soaking in a bit of culture, Mister Yankee.'

'I'm still so *not* a Yankee. Could you please read up about the history of the United States?'

'Yankee, Confederate who cares? I'm going to Venice on the Orient Express with my fiancé.' She grins from ear to ear.

'He must be a very patient man,' Sebastian smiles.

Constance air-kisses him across the table. 'And good-looking and kind. Not to mention very sexy!'

The warmth in her chocolate-brown eyes makes Sebastian's heart do a somersault. He blushes despite himself, which in turn makes Constance blush too.

'What a great guy!' jokes Sebastian to dispel their sudden awkwardness, but Constance has already changed topic.

'I must tell Philly about us!' She beams and digs her phone out of her bag.

> ***Myname.sNotConnie*** *@FitnessPhilly289 –*
> *Phil! Any smoothie tip for soon-to-be*
> *Mrs IRL?*
> ***FitnessPhilly289*** *@Myname.sNotConnie –*
> *Bout time! God is good. Congratulations*
> *from me and Wayne!*
> ***Myname.sNotConnie*** *@FitnessPhilly289 – My*
> *head's still spinning!*
> ***FitnessPhilly289*** *@Myname.sNotConnie –*
> *Make my cacao and avocado serenity*
> *smoothie. And send pictures…*
> ***Myname.sNotConnie*** *@FitnessPhilly289 – Of*
> *the smoothie?*

> ***FitnessPhilly289*** *@Myname.sNotConnie – Of Venice, you silly.*
>
> ***Myname.sNotConnie*** *@FitnessPhilly289 – How do you know where we're going? God's tracking our GPS?*
>
> ***FitnessPhilly289*** *@Myname.sNotConnie – 1) Wash your mouth, missy. 2) Who do you think stopped IRL from buying you an ugly ring?*
>
> ***Myname.sNotConnie*** *@FitnessPhilly289 – It's a conspiracy!*
>
> ***FitnessPhilly289*** *@Myname.sNotConnie – U 2 young 'uns need all the help you can get. Ciao! xoxo*

'You told them!' accuses Constance, thrusting the phone back into her bag. 'You spoilt my surprise.'

Sebastian puts his hands up in defence. 'Couldn't it count as just another surprise?' he laughs.

'I'm going to give *you* a surprise. You just wait and see how you like it!' she grumbles. She breaks a shortbread in two, shoves both pieces into her mouth and chews vigorously.

'See, you're in a mood,' he says. 'You didn't sleep enough.'

'Shut up, I'm reading!' She opens her guide book at the page she dog-eared.

They're silent for a while until he asks, 'Do you reckon there's anywhere to get married in Venice?'

She throws him a quick glance. 'Asking for a friend?'

He smiles. 'Something like that.'

'One hundred and thirty nine churches at the most recent count. It's in the guide,' she replies with a reluctant smile.

'We could ask the Doge to officiate.'

'Last one abdicated in 1797 and died in 1802.'

'Imagine the tabloids. Married by the ghost of the Doge of Venice. That would beat the Clooneys' wedding!'

'You are making zero sense, mister.'

'At least I'm not reciting the guide book.'

'Nothing wrong with educating oneself. If you didn't want me to take in the culture, you should have taken me to Canada and bought me snow shoes instead of books.'

While Sebastian is left to wonder whether that might have been the better option, Constance turns her attention to the view of the Venice skyline rising out of the Lagoon.

The rest of the journey is punctuated by Constance's oohs and ahs, interspersed with whole sections of the guide book she has memorised.

When they disembark at Venice Santa Lucia, she throws her arms around his neck, enraptured with the high metal arches of the station ceiling, which she describes as a 'feat of engineering', and Sebastian fears his huge reserves of patience are about to be tapped.

66
1 JULY - FONDAMENTINA DE L'OSMARIN, VENICE, ITALY

*T*he gentle lapping of the water against the ochre and red buildings bordering the canal is a welcome change from the noise of the crowds they left behind on St Mark's Square.

The Italian summer heat reverberates in the narrow streets, like sound caught in between cymbals.

After winding their way away along the decaying elegance of the Venetian palazzi and investigating the various tourist hotspots, Sebastian and Constance have discovered the city's tiniest bridge: Ponte del Diavolo. They rest their elbows against the rusty balustrade while gazing into the opaque jade-green water.

'It means "Devil's Bridge",' explains Constance, pointing at the carved stone street sign. 'There are actually two in Venice. The other is in Torcello, and unlike this one, it doesn't have a parapet.' She takes a giant lick of her *gelato*, and her upper lip acquires a thin chocolate moustache.

Sebastian smiles with indulgence. 'I never have to read another guide book in my life.'

'How do you even put up with me?' She bites off a chunk

of the waffle cone and soon realises her mistake when her ice cream drips onto her hand.

Sebastian retrieves from his Armani Bermuda shorts pocket the napkin he took from the street vendor for just such an occasion. He wipes the brown smudge off her hand.

'I'm uniquely equipped to deal with you. Have you never noticed?'

'With a ready supplies of paper towels?' she grins.

His eyes sparkle with amusement. 'I meant superhuman self-control! My former incarnation as a good Baptist boy helps me take care of you. From the beginning, I've treated you the way my mamma would have expected me to treat my future wife. I reverted to type.'

In the perpendicular canal, a gondola glides by. The bored gondolier spoon-feeds tourist-friendly titbits in broken English to a young couple and their selfie sticks.

Constance would love a picture of Sebastian and his unearthly golden glow, but she knows no pixel could do it justice.

Wishing she had her pencils and sketchbook with her, she settles for feasting her eyes on his un-capturable handsomeness until the boat and its occupants are out of sight and she can speak again.

'So you do mean it when you say, "no sex before marriage"?'

'Of course. It's hard, but it has the advantage of making couples feel secure in their relationship before becoming intimate. It's exactly what you need.'

'I never thought of it like that.' She leans her face against his thick biceps, unwittingly transferring a chocolate mark onto the straining sleeve of his white linen shirt.

The distinct whiff of dirty canal water mixed with his Chanel aftershave is an intoxicating fragrance.

'However rubbish sex will be at first, once we're married, we're stuck together,' she says.

He chuckles and tucks a dark curl behind her ear before it can attach itself to her ice cream. 'I wouldn't have chosen those specific words, but yeah, that's the idea.'

'You won't be able to get rid of me even if I'm terrible at bedroom gymnastics.'

He runs his hand through his hair. Dampened by the Venetian humidity, it sticks up in a photoshoot-worthy quiff. 'You will be bewitching, I can tell. I find your particular brand of spontaneity and shyness a potent aphrodisiac!'

He presses his lips to hers and tastes the sweetness of her mouth with a sneaky flick of his tongue.

'Wait a minute,' interrupts Constance, spattering ice cream down the front of her flowery dress. 'Good Baptist boys don't kiss like that!'

'Look away now, Mamma!' Sebastian laughs.

He throws the sticky ruins of her gelato into the canal, wraps her tight in his arms, and gives her a leisurely kiss that makes her knees buckle and her body burst into flames.

67

2 JULY – CONSTANCE'S HOUSE, HENLEY-ON-THAMES, UK

On their return to London, neither Constance nor Sebastian could face the long flight back to LA, and she held him to his promise they would stay at her house instead of checking into an expensive hotel.

So, on the evening of their arrival back from Italy, they are playing Uno and drinking champagne, sitting cross-legged on the carpet in Constance's cream sitting room.

'I can't believe you don't know any other card games,' complains Constance, with a now habitual glance to the sparkling ring on her right hand.

'I know Old Maid.'

Constance puts up an impatient hand. 'Just stop talking.'

'Your turn,' says Sebastian.

'Gawd, I'm so bored!'

'Do you want to go for a walk?'

'It's the Henley Regatta. Someone is bound to recognise you and make a fuss.'

Sebastian still tries hard to be helpful. 'TV perhaps? Must be something on Netflix.'

Constance doesn't even reply. She looks grumpily at the

room. 'I don't like this house any more. I don't like being here.'

'Is that why you're pitchin' a fit? Let's just go back to London tomorrow, get a hotel.'

Constance's tone turns waspish. 'Stop it with your solutions! I've had enough of your American positivity. Our lives suck! We shouldn't be sitting here like idiots playing cards. We should be having sex.'

Sebastian gives her a searching look. She's clearly just getting started, and trying to stop her now would be as wise as sticking a hand into a lawnmower.

She groans. 'It's because of me we're not. I'm angry with myself. Sometimes I want to shake you and say "*Be angry"*! I want you to berate me for being such a coward, for being such a *princess*!' She throws her cards on the floor.

'Whoa! Hold your horses. It's not because of you.' Sebastian grabs her wrist. 'I told you. I'm the one who wants to wait. Why should I be angry about a decision I made?'

She opens her mouth to respond, but he cuts her off. 'If you wanna know, I *am* angry you're thinking so little of yourself. And I'm fed up with being the only one looking for solutions.'

Constance finally meets his eyes. 'I was awake half the night worrying about the wedding,' she confesses in a small voice.

His eyes widen in surprise. 'What about the wedding?'

'I never thought I would get married, so I'm years behind the average fiancée! I don't know the first thing about table arrangements, flowers, dresses! I was researching cap sleeves on Google at four o'clock this morning.'

'Why? Who do you think is going to attend?'

'All your friends, Hollywood people. My mother. Whatever I wear, she'll think it's "common".'

'We don't have to invite anyone you don't want to.'

'I think I have great-aunts on my dad's side. We're going to have to have the wedding in England, because they won't want to travel.'

'You're worrying about the travel arrangements for relatives you're not even sure you have?'

'And who's going to be my bridesmaid? I don't have any friends apart from Philly. But if I ask her, my mother will be livid.'

'Wait a second—'

'And Rupert is going to want to walk me down the aisle. What will my father say?'

'What about a small wedding, just us, then?'

'But your big Tennessee family?'

'I don't care.'

'And the wedding cake. You have to book months in advance.'

Sebastian rolls his eyes and smiles. 'Okay, stop. Come here.'

He waves her over and open his arms. She scoots into his embrace and hides her face in the crook of his neck. With one arm Sebastian is holding her close, while he picks up the champagne bottle she knocked over in her haste.

He strokes her hair. 'You're driving yourself nuts. Put it out of your mind, we haven't even set a date yet. Think happy thoughts.'

She closes her eyes and breathes in the smell of his aftershave just in the nook behind his ear.

'All better?'

'Not really. Now I'm worrying about selling my house.'

He puts his hands on her neck and pretends to strangle her, but it doesn't even raise a smile.

'I don't want to live here any more. It's like being locked in a dungeon with my worst memories.'

'I'm sorry.' He kisses her jaw.

'And there's the estate agents' fees.'

Sebastian holds her closer and kisses her ear lobe. 'What about them?' he murmurs against her neck.

'I might try to market the house myself to save money. Maybe ask around. Try for a private sale.'

Sebastian is curling a lock of her hair around his index finger, savouring the silkiness of it. 'How will you feel once you've sold it?'

'Free,' Constance replies without hesitation.

'That's good.' He pecks the corner of her mouth.

'Then we can move on, go somewhere new.'

Constance kisses his neck to the jawline. He closes his eyes in delight. 'You're going to be spectacular.'

She nuzzles his neck. 'Hmm. What?'

'You're going to be fantastic at sex. I can tell.'

Constance brings her hands to hold his face while she nibbles her way down his neck to the collarbone. He moans softly.

'Am I doing well?' she asks.

'This is already the best sex I've ever had.'

'Liar,' laughs Constance.

Sebastian runs his hands up and down her back slowly. 'Honest word. I'm in heaven.'

'Better than cards?' whispers Constance.

'Oh yes.'

'So what do we do now?'

'Sorry?'

'What would you do with a normal girl?'

Sebastian frowns at her choice of words. 'I would say, "Sorry, not happening," and I would go home to you.'

'You know what I mean.'

'Yes, I know what you mean.' He stands and straightens his clothes.

'What are you doing?

Sebastian replies with a devilish grin, 'Sorry, not happening,' and marches up the stairs to the spare room as Constance looks aghast.

68

3 JULY – CONSTANCE'S HOUSE, HENLEY-ON-THAMES, UK

Constance enters the room where Sebastian sleeps and her irritation enters with her.

'I can't believe you won't sleep in my bed!' she gripes. 'I feel we're going backwards.'

'Go away, I'm sleeping.'

'Why won't you?' she insists. 'You made me feel all *funny*. And now you're abandoning me.'

Sebastian pulls the duvet further up his face and mumbles something unintelligible.

'Are you trying to punish me?' Constance asks.

Sebastian stirs awake. 'What—*What*?'

'Well? Are you?'

Sebastian rolls his eyes. 'You're just yanking my chain. Go back to bed!'

Constance sits down beside him. 'Why are you doing this? You're driving me mad.'

Sebastian stretches one arm out of the duvet, wraps it around her neck and pulls her down to him, a move that would have sent her running for the hills only a few weeks ago.

'Don't be such a baby,' he says.

'Stop ignoring me! I am upset.'

Sebastian speaks through the tangle of her hair. 'It's the middle of the night.'

'Why? I want to know why!'

Sebastian finally sits up and stretches. 'Okay. Why did I go to sleep here instead of with you? Because you were talking nonsense about "normal girls". Who cares about them? Whoever *they* are, for I sure never met one.'

'You know what I meant.'

'Yes, and I didn't like it'

'So, you just give up on me?'

'On the contrary, I'm going to phase two. It does you good to want me. Otherwise, I'm always coming closer and closer, and you have no time to realise you want to come closer too. So now you're frustrated and thinking how much better it would be to always sleep in the same bed. And that's another little step in the right direction.'

'I hate it when you go all evil mastermind.'

'Says the girl with the secret plan. Anyway, how do you think I've lasted so long courting you? I get you. Sometimes you're just too impatient! You need to wait, let time do its thing.'

Constance sulks.

'Do you think I want to say no when you're *offering* me sex?' he asks. 'I say no because it's better in the long run. I'm carefully playing the cards I've got in the game in front of me.'

'You sure that's the only reason?'

Sebastian lies back down. 'Yes. Now quit your whinin'. You can sleep here. *But we're not having sex!*'

The tension leaves Constance's face like water circling a drain. It bubbles then disappears. She giggles and snuggles down next to him.

He pulls the duvet over them both and presses his face into

her hair, filling his lungs with her vanilla and orange blossom perfume.

Constance smiles. 'You're so *mean.*'

'That's right, baby. Good night.'

69

3 JULY – CONSTANCE'S HOUSE, HENLEY-ON-THAMES, UK

Constance is cooking breakfast in her small kitchen flooded with light.

She's singing 'You Are My Sunshine', but every few seconds she stops to speak. 'Table, two steps.' More singing. 'Fridge, three steps.' More singing. 'Microwave, four steps.' More singing. 'Sink, five steps.'

When Sebastian enters the room in a pair of tight boxers and a well-worn LA T-shirt, still smelling of man musk and not yet of Chanel, she stops her singing abruptly and blushes.

'What you're doing?' he asks.

'Can't a girl sing in her own kitchen without the Gestapo interrogating her?' she smiles.

She goes on her tiptoes to kiss the angle of his jaw. 'You are my sunshine,' she sings to him, and he bends her back in a tango hold.

'Coffee?'

'Here,' she says, handing him a steaming mug of black coffee. He looks like he needs it. The zigzagging between time zones is not doing him any favours. She can't remember the last time she saw him looking rested.

'Saving your performance for posterity?' he winks, pointing towards her phone displaying the audio recording app.

'Says the guy forever associated with *Slow Motion*,' she snarks, naming his least successful movie.

'Okay then,' he smiles, 'moving on!' He grabs her by the neck and kisses her hair. 'I love your crazy curls!'

He sits at the table with a tub of yoghurt and his black coffee. He eats but never stops watching her. She puts a knitted tea cosy in a large plastic box balanced on her hip.

'What are you doing?'

'Packing.' She squeezes past the table at which he is sitting, and the corner of her box catches the side of his cup spilling the coffee onto the table.

He only has time to pull his chair back to avoid the hot liquid. By then, Constance is already gone.

So, Sebastian wipes the table with a cloth and sighs.

Then he takes what little is left of his coffee to the dining room where he perches in a tired cream damask armchair.

At random he picks *The Little Prince* by St Exupéry from a nearby shelf. He has time to read half of it while Constance is banging furniture upstairs.

When she returns with a second lidded plastic container, she looks in Sebastian's direction, but he keeps his attention on his book. She goes back upstairs and brings back a third container. She glances at him, but he still ignores her. She goes to fetch a cardboard box. On her way down, she stares angrily. 'Don't help me or anything.'

'Hush,' he says. 'This is a must-read when you're taming a wild thing.' He winks at her winningly. She blushes and plops onto his knees, crushing the book under herself.

'Sometimes I forget how truly good-looking you are.'

'Is that a colloquialism for *I'm really sorry I nearly burnt your dick off*?' he jokes.

'The coffee was an accident.' Constance shifts in his lap to a loud rustling of paper and leans her head on his shoulder. He wraps his arms around her. 'So, you're in a good mood now?'

'It feels good to make decisions.'

They hold each other in peaceful silence.

'What are those boxes?' he asks eventually.

'The stuff I want to take with me. I've changed my mind. I'm going to get an estate agent to sell the place for me then some house-clearance people to take the rest away.'

'Everything else?' Sebastian exclaims in surprise.

'Says the guy who had all his stuff in storage six months ago.'

'Fair point.'

'I can do it all from LA.'

'Great. Let's Fedex your boxes to America, sell your car at the nearest garage and get a hotel in London for tonight.'

'No! Not Oggie, she will always remind me of you. Dripping wet and all distraught. I'll find a nice cosy garage somewhere for her to sleep until I can ship her over to America,' she says quietly. She wraps her arms tighter around him and kisses his freckles.

'I've so outgrown this place. I can't wait to leave it all behind.'

'Well, I'm taking my book. Now you've sat on it, I'll treasure it for ever.'

'Shut up, you ninny.'

'That's a new insult,' he smiles.

'I love you so much.'

'I know.'

70

3 JULY – OVER THE ATLANTIC OCEAN, BETWEEN LONDON UK AND LOS ANGELES, CALIFORNIA, USA

*C*onstance and Sebastian sit in First Class on a British Airways flight to LAX. They each have their own berth with a fold-out bed.

Meals have been served then collected, and a delicious aroma lingers over the pervading scent of plastic.

They're both waiting for the optimal jet-lag-busting bedtime, which they've calculated is in thirty minutes.

Sebastian sits in the aisle seat, reading the news on his phone, wishing he could speak to Regina and check on the progress of her investigation.

Constance looks out of her window wishing she could paint the mottled white sky and trying to decide which Impressionist painting it reminds her of most. Perhaps a Monet or a Sisley? A Pissarro at a push.

She's pulled out of her happy reverie by Sebastian's nervous clearing of his throat.

His face is pale and the few hours of sleep he got in her spare room have done little to reduce the dark circles around his eyes. As he feels her watching him, he attempts a smile.

Scrambling for something to cheer him up, she says the

first thing that crosses her mind. 'Wouldn't you like to buy a house together?' she asks.

'Another one?'

'Fifty-fifty this time.'

'Perhaps.'

'Somewhere just us, secluded and quiet, where you won't get recognised or hassled. The opposite of LA.'

'First I need the money Tony owes me. If he suspects I'm gunning for him, his lawyers will tie it up in so many knots that we'll never see a dime. The only way is to expose him as an abuser and embezzler.'

'We have to play our cards very close to our chests.'

Sebastian turns to face Constance with a stern look. 'There's no "we" when it comes to Tony. I don't want you anywhere near him.'

'No, I understand. But I can be your *consigliere*. You know, like in *The Godfather*.'

'You can call it what you like if it means I handle it alone.'

'I get it.' Constance returns her gaze to the window.

The clouds stretch like an endless duvet beneath the plane. 'We're flying over a storm. Crazy to think all the generations before us never knew how small a storm really is. No matter how scary and dark it seems from the inside, it's finite.'

'Life lesson right there.'

'Sometimes I think I've taken a rainstorm and turned it into a hurricane.'

'What do you mean?'

'That first boy dropped me in a hole, but I kept digging. I chose to have sex for the wrong reasons. My current problem is more to do with the violence I did to myself rather than the harm done to me.'

Sebastian nods quietly and takes her hand. She looks out the window. After a long silence, he speaks. 'You need to forgive yourself. Whatever the reasons why you got hurt, you have the right to heal.'

'The only way is to turn the bad into something good, then I can let it go.'

'Sounds like a plan,' he smiles.

'It does, doesn't it?'

'Perhaps you should talk to Pastor John.'

'I will.'

While Constance admires the cloudscape, Sebastian returns to his own thoughts.

He's turning in his mind all the hare-brained plans he's come up with since that day in O'ahu when Tony's giant caterpillar of a hand crept over Constance's breast.

They haven't amounted to much. Tony's behaviour, like that of so many other powerful men in any walks of life, is an open secret. The aura of impunity that precedes, surrounds and follows him is his best shield. Watching him get away with the unacceptable, the immoral, and the illegal is gagging victims more effectively than any crooked lawyer.

It is easier to accept his abuse as part of the Hollywood game they've all agreed to play. A twisted self-punishment for their unbelievable luck in making it this far in Tinseltown, when so many, no less talented or motivated, have failed.

They put up with men like Tony so they can feel better about earning five hundred times the average First World income.

He hopes Regina, with her terrier-like drive and her encyclopaedic knowledge of the underbelly of Hollywood, will come up with the goods.

Gloomily, he wonders what Wayne would make of his reliance on a woman to fight his battles against injustice. Probably not what he had in mind when he urged Sebastian to step up and be a man.

As his watch pings to remind him his carefully calculated bedtime has come, Sebastian reclines his seat into a cot and pulls the blanket over his head.

Despite the comfort of their First Class berths, sleep eludes him. His mind overflows with the questions he wants to ask Regina and the answers he hopes she will provide. The gnawing in his gut makes him restless.

Unbeknown to him, Constance is hatching plans of her own in the next booth, and she is much more optimistic. She knows no one will see her coming while, under the cover of her harmless appearance, she commando-crawls towards her target.

71

4 JULY – SEBASTIAN'S MANSION, PACIFIC PALISADES HILLS, LOS ANGELES, CALIFORNIA, USA

*A*fter being stuck in the I-405 North logjam, Sebastian and Constance's cab is now inching forward on the I-10 West.

Constance looks out the window to the streams of pimped-up SUVs on their enormous tyres, lining the lanes, and the access ramps as far as the eye can see. She imagines poor little Oggie would look like a Lilliputian in this monster-truck traffic.

Returning to LA has taken its toll on Sebastian. He couldn't get to sleep in the plane, and the ever-present Californian sun hurts his eyes. He worries that unless Regina discovers something useful, he'll turn up empty-handed at a knife fight.

It's all very well and good him telling Constance he will handle Tony, but now he has to find a way to do it or lose face. Worse, allow her to believe that he is not strong enough to protect her.

He's stuck between wanting to defeat Tony and the fear that people will know what he's had to put up with over the years, all the humiliations and debasements that are part and parcel of any association with Hollywood's OG Horrible Boss.

The pain in his stomach will not go away.

As they turn onto Ocean Avenue, the scenery improves and he works up the courage to call his agent.

'Hi Regina, so did you speak to Mal-Mal?'

'Took me days of cajoling before he spilt the tea. I had to give him a foot massage.'

'Oh shit, Reggie. I'm sorry. Anything interesting?'

'Dead end. Turns out Mal-Mal's palatial new house was indeed purchased by an out-of-court settlement but not one reached with Tony. He was very clear on that. He was fuzzier on what he had to do to get there. I wouldn't be surprised if he'd engaged in some nicely orchestrated piece of blackmail.'

'Huh,' says Sebastian, not to alert Constance that anything is wrong.

'So unless you want to stick your head above the parapet and take your own ass over to some chat show, you're going to have to wait for Jack, Jim and Johnny to do the dirty work for you.'

No one could ever accuse Sebastian of being vindictive but waiting for his former mentor to succumb to his excessive whisky drinking is not Sebastian's idea of revenge.

Regina was the last cartridge Sebastian had in his magazine. His last chance of achieving his goal without getting his hands dirty.

'Thank you for what you did, Regina. I really appreciate it. I'm going to have to take it from here. You might want to damage-control your exposure to Tony Da Ricci.'

He hopes his confident tone will fool Constance and help her believe he can handle this.

'Roger that, kiddo. I always thought you were a simpering fragile flower, perhaps I was wrong.'

And on this vote of confidence of sorts, Regina ends the call.

As they head up San Vicente Boulevard towards Pacific Palisades, a well-earned sleep, and a splash in the pool, both are silent.

When the taxi pulls off Fermo Drive, Constance is the first to see it. It is a bold red sign with white capital letters that reads 'Foreclosure' and underneath in smaller black print 'Bank owned'.

Constance's first reaction is to check the house number on the side of the gate. She struggles to make sense of what she reads. 'Is that the right house?' She stands on the pavement and checks the neighbouring gates, but this is the only one that looks anything like what she remembers.

Sebastian is already busy holding the taxi/cab. 'Get in,' he says, his voice flat. He is rattled at the look on her face and the speed at which she obeys.

Back in the relative safety of the cab, Sebastian calls Brandie, his personal assistant.

'It's Seb, find us a hotel. LA. Near the Fermo Drive house. Right now.'

Then there's a pause.

'What do you mean you can't?' His tone makes Constance's ears prick up, but she avoids his gaze.

In the silence that follows, she can make out Brandie's reply. 'Tony says I'm not to work for you any—'

Sebastian disconnects the call before the assistant has a chance to finish her sentence in the hope Constance has not heard the fateful words Brandie spoke.

Constance's British good manners prevent her from admitting to eavesdropping on something that wasn't meant for her, and impassively she pretends to be none the wiser.

'Nearest motel,' Sebastian says to the driver.

One stolen glance at his face convinces Constance now is not the time to ask questions about how exactly a fully paid-for house can end up foreclosed. *Dirty lawyers!*

Sebastian can't bring himself to look at her, but he seizes her hand and squeezes her fingers. 'I am going to destroy him.'

72

4 JULY – HOTEL, BRENTWOOD, LOS ANGELES, CALIFORNIA, USA

The only hotel still accepting guests on Independence Day is an uninspiring three-star off Sepulveda and Sunset Boulevards.

On the drive to the motel, Sebastian feels numb.

He wilts under the driver's gaze. No doubt the news of his 'eviction' will be all over the airwaves in no time. No matter how discreet he'd kept his address, there is no question the driver understood exactly what had just happened.

Constance yawns as she unlocks door of the crummy room they were lucky to get. Her body is travel-sticky, and the blistering heat between the controlled temperature of the cab and the AC at the reception desk was enough to cover her in a sheen of sweat.

She deeply feels the right to shower should be enshrined in the American Constitution, and she desperately wants a few hours' sleep.

'What time is it?' she asks.

'Eleven o'clock in the morning, London time,' replies Sebastian, dragging behind him a couple of unwieldy suitcases.

'We haven't slept in twenty-seven hours. We have to get some rest before we can deal with this shitstorm.'

'I can't sleep,' he says.

'You're dead on your feet. We need clear minds to make a plan.'

'I'm just going to have a shower. You sleep.' Constance would have loved to scrub the journey from her skin before getting into bed, but Sebastian looks so distraught, she lets him go first. By the time her head rests on the pillows, she's asleep.

As Sebastian lets the hot water wash away the grime of the day's travel, fear and rage roil in his gut. He's got no money, he's got no house, and without Tony, he has no career.

The taps complain loudly at the excessive force he uses to turn the water off. And part of the shower curtain tears off the pole when he exits the cubicle.

He doesn't bother drying his hair and steps into the bedroom, a small towel wrapped around his waist, dripping all over the carpet.

Constance is snoring softly, her fists loosely curled by her ears, like an overtired child. The urge to protect her, to please her, overtakes him and a wave of self-disgust at his failings is like a bucket of cold water thrown in his face.

Without thinking he throws some clothes on and steps into the moist evening heat. The sweat he's just washed away returns with a vengeance.

The pain in his throat is a nice change from the one in his gut.

He walks aimlessly and ends up at the pool. It is half the size of the Pacific Palisades pool, slightly murky and smelling strongly of chlorine.

Sebastian is back where he was when he met Constance in a silent face-to-face with the water. Reviewing in his mind what he can do to extricate himself from Tony's grasp. To re-establish control over his life.

There is no way to discreetly destroy Tony behind the scenes. He's going to have to come out and do it himself. In the full glare of the media. One man against Tony's carefully constructed fraudulent business empire.

Exposing Tony will create a splash that will get the whole movie industry wet.

He himself will get drenched, and everyone will know how weak he has been. For the whole word to know that – for Constance to know that – will be excruciating.

Could she still love him and respect him if she knew the litany of small humiliations he has swallowed over the years? Would he be unemployable? Would the glitterati whisper behind his back at award ceremonies? Would he even be invited to those without Tony's patronage?

He stares at the soupy pool water like he eyed the Thames that day in February before Constance. A prisoner of his own self-loathing, even more than of his sadistic boss.

Step up, be a man. Be the man she needs.

'I won't be able to drown you without getting wet. But you know what, Tony? I am not afraid to jump.'

He steps off the ledge and leaps fully clothed into the water, the splash resonating in his ears and the chlorine stinging his nose.

The ripples expand across the pool surface, then the water returns to its normal smoothness. At the bottom, Sebastian listens to the blood pulsing in his ears until his lungs scream for air.

Yes, he has what it takes to get justice for himself and for all of Tony's victims. Despite the years of loneliness and shame, despite the threats and machinations, Sebastian finds he still has the courage to do what's right.

You can't go wrong by doing the right thing.

He pulls himself out of the pool, his clothes dripping, and sits on the edge of a sun lounger to tip the water out of his sneakers.

After a few minutes, savouring the taste of his newfound resolution, he strolls back into the building and up to his room.

Without even removing his sopping clothes, he stretches on the bed beside Constance, and promptly fall into a righteous man's sleep.

73

4 JULY – HOTEL, BRENTWOOD, LOS ANGELES, CALIFORNIA, USA

It is the cold that wakes Constance, then the fear she might have wet herself in her sleep.

She blinks away the exhaustion that half an hour of shut-eye has left undiminished, and sees Sebastian pale-faced and soaked, lying next to her, stinking of chlorine.

Her first thought is that he is dead, and she holds her hand to his nose. *Alive.*

With his rusty hair plastered to his face and his sodden clothes clinging to the hard lines of his body, he is the picture of the man she rescued from Battersea Bridge, and her heart booms against her chest.

He's done it this time. He's tried to drown himself.

Through her stupor, she realises what the recent weeks have held for Sebastian.

A nightmare shoot in Burbank. A break-up over a stupid fake pregnancy. Days alone in Hawaii. Then an accident that almost cost him his life and a long stay in hospital. The anger at being replaced by another actor. His money stolen, his house foreclosed.

This is the sum total of all the woes she neglected to notice while he stoically indulged her every whim and patiently rode out her every mood.

No wonder he didn't turn to her and tried to drown himself while she slept. She's been the worst fiancée, the worst friend.

As she changes into dry clothes, a simple pair of white shorts and pink vest, she resolves to step up to the plate.

Her man needs her, and like Philly said, she's not the kind of girl to leave her man to fight his battles alone.

After sending a quick text to Pastor John, she leaves a note for Sebastian.

Silent as the grave, she slips out of the room.

74

4 JULY – HOTEL, BRENTWOOD, LOS ANGELES, CALIFORNIA, USA

Sebastian dreams he is lost in a white-out, and he wakes up with a jolt. The combination of wet clothes and AC cranked up to the max recreated some pretty believable blizzard conditions. His teeth chatter and his fingers tremble as he unbuttons his trousers.

He knocks on the bathroom door. 'Constance?' No answer. He struggles to pull his T-shirt over his head and shucks off his jeans. He peels his socks before stepping into the shower cubicle.

The warm water is glorious against his skin and halts the slow hypothermic shut-down of his brain.

He expected Constance to be fast asleep next to him. Where can she be?

He takes his time, scrubbing his skin and washing his hair with the lemon-scented courtesy shampoo. In the rising steam, he lets the glow of his new resolution cleanse his spirit of guilt, shame and helplessness, just as the water washes off the harsh stink of chlorine.

First thing tomorrow, he'll deal with Tony. But for now he

wants to hug Constance until she wriggles and giggles, and go back to sleep with his face in her curls.

When he returns to the bedroom, towelling his hair dry, Constance is still not there.

He pokes his head out the door, expecting to see her getting ice or a chocolate bar from the vending machine.

No ice box. No vending machine. No Constance.

Unnerved by her continued absence, he checks the cupboard, and looking back at him is her pink wheelie suitcase with her sunglasses tucked in the front pocket. His stomach contracts.

Her purse. Where is her purse?

No matter where or how well he looks, Constance, her purse and her cream Converses are gone.

G.O.N.E. Gone.

And that's when he sees the folded hotel letterhead, and the words Constance wrote in a hasty scribble.

'I've gone to sort everything out. Please don't do anything stupid. I love you so much. Your C.'

A thunderbolt from Mount Olympus would strike less fear in his heart. Without a shadow of a doubt, he knows where she's gone.

And, without a shadow of a doubt, he knows she's in danger.

75
4 JULY – TONY'S MANSION, HOLMSBY HILLS, LOS ANGELES, CALIFORNIA, USA

'Good evening, Mr Da Ricci. I hoped you might be home,' she smiles, her cheeks aching with the effort.

Constance had forgotten how creepy Tony looks with his Botoxed face and rapper clothes. The iciness of the eyes and the warmth of the smile wrestle in a duel to the death between truth and lies.

She swallows her fear and steps into Tony's hacienda-style villa. Everything about the building screams Hollywood royalty. It's only a few automated gates away from the Playboy Mansion.

She wonders how many of the dozens of geranium-lined windows have been purchased with Sebastian's hard-earned money.

Her cream Converses squeak on the polished marble of the two-storied lobby.

'Come in,' croons Tony with the mellifluous voice and gentleman-like manners of a psychopath. 'A pretty Redcoat, on Independence Day! To what do I owe the pleasure of your unannounced visit?'

He reaches for her handbag, but she hugs it against her

body, and he turns his attention to her shoes. As she blinks her incredulity, he unties one of her Converses, holding her foot for much too long.

Constance's mouth is as dry as the Mojave Desert, but cold chills travel down her spine. 'Please release my shoe,' she says as firmly as she can.

'Oh chill, Connie, I'm not one those foot fetishists.' His voice echoes in the cavernous entryway, making him sound like a real-life ogre. If the acoustic is meant to frighten his guests-slash-victims, it's working.

When both her feet rejoin the ground, Constance retrieves her literal and figurative balance. 'I've come to talk about the money you owe Sebastian.'

Tony's face morphs from brazen mischief to glacial contempt. 'What's it gotta do with you?'

'You owe him five and a half million dollars, it's time you paid up.'

'And you little gold-digger thought you'd come into my house and speak to me like that? Can't your pussy of a boyfriend come and talk to me man-to-man?'

'He doesn't know I'm here,' says Constance, exactly as she rehearsed.

Tony's face changes again to that of a truculent, avuncular business mentor. 'You're the business head of the two, aren't you, doll?'

'I'm the one here asking for what you owe.'

'Do you know what happens to English vixens on a day like today?'

'They get what they want,' she replies with a decent attempt at confidence.

'Yak, yak, yak, blabber, blabber.' He waves his hands in the air. 'And what are you going to do for me?'

'Nothing. Sebastian's worked for his money already. If you don't hand it over, it is theft.'

Tony stares at her for what seems like an eternity, and Constance's insides turn to ice. Then out of the blue, he lets out a cry of rage and rushes her. In her haste to get away from him, she falls backward into one of the entrance-hall Louis XV armchairs.

He's already on her. He grabs both the upholstered armrests, pinning her into the seat, and leans his face close enough to hers that she can see the burst capillaries in his eyes and smell the Scotch on his breath.

'I don't owe that piss-ant anything. He owes me!'

Constance closes her eyes in disgust. Her body is screaming against his intrusion into her personal space, but unlike many of Tony's victims, Constance is used to those feelings and experienced at hiding them.

Her face is smooth and her voice steady when she replies. 'Hurting me isn't going to change a thing, Mr Da Ricci. You'll still owe the money you owe, and I will have something over you.'

'Something over me? Do you think you will be the first little girl to go whining about something or other I've said or done? I have met my share of jealous, piss-streaked women who don't appreciate a man. Look who you shacked up with. An overgrown little boy with a paper-thin ego. You want to sue me, get in line! My lawyers will destroy you, you pathetic money-grabbing whore.'

'Fine, we'll sue you for it, then. Now let me go.'

'Oh I don't think so. I think you owe me an apology.'

'Not happening.'

'Do you know what I can do to Seb, if you cross me?'

She stares at him.

'Destroy his career, have him accused of statutory rape, plant drugs on him. And that's just for starters.'

Constance swallows and says as brightly as she can. 'Sounds like heaps of fun, I'm sure, but two can play at that game, then everyone is covered in mud. Those in glass houses shouldn't be throwing rocks, Mr Da Ricci.'

'Shut up, you little bitch,' he groans and grabs her around the waist, lifting her off the floor with ease. As he marches towards the stairs, panic floods Constance's mind and her limbs go weak.

Fight! Don't let him lock you in a room.

A fresh jolt of fear gives her the energy to buck against him, and he drops her onto the stairs.

Pain shoots through her body like a lightning bolt, and her eyes fill with tears. She kicks frantically, but he straddles her and without warning sticks his hand between her legs, where nervous sweat has drenched her panties.

His eyes change. 'Oh you sneaky little whore, you're not here to ask for money, are you? Feel how wet you are for me.'

This new assault galvanises her, and she regains her cool poise. 'Take your hand out of my crotch,' she says as if she was asking him the time.

'You need a good fuck, don't you? To relax you, release the tension. You try so hard to do everything right, be a good girl, draw pretty pictures, keep your nose clean. But sometimes, when you're alone at night, you dream of a real man. That will tear your clothes off and ram you until all your stupid little ideas are gone. I know your type.'

'You couldn't be more wrong. I don't want to have sex with you.'

'That's what they all say. At first. But once you apply enough pressure, they change their tune. Like you'll change yours.'

He drops his trousers and exposes himself. She hadn't thought of that and closes her eyes tight. Too late. The image is branded inside her closed eyelids.

'You want Seb's money, fine. You follow me to bed right now and it's yours.'

'What?'

'You heard me. You let me put my cock inside you, and I'll give you a cheque for five million dollars. In. Your. Name. Best offer you'll ever have for your skinny ass.'

'Get your genitals out of my face and put your trousers back on.'

'Or what?'

'You take your chances, and I take mine.'

He smirks at her.

'Let me stand up,' she says. 'Let me out of here.'

'I don't think I will,' he growls. She can see on his ugly maw he thinks he's won. This is the moment she has been waiting for.

With trembling hands, Constance reaches into her handbag. As her fingers touch the textured plastic, she calls on the fear and anger of years of trauma to steady her grip. Her eyes in his, she tasers Tony in his naked groin.

He howls and stumbles backwards, down the stairs, his trousers around his ankles.

Her legs struggle to carry her and she hangs on to the handrail for dear life.

Thanking her careful preparations for her choice of footwear, she runs down the marbled hall and throws the door open.

The heat of the evening sun clings to her sweaty skin as she stumbles onto the stucco porch. Blinking tears, she makes out a familiar vehicle pulling into the property.

As the car comes to a screeching halt on the gravelled

drive, a door is flung open and she lands, dishevelled and her clothes in disarray, into the passenger seat.

'Drive! Drive,' she shouts. Then and only then does she burst into disgusted sobs.

A manly hand grabs hers. 'Constance, what's happened?'

Fighting waves of nausea, she looks into Pastor John's eyes. 'Please take me to a police station,' she hiccups.

No matter how often he's faced the victim of a serious assault, he hasn't got used to it, and the Pastor's voice trembles as he asks, 'Are you hurt?'

Constance's eyes blaze when she answers. 'I won, Pastor. I won.'

76

4 JULY – POLICE STATION, ECHO PARK, LOS ANGELES, CALIFORNIA, USA

Night is falling over Los Angeles. The remaining rays of the sun leave orange gashes across the indigo sky.

Inside a police station whose name she's already forgotten, Constance hangs for support to the sides of her plastic chair. Her tears leave a wet polka-dot pattern on her skimpy white shorts.

She wishes Pastor John had accompanied her into the office, for the female police officer on the other side of the desk is showing zero signs of empathy.

You did go looking for trouble and you found it.

The voice in her head sounds a lot like her mother, and it isn't easy to silence.

'So, you had planned to record him on your phone all along?' asks the officer for the third time.

'I wanted him to admit on tape he owed Sebastian money. I didn't think he would assault me.'

'He does have a reputation,' the older woman says slowly.

You're an idiot. What did you think would happen?

Since the police believes she's brought this on herself,

Constance decides to confirm their suspicions and play her 'maximum naivety' card.

'I thought he was only after actresses,' she sniffs. 'You know? Beautiful women. I didn't think he would trap *me* in his house and—' She bursts into fresh tears. 'Expose himself, and try to rape me.'

The police officer fills in her form dispassionately, ticking boxes and crossing out text with a leaky pen that leaves smudges across the recitation of Constance's victim account.

'What's going to happen now?' she whispers.

'The report is going off to the DA, but I'm not going to lie to you, Mr Da Ricci is a powerful man. You probably need to hire a lawyer. It will be slow and expensive, and I don't know what will come out of it. Besides, your boyfriend might not want the publicity.'

Constance bites her tongue and stares at her shoes to hide the anger growing in her chest. It wouldn't do to assault a policewoman. *Stick to the plan, Constance.*

'Can I get a copy of my statement, please?'

'As the alleged victim of a sexual assault, you have two years to mail a written request to Records and Identification. The first copy is free of charge.'

The woman stands to terminate the interview. As she is shown out of the room, Constance wonders what she's expected to say.

Thank you?

Fortunately, the minute she steps into the neon-lit corridor, Pastor MacKenzie is there, his arm respectfully hovering above her shoulders.

'Come, let's go back to Trevor.' He silently guides her towards the exit. The coolness of the night hits her and her shivers redouble.

Finally safe inside the Pastor's car, she releases a shaky sigh.

'What now?' she asks.

'As we discussed, I recorded what you told me on the way over here and put it through my speech-to-text app. My buddy at the precinct's just printed it out for me. It's ready for you to sign.'

Pastor John hands Constance a felt tip pen, and she signs her name at the bottom of the second statement she's made today.

This one will count.

She folds it into three and slips it in the envelope the Pastor provides. Across the front, she writes in big angry capital letters 'Tony Da Ricci'.

'It's time for the Wrath of God, Miss Constance,' says Pastor John, his eyes in hers.

'Amen,' she replies, and she gives him the envelope.

She takes her phone off silent mode, and immediately it buzzes in her hand like an angry hornet. She scans the twenty-three messages she's received from Sebastian.

77

4 JULY – POLICE STATION, ECHO PARK, LOS ANGELES, CALIFORNIA, USA

Sebastian's texts get progressively more frantic.

'Don't go to Tony's.'
'If you're at Tony's, leave now.'
'I'm coming for you.'
'I've called the police.'

Shaken as she is, she dreads calling him and opening herself to his wrath, but she keys in his number with shaky fingers.

He answers on the first ring. 'Where are you?' he asks in a breathless voice.

'Outside a police station.'

'Were you at Tony's?'

'Yes, but—'

'What happened? Are you all right?'

'I'm safe. I'm with Pastor John. He's going to drop me at the hotel, and I'll explain everything.'

'No. Go straight to LAX.'

Her stomach drops. 'What? Sebastian, no!' She bursts into tears. 'Don't leave me!'

There is a silence. 'I'm not leaving you, I'm asking you to meet me at the airport.'

'Where are we going?'

'I have a car there.'

'Oh okay.'

'I'm on my way now. I've got something to sort out. Call me when you get there.'

'I love you,' she whispers, but the line is already dead.

Constance ends the call, and her tears return. The fear she felt in Tony's house is nothing compared to what she suffers now.

If Sebastian is furious enough to leave her, she doesn't know how she'll survive. She braces herself for his next words.

Soon enough, her phone rings.

'So, what happened?' he growls in a voice that doesn't sound like his.

'I went to Tony's house to ask for your money—'

'You went for the money?' he shouts. 'What came over you? Why would you do something so stupid?' There is a pause, and his voice changes. 'Did he *hurt* you?'

'No,' she answers shakily.

'What did he do?'

She decides telling him part of the truth now will help to soften the blow she knows she has to deliver later.

'He threatened me and insulted me – and you,' she adds for good measure.

'Did he touch you?'

'He didn't rape me. Look, I'll tell you everything when I see you. Just know I'm safe now. Just keep your head.'

'Keep my head? You throw yourself in the hands of a

rapist, and you tell me how to react? Constance, I swear to God!'

On the whole, Constance is happy he is yelling. Anything but the cold fury of their first conversation.

'I love you baby, I just wanted to do right by you,' she whispers.

'We don't need the fucking money, Constance!'

'I'm sorry,' she says to placate him. And it does.

'I'm sorry too. How are you feeling?' he asks in a softened tone.

'I'm okay. A bit shaken,' she lies. 'Nothing I can't get over.'

'So why the cops?'

'I'm going after him, of course.'

78

4 JULY – LOS ANGELES AIRPORT, LOS ANGELES, CALIFORNIA, USA

*A*t their LAX rendezvous, Constance exits Pastor John's car like a bullet shot from a gun.

If only she can wrap her arms around Sebastian, everything will be okay. He won't be angry, and she will feel safe.

He hasn't yet closed the taxi's door, and she's already at his side, burrowing her face into his armpit. His scent unleashes a wave of relief.

As Sebastian pays the driver, Pastor John joins them in his loping cowboy stride.

'You've got a brave girl there, son.'

'Too brave for her own good,' says Sebastian, anger lingering in his tone. Nevertheless, he squeezes Constance to his side.

'I appreciate you helping her, Pastor.'

'I will pray for you two. You'll need all the help you can get.'

'Gee, thanks Pastor for the vote of confidence,' Constance pipes up, from underneath Sebastian's arm.

'I'm going to circulate this envelope throughout my

network. See if we can find a match.' He hugs them both in his long arms.

After they wave the Pastor goodbye, Sebastian turns to Constance and takes her face between his hands. 'What have you done?'

Rather than reply, she plants a kiss on the perfect bow of his upper lip. 'I'll tell you everything in the car. Can you just hold me for a second? Just hold me and don't say anything.'

'Let's hug and move, the car is just in the next row.'

As they turn the corner, the shock knocks the air out of her lungs. There's a green car with a short muzzle and buggy eyes winking at her.

'Oggie!' she cries.

She's so excited that instead of hugging the instigator of the surprise, she hugs the car.

79
4 JULY – OGGIE THE TWINGO, INTERSTATE 105 WEST, LOS ANGELES, CALIFORNIA, USA

'If you wanted to drive, you should have slept instead of going on some hare-brained undercover mission.' Oggie's manual gear stick screeches as Sebastian reverses out of the parking space.

Constance sits ramrod straight in the passenger seat, her cheeks scarlet.

'So not only did you go there on your own, on purpose, without telling me, but you *recorded* everything?'

'I knew I was the best placed – the most equipped – for that part of the plan. Remember? The one-two punch. That was the first punch.'

'How was that a punch?' he growls. 'He sexually assaulted you! You knew he would, but you went anyway! And now we have a recording of it – probably illegal and unusable – and a police report that will end up in some bent cop's trash can. What were you thinking? Did you even think about us? What that's going to mean for us?'

'But I did it *for* us!'

'You mean for the money? Do you know me so little that you thought I'd care about that? That I would want him to touch you, to expose himself, to push you around, to threaten you.... For money?'

He runs a hand through his russet hair, and exhales through his nose slowly.

Step up, be a man.

'It was never about the money,' says Constance. 'Can't you see? It was a trap. Something to rile him up. I knew once he believed I was motivated by money, he would think me in his power. Think he could shut me up by paying me. And it all happened as I'd planned. He opened his revolting gob, and all sorts of self-incriminations came tumbling out. And now we have that to use as we see fit. We've got something over him. The grain of sand that stops the machine.'

Sebastian is stunned into silence. He looks at Constance as if he's never met her before.

'I meant what is it going to do to us?' he asks. 'Putting yourself again in a situation where you are sexually abused. We were doing so well, and this is going to set us back. Why did you do it?'

'It's *not* going to set us back. I took my weakness and turned it into a strength. How much more empowering can it get? The guys who abused me are beyond my reach, but I can bring Tony Da Ricci down, as a warning to men of his ilk we are not the defenceless victims they think we are. I knew I could handle Tony and his threats and his roving hands. I was prepared. Life's shaped me for that moment.'

'I can't decide whether you're completely insane or fiendishly clever.'

'Take your pick, it doesn't matter. We've got him.'

'How? The police aren't going to do anything.'

'This is where the Wrath of God comes in.'

'You realise you sound crazy, right?'

'Just listen, would you! The Pastor told me about this

system where victims of a person they're scared to publicly accuse write a statement they seal in an envelope with the abuser's name on it. Then they entrust it to a safe organisation, a university or a church, and specify the time when it is to be unsealed. Usually, they wait until enough envelopes are gathered with the same name on it. Then all the envelopes are opened at the same time, and a group complaint is made by all the victims together. Strength in numbers.'

'So you did all this for an envelope with Tony's name on it?'

'How many other envelopes in his name exist already? Other victims who have never spoken out, just waiting for the right time to take him down.'

'And when they know they're not alone—'

'The dominoes will fall.'

He stares above Constance's head while he processes the information. 'So, it was never about the money.'

'I doubt you'll ever see a dime of it. He's probably spent it, and when the lawyers are finished with him, there won't be any money left to pay you back.'

His brow furrows. 'The tape could be enough to get me out of my contract on the moral clause. And out of any power of attorney.'

'See? You're free. You can get the Fermo Drive house back, you're still a Hollywood star, you can make twice the money for your next movie.'

Wayne's words ring in his mind. *The queen protects her king.*

All in one go, he sees what Constance has done for him. How she did the very thing that scared her most. The thing he could never have done himself.

The shackles that have held him in Tony's power for ten years fall off with a loud clank.

He takes her hand. 'Constance, I have to apologise to you. You have just given me my freedom, and instead of thanking you, I've berated you.' He kisses her fingers. 'Your work is done.'

He pulls off the Century Freeway onto the hard shoulder.

'You can leave it all to me now,' he says. 'I am going to drag Tony in front of the most powerful court in America.'

He opens up his Twitter account and shares the audio recording of Constance's visit at Tony's.

'This is how Tony Da Ricci treated my fiancée today. #metoo #nowheretohide'

He takes her in his arms, and whispers in her ear, 'It's done. It's over.'

Finally, she can drop the mask and show him shaken she truly is. She soaks up the warmth of his embrace and draws the strength she needs to confess her last worry.

'I've heard from the estate agent, they've just sold my house. We don't have a single home between us.'

'We're each other's home now.'

She empties her mind, focuses on their intertwined fingers and breathes a deep, long sigh of relief.

'Where are you taking me then?'

'Back to LA.'

'Aren't we driving the wrong way?'

He smiles. 'L.A, Arkansas.'

80

8 JULY – "LONG ACRES", MARION, ARKANSAS, USA

*A*fter five interminable days driving east on the Interstate 40, four nights in roadside motels and two engine repairs – one in Flagstaff, Arizona and another in Amarillo, Texas–, Oggie chugs into the Long Acres dirt road.

Constance, who stayed up late into the night to watch TV footage of dozen of Tony's victims coming out of the shadows, is fast asleep in the back seat and snores softly.

The Johnsons' property looks ethereal in the mid-morning light, as heat rises from the grass in tiny streamers of distorted light.

Sebastian deploys all his scant driving skills to manoeuvre the car around the potholes in a vain attempt not to wake Constance. Unfortunately for Oggie, the Swiss-cheese pattern claims an early victory.

'Huh, what? What?' she shouts when her head hits the moulded plastic armrest.

'Wakey-wakey. Time to bring the snoring concerto to a close.'

'A concerto has several instruments, you doofus!' mumbles Constance, in her typical early-morning irascible mood.

'Then you must have been hiding a second set of pipes under your shirt!' he laughs.

'Hilarious.' She sits up and runs her fingers through her tangled hair. 'I think that's finished Oggie,' complains Constance. 'Twenty-six hours' drive from LA! This country is seriously too big.'

She checks her reflection in the rear-view mirror, and her worst fears are confirmed. Her hair does look like an expensive mop. No question.

While she frets about her appearance, Sebastian prays Philly and Wayne have had time to organise for their arrival.

When he phoned from a petrol station in Albuquerque, New Mexico, Philly shrieked for a full minute, and he had to speak to Wayne instead. The delicate business bringing them back to Long Acres would have been better communicated to his wife, but she was otherwise engaged in her fit of squealing.

Sebastian is left to hope Wayne's law enforcement training taught him to absorb details, despite the pandemonium created by his better half.

As they drive up the dirt road, Constance notices the garlands decorating the fences. 'Gawd, do they think it's still the Fourth of July or something?' she comments.

'Or something.'

'Trust Philly and Wayne to go over the top.'

The downward lines on either side of her mouth – next to the jersey impression her cardigan left on her cheek– tell Sebastian that on the scale of morning grump, Constance is scoring a solid eight.

His anticipation of the day ahead is dampened, and he is suddenly relieved that Constance's bad mood will soon be drowned by the Johnsons' tsunami of enthusiasm.

As they approach the house, he notes with satisfaction his request for a complete absence of explicit banner has been acted upon, but his plea against a welcoming committee utterly ignored.

A little crowd is assembled on the white front porch. Next to Philly and Wayne stand Regina in a subdued pink outfit, Pastor John in a smart dark suit, and even Haunani, from the hospital in Hawaii, looking very small and dainty without her larger-than-life nurse's uniform. They're all clapping loudly.

'Do they think we won the Olympics or something?'

'Or something,' says Sebastian again.

'Stop saying that. Goodness, you're so annoying in the morning.'

He only grins.

'Surprise!' shouts the welcome party.

As she gracefully disembarks, Constance asks the non-Johnsons, 'How did y'all know we were coming?' Sebastian smiles at her first ever use of the Southern pronoun 'y'all', which he spent years removing from his vocabulary.

'The Johnsons invited us,' says Regina defensively. Wayne elbows her in the side. 'To celebrate Tony's downfall, of course,' she adds hurriedly.

Haunani blushes pink. 'Philly and Wayne kindly gifted me some air miles.'

'And we were given some other very specific instructions,' winks Pastor John like he's got something in his eye.

'Y'all did it!' Philly squeals, squeezing Sebastian's cheeks and pulling Constance into a crushing hug, her eyes lit up like a Christmas tree.

Wayne offers Sebastian a manly handshake, but his voice wobbles when he says, 'Well done, son. Ya sure did step up.'

Sebastian keeps a straight face as he nods, but his throat feels a little too tight when he replies, 'Thank you, sir.'

Without wasting another second in pleasantries, Philly

grabs Constance by the arm. 'Now ya're coming with us, Miss Constance!'

Regina falls into step and provides extra propulsion by pushing Constance in front of her. Haunani follows quietly behind.

As she is half carried and half pushed up the stairs, Constance is too dumbstruck to say anything, and the sight of their destination does little to help her find her words.

The pink bedroom looks like an explosion in a fabric factory, with clothes, lace, frou-frou and ribbons strewn everywhere.

'We didn't know what ya'd like, so we got a selection!' trumpets Philly, beside herself with excitement.

'A selection of what?' manages Constance.

'Dresses…' replies her hostess.

'Oh, I brought some clothes, don't worry! We left LA in a rush, but I stopped to buy a couple of outfits en route,' says Constance.

Regina is the first to catch on. 'Do you really not know why you're here?' she asks suspiciously.

Constance looks from face to face, still at a loss. 'What are you guys talking about? Is it some kind of celebration?'

'He didn't tell her,' guesses Haunani, biting her lip.

The atmosphere in the room changes instantly, and Philly's unbridled joy turns to black fury. She sticks her head out the window. 'Ya didn't tell her?' she bellows at the men below.

'Nope,' Sebastian shouts back, and the three men burst out laughing.

'Pastor, I would have expected better from ya,' says Philly, her cheeks pink with indignation.

When she turns back to Constance, her expression is pitiful. 'I think ya'd better talk to your man, darlin'. He may have played a little *practical joke* on us all…'

The loud exchange has given Constance the chance to fully take in her surroundings. 'Hang on, Phil.' She grabs the older woman by the wrist. 'Are we supposed to get married? Here? Now?'

'That's the idea, genius,' snaps Regina, never a natural host for the spirit of compassion.

'And he didn't even tell me?' stutters Constance.

'Apparently not,' whispers Philly, on the verge of tears.

'I'm going to kill him. Sebastian!' Constance shouts out of the open window, but the only thing she sees is him, hands braced on his knees, laughing so hard he can't stand up.

'Your face!' he manages between two hiccups.

As she stomps down the stairs, she mutters to herself. 'With my history! He doesn't even ask for my opinion. Unbelievable!'

She manhandles Wayne – three times her size– out of the doorway. 'I'm going to skin him alive!'

'Don't let me stop ya, sweetheart,' he chuckles.

When she plants herself in front of a still-laughing Sebastian, she shouts, 'How could you?'

'How could I what? Give you a surprise?'

'But a wedding?'

'Save you weeks of poring over magazines and worrying?'

'But—'

'Give you the best-ever excuse not to invite your parents?'

This stops her in her tracks. 'That's actually a good point,' she admits.

'Would you prefer a big wedding with lots of people you don't know and the press at the door?'

'No.'

'So?'

'What if I wanted to organise my own wedding?'

'Yeah, right. You almost had a panic attack worrying about

cap sleeves. So, I'm sorry if it's taking you a while to realise it, but this is the absolute best way for us to get married while salvaging what's left of our sanities. Personally, I'd be happy to marry you in a trash bag at the back of a rainy alley. But it's all ready, here and now. No fuss. Philly has organised a dress for you and even created a special wedding smoothie. Plus, Wayne will walk you down the aisle.'

'Wayne said yes to walking me down the aisle?' Constance asks in a small voice.

'Sure thin', darlin'!' shouts Wayne from the safety of the house.

Constance's cheeks turn red. Sebastian cups them in his cool hands. 'Do you want to get married now or not?' he asks. 'It's still up to you.'

As she looks up into his eyes, her reluctance melts away. 'Okay, then.'

Sebastian smiles and drops a soft kiss on her parted lips. 'You won't regret it.'

'She said yes,' Wayne shouts up the stairs to Philly.

Philly's head appears at the window, she's still wiping tears of disappointment, but her enthusiasm is reignited. 'Come on, Missy,' she calls. 'Those dresses aren't going to try themselves!'

When Constance returns to the pink room, several dresses in different shades of cream are hanging from the picture rail.

'Hurry, darlin'. Ya don't want to leave your handsome young man waitin' at the altar for too long…'

'Yes, we don't have time to piss about!' grouches Regina.

'Language!' says an outraged Philly.

'Huh, my apologies, I guess,' mumbles Regina.

Haunani has kept her mind on the task at hand, and she silently presents a dress with a sparkly body and a wide poofy skirt that Constance waves off immediately.

'You should go for something less bridal,' interrupts Regina, and she holds up a light blue summer dress with mid-length skirt and bell sleeves.

'No, that's my outfit,' warns Philly, slapping Regina's hand.

Instead, she unwraps a pearl silk gown with vintage Victorian lace down the back and an elegant scoop neck. 'It was my mamma's. I thought perhaps ya would like to try it. She was just your size. The lace is very old, but it's modest.'

Constance's heart swells at the reverence with which Philly is handling the garment. The fabric is pristine as if untouched by time. 'She sewed it herself.'

Constance admires the tiny needlework and can't help caressing the bone buttons on the sleeves.

'A labour of love,' says Haunani, speaking for everyone.

The soft feel of the fabric and the nurse's simple words are like a balm soothing Constance's panicky feelings. She takes a deep, calming breath.

'Philly, it's beautiful. I don't care what I look like in it. If it was your mother's, I'm wearing it.'

Later, as she walks down the aisle hastily organised on the Johnsons' front lawn, Wayne's arm in a death grip, she gasps at the sight of a teary-eyed Sebastian, resplendent in a made-to-measure suit Regina brought for him from LA. The look on his face tells Constance the dress fits plenty well enough, thank-you-very-much.

When they finally meet in front of the Pastor, Philly starts sobbing softly.

Through her bliss, Constance takes in her dreamlike surroundings: the garlands and candles, the trees festooned with fairy lights and the gentle classical music emanating from somewhere behind her.

The white roses woven into the wedding arch smell beguilingly sweet, combined with the delicate fragrance of her favourite aftershave.

Sebastian looks like a carved Adonis, with his sun-kissed hair a burnished bronze, his green eyes glistening with emotion and his perfect lips waiting for her legally binding kiss.

When Pastor John, in his best thespian voice, reads out the traditional words of the wedding ceremony, Constance floats away on a happy cloud and loses track of time.

She hopes someone will pinch her when it's time to say 'I do'.

81
12 JULY – GATINEAU PARK, QUEBEC, CANADA

*S*ince they entered the park in their rental truck full to the rafters with hiking equipment, Constance has counted ten dragonflies in various arrays of colours, their luminescent wings fluttering in the summer sun.

Gatineau Park, near Ottawa, is one of these rare places on Earth where a supernatural peace seems to simultaneously rise from the ground and descend from the skies.

The air is pure, the colours true, and the silence alive with contented living things.

As they drive up a steep lane to their wood cabin, Constance and Sebastian exchange a look of excitement. Their home for the next two weeks is suitably secluded, hidden as it is behind a crescent of pine trees, and the view from the benches flanking the front door looks like a postcard.

Constance makes her way across the grassy area surrounding the cabin with huge snowshoes strapped to her flip-flops. 'This is the traditional design,' she explains. 'It's made of white ash and caribou-hide strips. This particular model is called the teardrop.'

Sebastian grins, 'Come here, you nerd.' He waves her over,

and she waddles towards him. 'You're nuttier than squirrel poop!'

He kisses her then trips her over mischievously, catching her just before she plummets to the ground.

Inside, the main room is cosy and flooded with the evening light. The tiny bedroom at the back contains a bed made in cheerful linen and nothing else.

Once they've dragged in their suitcases, there's hardly room to turn around. The rest of their equipment will have to remain in the car.

Constance, with a second pair of snowshoes under one arm and her art box in the other, struggles through the doorjamb.

'So glad we got those shoes,' she remarks. 'In case we get snowed in.'

'It's July.'

'Freak weather, you never know. You're always such a wet blanket.'

'What is it with you and blankets?'

She prods his biceps playfully. 'Gosh, you're so *hard*.'

Sebastian's mouth forms a perfect O of surprise. 'In case you flunked "Males 101", only ever say the words "*you're so hard*" if you plan to be dragged into bed immediately.'

'Is it like a code word?'

'Yep. It means "*sex me now!*" in universal man language.'

'You're so hard,' she repeats coyly.

In no more than a heartbeat, he's carried her to the bedroom and tackled her onto the bed.

She huffs when he lands on top of her, his face buried in her dark-coffee curls. The scent of vanilla and orange blossom does something to his groin.

'You're crushing me under your two hundred pounds of hard muscle,' she complains ruefully.

'Do not offend my sensitivities by implying my weight may be excessive.'

'The Victorians are back,' she giggles. Her arms circle his neck in a stranglehold, and she pecks the freckles on his cheek, relishing the familiar scent of 'Pour Monsieur' on his reddish stubble.

When she bites his earlobe, Sebastian takes in a sharp breath. 'Ouch!'

'Stop whining. I can't help myself, you're so handsome and sexy. And mine, all mine!'

'No sweat, help yourself. Take another bite.'

This time, she licks ever so slowly under his chin, and he lets out a strangled moan. 'I like it that I can turn you on so easily, it's like having magic powers.'

'It used to scare you.'

'It's got easier, as you always said it would. You've been right all along.'

She climbs on top of him and straddles his hips. She delights in his bulging muscles flexing and rolling under her tingling palms as she massages his broad shoulders through his cotton shirt.

'Even last time in Henley, you were right. I was too impatient; it was too much too soon.'

Constance rolls off and settles next to him to kiss him. She adds with a flirty smile, 'If you play your cards right, tonight might be your lucky night.'

'Here we go again, always jumping the gun.'

'Well, if you're going to be all mister-safety-first, I'm going to drown my sorrows in the bottle of welcome wine.'

'No, you're not,' says Sebastian, rearranging himself. He hooks his arm around her neck and pulls her into his chest. 'You are going nowhere. After what happened last time, I can't sleep and leave you unsupervised. You might find another sex predator to entrap.'

'Or I might singlehandedly reform the American weight unit system.'

He laughs. 'Either way, you're staying right here, Mrs Anders.'

'Mrs Wilkinson-Anders, you mean.'

He shuts her open mouth with a soft kiss and kicks off his shoes. 'What was going through your mind the day we met?' he asks.

'I felt I *had* to help you. Once you were dry and not looking like a drowned cat, I started feeling the attraction. And it wasn't just because you look like a bloody movie star. We connected like I'd never connected with anybody before.'

He kisses a trail from her ear to her cleavage, raising goosebumps along the way, and lifts her vest to give himself better access.

She speaks through the fabric bunched up on her face. 'And I could tell it wasn't one-sided. I started feeling very uncomfortable and frightened. I wanted you and I knew I couldn't have you.'

'And look at you now,' he chuckles. She obediently lifts her arms as he pulls the vest over her head.

'I was trying to push you away, and you weren't having any of it. Then when I told you we couldn't have sex, I was devastated. I thought I'd never see you again.'

He grabs her chin and explores her mouth with his tongue until her toes tingle.

'It wasn't like that for me,' he says, unzipping her shorts and shimmying them down her legs. He places a warm hand on her stomach, and her muscles relax at the exact same time that her nerves snap to attention.

'I thought we could be together right from the start. Even

in your car, while I was still dripping on your backseat, I was thinking if I could be with a girl like her, my life would be worth living. By the time we were at your house, I was already determined to pursue you. When you said you didn't like sex, all brave and shy, I thought about marrying you.'

Her eyes blink open. 'What?'

He traces the contours of her lacy pink bra with a reverent finger. 'Yes. And I thought about it a lot afterwards, but I didn't want to spook you.'

She turns onto her side to face him and takes good note of the recent expansion in his crotch area. Even last month this would have sent her running for the hills. Today, it fills her with proprietary pride.

She lets out a small sigh. 'Kiss me.'

'No, *you* kiss me.'

When Constance touches her lips to the skin above his heart, his whole body shivers and he lets out a long exhale.

'Did I do that?' she asks.

'Yes, ma'am.'

'Cool,' she grins. She nibbles his neck to the jawline, and he closes his eyes in delight.

With tremors in her hands, she holds his face and kisses her way down his neck to the collarbone. He moans softly.

'Am I doing well?'

'This is already the best sex I've ever had.'

'Liar,' she laughs.

Sebastian runs his hands up and down the milkiness of her back slowly. 'Not a word of a lie. I'm in heaven.'

'Me too.'

Sebastian pulls back to watch her face. 'Really?'

'Really,' confirms Constance bashfully.

Sebastian sinks deep into the chocolate of her eyes. 'You're so beautiful. You take my breath away.'

'It's strange,' she says, 'how we could become close so quickly, and how there is still so much distance to cover to bring us properly together.'

'What distance?' He gestures to his lap and she straddles him while he unhooks her bra with deft fingers. 'In all the important things, being together is as easy as breathing.'

As the *girls* are freed from their lacy bonnets, he gasps at the sight of her perfect perky breasts.

His hooded eyes follow her gentle curves, and he swallows before diving into her cleavage with the relish of a man starved of bosoms.

He palms her bare breasts and pecks and pinches his way from one to the other and back again. Her head falls back, and he secures her to his chest with a strong arm.

Heat radiates from his body into hers. 'Before you know it, sex will be easy too,' he says.

'I hope so,' she murmurs.

This is not the enthusiastic response he was hoping for, but she is unbuttoning his shirt and sliding it off his tanned shoulders.

Her light touch sends his heart into overdrive and for a moment he can't think.

With a tilt of his hips, he lays her back onto the bed. Constance lies rigid. 'I'm so nervous all of a sudden.'

He stops. 'No plan, no schedule. No obligation. We do what's good for both of us. Either of us wants to stop, we do. We talk, we hang out, we go to sleep. It won't be weird.'

They look at each other in silence.

She plasters a smile onto her face. 'You're not getting any younger. I'd like some of that tasty meat while it's still fresh.'

He sees through the thin veil of her confident grin. 'You're scared.'

'I'm always going to be scared the first time. Just don't hurt me.'

'Of course not. What are you going to say if you want to stop?'

'Stop.'

'And if it's going too fast?'

Constance pretends to think about it. 'Pineapple.'

Sebastian laughs. 'Okay then. Bucking bronco!'

Constance, only half-joking, coos, 'Oooh I'm *so* scared!' Just in case, she grabs the pine plank that forms the headboard. Her hand looks so small against the thick wood that his heart melts.

Just as he is about to tell her, she whispers, 'When I look at you it makes my insides go funny.'

'Me too. I have a platoon of dragonflies in my stomach,' he chuckles.

'And an elephant in your pants,' she jokes.

He kisses her deeply and wriggles out of his shorts. As soon as they are front-to-front and skin-to-skin, Constance grows still.

After a split second of hesitation, he lifts himself off her and settles down at her side.

He struggles to calm his breathing.

'What happened? What did I do wrong?' she stutters, eyes wide.

'Nothing. You just look like a rabbit in the headlights. I'm not doing anything with you if you're that frightened. There's plenty of time.'

He'd hoped his tone would be appeasing, but Constance shuts her eyes tight and bursts into tears. 'You've ruined it. Why did you stop?'

Startled at her reaction, he does his best to smile. 'I'm keeping some fun for later,' he says in a conciliatory tone.

'Don't treat me like a freak.'

'I'm just being a patient, considerate husband.'

'Come back and finish it!'

'I will as soon as you've calmed down.'

'Don't tell me to calm down!'

Sebastian looks at her as if he's working out a complicated puzzle. She punches the pillow in frustration. He reaches out to her slowly, but she bats his hand away with tear-filled eyes.

'Baby, don't cry.'

She hits his chest, right in the solar plexus, and he winces. 'I need you to carry me over the last hurdle, not abandon me in front of it.'

'Why don't you take your time—'

'I don't want to take my time. I want you to make love to me now.'

'You're obviously not ready. You will feel very silly about this one day, you know,' he says.

'I don't care. Shut up and do it.'

As he still hesitates, she says, 'You promised. No matter what. If I asked you, you would make love to me.'

'Are you saying this is the Call?' he asks.

Constance says resolutely, 'It is the Call.'

Despite his misgivings, Sebastian nods. 'Yes, ma'am, reporting for duty.'

His little joke sounds in poor taste as soon as it has left his lips, but Constance doesn't object and she pins him in place with eyes blazing with anticipation and fear.

He sends his boxers flying into orbit and settles between her legs. Fascinated by what he sees, he nevertheless makes himself glance at her to seek some confirmation he's doing the right thing.

Her little chin goes up and down once. Permission granted.

So, he brings her calves around his waist. He tears the pink string on the side of her thong and throws it over his shoulder. Bowled over by her nakedness, he freezes with the look of a man stabbed in the chest.

'Do it,' she says, in a businesslike tone that breaks his heart, then her expression softens. 'Please, I want you to.'

His eyes beam the same green as the water underneath all the bridges they've ever stood on together.

At his neck, his pulse jumps into a higher gear. Her insides squeeze in response.

The desire for intimate connection is entirely new to her, but the animal part of her brain recognises it for exactly what it is – the fierce, irrational longing that has kept the Earth populated for a hundred thousand years. It burns the fear out of every single one of her cells.

He reads the mood shift on her face and his frown disappears, replaced by a roguish smile. 'Not until you beg loud enough to scare the dragonflies for miles around.'

Caged between his golden forearms, she laughs a happy musical tinkle that lifts his heart and stokes the blaze in his groin. 'We'll just have to see about that.'

'I've got a few tricks up my sleeve,' he whispers hoarsely into her ear.

'Don't tell me, show me.'

He wraps her in his arms, and she melts in his embrace. At long last, they're perfectly aligned.

'Hang on to your fox hat, *Connie*, because now we're having sex!'

82

12 AUGUST – OUTSIDE RIPLEY, TENNESSEE, USA

*C*onstance is driving her faithful Oggie across the Memphis–Arkansas Bridge.

The traffic is fluid, the sky above royal blue. Below the old bridge, the Mississippi River stretches murky green under the sticky Southern heat.

Whereas Oggie's heating system works perfectly well, she was never fitted with air conditioning, a precaution somewhat unnecessary in the British climate.

All the windows are down and air is billowing through the car, but the heat has turned Sebastian and Constance's clothes into clinging wet rags.

Constance's white broderie anglaise summer dress sticks to her thighs like a second skin.

Sebastian sports sweat stains down the back of his 'Born In Tennessee' T-shirt Philly insisted he wore on his final trek home.

Constance and Sebastian left Long Acres and the Johnsons half an hour ago, and they've already passed the blue 'Tennessee – Welcome Center' sign.

The 'Mighty 990' KWAM Radio is on full volume, and

Constance sings along to 'Carry On My Wayward Son' by Kansas.

'This is the song for you!' she shouts over the music, shaking her curls to the beat, before diving back into the chorus. 'There'll be peace when you are done…'

Sebastian smiles, but he's not sure there'll be any peace for him at the end of this road.

As the music gives way to a news bulletin, Constance lets out a glass-shattering shriek. Sebastian pricks up his ears.

'We've just got news Tony Da Ricci was arrested by the LAPD late last night, in full view of the press photographers, as he stepped out of a glamorous Hollywood party at an undisclosed location. Our correspondent, William Dawson, is currently standing in front the disgraced movie mogul's Holmsby Hills house, a few yards away from the Playboy Mansion. I bet Tony Da Ricci won't feel like a playboy in the county jail tonight… Over to you, Will.'

Constance's face is a perfect impersonation of the surprised emoji, frozen wide eyes and open mouth.

Sebastian swallows his shock just enough to speak. 'We did it, baby. We destroyed him,' he whispers.

Constance almost breaks his fingers with her iron grip and misses only a beat, before bursting into song again.

'Tony Toad is going down, down, down!' she chants in every octave, while jiving in the driving seat.

Sebastian's reaction is more subdued. Tony has been an essential part of his life since he was a teenager, and Constance's jubilation is not echoed in his heart. Ten years of his life will forever be besmirched by an unwashable stain of trauma and guilt.

When they come off the bridge, Sebastian's breathing becomes increasingly shallow. 'Take Highway 51,' he says, his throat tight, because that's the road his father always took when they were driving home.

Slowly coming down from her revenge high, Constance notices his pallor. She strokes his biceps.

'I wonder what state it's in,' she says, not to leave him alone with his thoughts.

'Probably a ruin.'

'How long since it's been lived in?'

'Sixteen years.'

'I can't believe you've never been back since. You lived nearby at your grandma's.'

'It was too sad at first, then it got harder and harder to look back on the only happy time in my life. Besides, even at the time, it was even more derelict than my grandma's house.'

'When I think how long I lived in my childhood house, even after it got filled with bad memories…'

'Too long. I'm happy it sold so quickly.'

She nods. 'Pretty neat we can fix up your childhood home with the money from the sale of mine.'

'"Pretty neat"? Look who's talking Southern now,' he grins.

Despite the butterflies that fill her stomach every time he smiles, she ripostes, '"Pretty neat" is standard English, I'll have you know.'

The bubble of sadness in his heart bursts at the sight of her schoolmarmish expression. 'Yeah, yeah… Whatever,' he laughs. 'You're the language expert, the condom disposal expert and the snowshoes expert. Plus, of course, the sick bucket expert…'

Her cheeks turn pink, and her eyes blaze in indignation. 'How many times? It was our first date. I was *nervous!*'

The wet tendrils stuck to the nape of her neck make him

want to stop the car and rid her of her clothes on the back seat. His melancholy mood is forgotten.

Glad she was able to drag him out of his tizzy, she keeps the conversation going. 'How much longer?'

'Ripley is an hour away now, plus an extra fifteen minutes to get out of town. I hope Oggie will cope with the dirt road. It was like a rollercoaster when I was a child. Fat chance it's improved since.'

'Now she's survived the Long Acres' drive, Oggie can get through anything.'

Despite Constance's optimistic predictions, the last mile almost signs the death warrant of Oggie as a roadworthy vehicle, and when they get out of the car, Sebastian and Constance feel they've just fallen off a rodeo bull.

At the sight of the house where he never was anything but a much-loved younger son, Sebastian has to hold back tears.

He doesn't see a dilapidated house. He sees his parents on the porch and two little boys playing hide-and-seek. He sees the happy childhood that was over much too soon.

What Constance sees is quite different. As most British people, she fancies herself as a bit of a real-estate expert. (All those property porn programmes she watched in her cream sitting room must count for something!)

She sees the architectural equivalent of a beautiful Victorian damsel in distress. She gasps at the elegant patrician structure, cladded in ivory weatherboard, complete with bow windows and roof dormers. She swoons at the gorgeous covered patio and the intact original porch.

This is the kind of building you could never get tired of drawing.

Everywhere the paint is peeling, and yellowing grass grows in the gutters, but she can already imagine the hardwood floorboards and the nineteenth-century fireplaces and staircase.

And just like that, she falls just as much in love with his ruin of a house as she is with him.

'This is my house,' she declares. 'This is the house I was always meant to have.'

'This is *our* house,' he says. 'We're finally home.' He chokes on the lump in his throat.

Now he's back where he started, with Constance's hand clutched in his, he feels like a brand new man, cleansed and renewed.

He is done, and there is peace.

'It's been quite the adventure, hasn't it?' says Constance, stepping into the circle of his arms.

He grins and squeezes her to him. 'It's only starting, baby.' He smells of his sweat, which recently became her new favourite fragrance.

'I can't wait to have sex in every single room in this house,' she giggles.

'We may have to stick to the downstairs until the roof is repaired!'

'Let's start with the hallway.'

'Is it the Call again?'

'It *is* the Call. Again.'

'At your service, ma'am.'

'I should think so, you've waited long enough,' she grins.

'Good things come to those who wait.'

'And to those who rescue famous actors on Battersea Bridge.'

'That too.'

🐾

THE END

For book swag, news and new release dates, sign up for Venezia's Friend Zone at www.facebook.com/veneziaphillipsromance, and follow @veneziaphillipsromance on Instagram.

Venezia will straight up love you forever if you leave a review on either Amazon or Goodreads.

ABOUT THE AUTHOR

A certain Mrs Phillips, whose legal name may or may not be Venezia, lives near London, UK, with an assortment of humans and canines who she successfully keeps alive, and who in turn successfully keep her sane.

She writes witty romantic comedies she dubs 'books to chuckle and swoon'.

Her next book, "We're NOT Having a Threesome!", another stand-alone romance, comes out in 2021.

For book swag, news and new release dates, sign up for Venezia's Friend Zone at www.facebook.com/veneziaphillipsromance, and follow www.instagram.com/veneziaphillipsromance.

Venezia will straight up love you forever if you leave a review on either Amazon or Goodreads.

ACKNOWLEDGMENTS

Venezia sails a small ship, so the list of the people she would like to acknowledge is not as long as some. Her thanks are all the more heartfelt.

The following people have gone above and beyond the call of duty and delivered some sterling work despite tight deadlines.

In chronological order:

- MiblArt, and the lovely Mary for the book covers and images (@Miblart)

- Catherine Rubinstein, my invaluable editor extraordinaire, who worked through the 2020 UK Lockdown.

- Liz Bodin, Editor-in-Chief at EB Editorial Services, for her fantastic beta-reading and feedback (@eb.editorial).

Give them some love on social media, they deserve it!

Plus, there is of course a certain bookclub group, but if Venezia goes there, she'll just cry. So, thank you ladies, you're the best!

For book swag, news and new release dates, sign up for Venezia's Friend Zone at www.veneziaphillipsromance.com/contactus or at www.facebook.com/veneziaphillipsromance, and follow www.instagram.com/veneziaphillipsromance.

Venezia will straight up love you forever if you leave a review on either Amazon or Goodreads.

Printed in Great Britain
by Amazon